KADE

Kade

Madeline Baker

Kade

This book is published on behalf of the author by the Ethan Ellenberg Literary Agency.

You can reach the author at:
Author website: www.madelinebaker.net
Email: darkwritr@aol.com

Reckless Heart
Reckless Love
Renegade Heart
Shadows Through Time
Spirit's Song
The Angel and the Outlaw
The Spirit Path
Under a Prairie Moon
Under Apache Skies
Unforgettable
Warrior's Lady
West Texas Bride
Wolf Shadow

Maiden's Song
Masquerade
Midnight and Moonlight
Midnight Embrace
Night's Kiss
Night's Master
Night's Mistress
Night's Pleasure
Night's Promise
Night's Surrender
Night's Touch
Quinn's Lady
Quinn's Revenge
Sandy's Angel
Seasons of the Night
Shades of Gray
Sunlight Moonlight
Surrender the Dawn
The Captive
The Music of the Night
Twilight Desires
Twilight Dreams

DEDICATION

*To my cousin, super line editor Susan Spiceland,
for editing the final draft.
And
To Kimberly N. Eldridge
for helping me decide on my hero's name.*

TABLE OF CONTENTS

CHAPTER ONE

South Dakota
1873

He stared up at the vast blue vault of the sky. He had always known this day would come. Any man who lived by the gun usually died that way. Even now, blood from the gunshot wound low in his left side was leaking through his fingers, soaking into the dirt beneath him.

Only a matter of time, he thought. He might have had a chance of finding help if the posse hadn't shot his horse out from under him. But maybe that was a good thing. When a warrior died, the People killed his favorite mount so the warrior's spirit wouldn't have to walk to the happy hunting ground. Kade grunted softly as he glanced at the dead mare. At least he had a good horse to carry him to the land of spirits.

Resigned to his fate, he closed his eyes and waited for death.

Norrie McDonald shaded her eyes against the setting sun as she watched a trio of vultures circling overhead in the distance. Something had died. Probably one of their calves or perhaps a cow. A deer, maybe.

Clucking to her horse, she headed that way to check it out. If it was a wounded animal, she would put it out of its misery.

She didn't see anything until she crossed the shallow river. And there, partially hidden by a boulder, she found the source of the vultures' interest.

Reining her mare to a halt, Norrie stared down at the man. He looked Indian but he was dressed like a white man, right down to his worn leather boots. He'd been shot. Blood caked his shirt front and stained his hands. Flies swarmed around him. He wasn't moving.

Leaning forward, her arms folded on the pommel of her saddle, Norrie tried to decide what to do. She didn't have a shovel, so she couldn't bury him. And she certainly couldn't lift him onto her horse and take him back to the ranch. Heaving a sigh, she decided to ride back to the Lazy Double D and send a couple of the hands out to dig a proper grave.

She was about to head back to the ranch when she paused. Maybe before she left, she should make sure he was dead.

Dismounting, she knelt beside him, her fingers searching for a pulse.

At her touch, a low groan erupted from his throat.

Startled, Norrie scrambled to her feet and backed away.

He stared up at her a moment, then licked his lips. "You got any water for a dying man?"

With a curt nod, Norrie retrieved her canteen. Kneeling beside him again, she removed the cap, then lifted his head and held the canteen to his lips. He drank greedily before closing his eyes again.

Norrie recapped the flask and slung it over the pommel of her saddle. "Can you get up?"

He looked at her through heavy-lidded eyes as cold and gray as storm clouds. "I don't know."

"Well, I can't lift you." Taking the bandana from his neck, she folded it into a thick square, then pulled his shirt from his trousers and pressed the pad over the bullet hole. "Can you sit up?"

He grimaced in pain as she helped him.

"The bullet's still in there." After ripping a long strip from his shirttail, she wrapped it around his middle to hold the bandage in place. "You're gonna have to help me," she said, gaining her feet. "Unless you want to feed those buzzards."

He glanced upward. Took a deep breath, and grasped the hand she offered.

Norrie wasn't sure how they managed it. He was a big man, broad-shouldered and long-legged, but somehow she got him on his feet. With his arm draped heavily over her shoulders, she walked him to her horse and gave him a boost into the saddle. Putting her foot in the stirrup, she swung up behind him, then leaned forward and grabbed the reins.

It was five miles back to the ranch, she thought as she wrapped one arm around his waist. She just hoped he stayed conscious until they got there.

"What the hell!" Old Tom exclaimed when she reined up in front of the veranda. "Who the devil is that?"

"I don't know. Help me get him into the house."

Between the two of them, they managed to get the stranger into Seth's bedroom.

"Tom, I want you to ride into town and get the doctor."

Grumbling under his breath, the old cowboy limped out of the room.

Norrie stood beside the bed, her hands on her hips as she regarded the stranger lying in her brother's bed. She couldn't help noticing that he was handsome in a rough-hewn sort of way as she unbuckled his gunbelt, dragged it out from under him and dropped it on the ladder-back chair beside the window. His hair was long and thick and black, his skin the color of copper. A faint white scar ran from the outer edge of his left eye to the corner of his jaw.

Taking a deep breath, she unbuttoned his shirt so she could remove it. No easy task, big as he was, unconscious, and unable to help. She couldn't help staring at his scars—a puckered one on his right shoulder, a long narrow one she thought had been made by a knife ran diagonally across his chest. Her fingers brushed his bare skin as she traced another scar she couldn't identify. It wasn't a bullet wound and it didn't look like a cut from a knife. His skin was smooth and cool, his stomach ridged with muscle.

She washed the wound as best she could, bandaged it up and removed his boots, then averted her gaze as she tugged off his pants. Next, she covered him with an old quilt, hoping all the while that the doctor would get there before it was too late.

Kade woke expecting to find himself in hell. The life he'd led certainly didn't merit heaven. A quick glance around made him think he was nearer paradise than perdition. The room was good-sized and square, with white walls, and colorful rag rugs on the floor. The bed beneath him was soft, but not too soft. Morning light filtered through the lace curtains at the window.

So, where the hell was he? And how had he gotten there?

At the sound of the door knob turning, he reached for his gun, only it wasn't there. Neither were his pants. His eyes narrowed as the door swung open and a woman carrying a covered tray stepped into the room.

She was a pretty thing, with a mass of curly, dark-brown hair tied back with a red ribbon. Her deep-green eyes looked wise beyond her years. A smattering of golden freckles were sprinkled across her nose and cheeks. She wore pants that outlined a pair of long legs, and a plaid shirt that left little doubt that she was all woman.

Careful to stay out of his reach, Norrie moved closer to the bed. Her patient had looked like death warmed over last night. And didn't look much better today. "How are you feeling this morning?"

"I've been better. And worse. How long have I been here?"

"Three days. Doc Williams dug a bullet out of your side. He said you were lucky to be alive."

He grunted softly. "Who are you?"

"I'm the one who saved your life," Norrie retorted. The doctor had said as much last night. "Who are you?"

"My old man called me Kade."

The way he said it made her wonder if it was his real name. "Do you know who shot you?"

"Not exactly."

She lifted an inquiring brow.

He shrugged. "Could have been one of a dozen."

"You had *twelve* men chasing you? What did you do? Rob a bank?"

"Not this time."

Norrie stared at him. Was he joking? Or had she rescued a wanted man?

He glanced around the room. "Where's my Colt?"

"I put it away."

"Afraid I'll gun you down?"

"The thought crossed my mind," she said with asperity.

"I've never shot a woman. Yet." He jerked his chin toward the tray. "Is that for me?"

"What? Oh, yes." Setting the tray on the table beside the bed, she lifted the cloth, revealing a plate of bacon, eggs, fried potatoes, and a cup of coffee.

"You got a name?"

She wanted to refuse, but it seemed childish. "Norrie. Do you need anything else?"

He shook his head as he reached for the tray.

"You're welcome." Turning on her heel, she marched out of the room.

"Not only an outlaw," he heard her mutter before she slammed the door behind her, "but an ungrateful one at that!"

Connor McDonald stared at his daughter across the break-fast table. "I still can't believe you brought that outlaw home while I was gone. By all the Saints, daughter, what were you thinking?"

"I couldn't just leave him out there to die, could I? Besides, we don't know he's an outlaw."

Connor snorted. "The man's on the run, anybody can see that. You should have taken him into town and let the sheriff deal with him."

"He would have bled to death before I got there!"

"Good riddance, I say. We've got enough problems without you bringing more home. Where's Seth?"

She shrugged. "He went into town last night and hasn't come back."

"Probably sleeping it off at Truvy's place," her father muttered.

"Probably." Norrie liked Truvy Owens. She had been widowed young and ran the boarding house that had belonged to her husband. Truvy had a soft spot for Seth and she often let him stay the night whenever he'd had too much to drink. Which was far too often, Norrie thought bleakly.

"Doc say how long the stranger would be laid up?"

"A week. Maybe more."

Her father scowled his disapproval. "Do you know who he is?"

"He said his name's Kade."

Connor stared at her, his expression thoughtful. "I've heard that name somewheres. Can't recall just where. But it'll come to me. In the meantime, you watch yourself around him."

After clearing the table, Norrie went to collect the stranger's dishes. She had hoped to find him asleep. Instead, he was sitting up in bed, staring out the window.

His gaze swung toward her when she stepped into the room.

A shiver ran down Norrie's spine when he turned those cold, gray eyes on her. There was something in his expression, something dark and haunted and dangerous. And then it was gone and a lazy smile twitched his lips.

"Can I get you anything else?" she asked, stacking his cup and silverware on his plate.

"Another cup of coffee would be nice."

"Is that all?" she asked, her voice cool.

"I don't know." His gaze moved over her from head to heel, making her shiver everywhere it touched. "What have you got?"

"Nothing you'll ever get your hands on!" she snapped, and fled the room, slamming the door behind her.

The sound of his amused laughter chased her down the hallway.

The girl, Norrie, was a feisty thing, Kade mused. Pretty, too. And a damn good cook. Taking a deep breath, he threw back the covers and eased his legs over the edge of the bed. Hands braced on the mattress, he stood, wincing as a sharp pain lanced through his left side.

He stood there a moment, taking in the room at a glance while he waited for the pain to pass. Where the hell were his clothes? And his gunbelt? He needed to be on his way before the law came looking for him.

The law! He cursed under his breath. They hadn't seen fit to convict the man who had killed his brother in cold blood, but that was no surprise. No jury this side of the Mississippi was going to hang a white man for killing an Indian. So, he had taken the law into his own hands. That had been five years ago.

And now, after that dust up in Cheyenne a few days back, he was on the run.

Again.

Hearing footsteps in the hallway, he pulled the sheet from the bed and wrapped it around his hips. Took a deep breath. And opened the door.

He had hoped to find his pretty nurse.

Instead, he came face-to-face with a tall, gray-haired man who regarded him through inhospitable brown eyes.

"You must be feelin' better," the old man said, his voice flat.

Feeling vulnerable as hell, unarmed and wearing only a sheet, Kade nodded. "Are you lookin' for something?"

"My pants. And my gun."

"You any good with that hogleg?"

"Why? You got someone who needs killin'?"

"I might, if I ever find out who's been stealing my cattle and fouling my water."

"Afraid I can't help you. I've got troubles of my own."

"You look like a man on the run," the old man remarked, scrubbing his hand over his jaw.

"Then don't slow me down."

"My daughter saved your life. I'd say you owe me one."

"What are you asking me to do, exactly?"

"Just hang around and keep your eyes open. You look like a fella who knows how to read trail sign."

Kade's eyes narrowed. "What are you implying?"

The man shrugged. "You've got some Injun in you."

"So?"

"I'm just saying, your people are good trackers. The ones I'm looking for are good at not leaving any sign. Maybe you can see what I can't." He cocked his head to the side. "You're looking a little peaked. I'm thinking you should probably crawl back into that bed and get some rest."

"I'm thinking you're probably right."

"You want some help?"

"I can manage." Feeling light-headed, Kade turned and headed back to bed. The old man obligingly shut the door for him.

Dropping onto the mattress, he closed his eyes, his mind replaying his conversation with Norrie's father until he fell asleep.

It was late in the day when Norrie opened the door to Seth's room and peeked inside. She had expected to find Kade asleep, but the bed was empty. Had he left? Not likely, she thought with a shake of her head. If he had, he must have taken off in the nude, since his clothes were in the laundry basket in the kitchen, waiting to be ironed.

Alarm skittered down her spine when a shadow passed in front of the window. She was about to fetch her father's rifle when she realized the shadow belonged to her patient, who was slowly pacing back and forth on the side porch. What on earth was he doing out of bed so soon?

Norrie hesitated a moment, then hurried outside. She came to an abrupt halt when she saw him pacing toward her clad in nothing but a sheet. Face burning with embarrassment, she quickly turned away.

"Something you wanted?" he asked, obviously amused by her reaction.

"I...um...just wanted to see if you were...um...hungry. Supper will be ready soon."

"Starved."

It took every ounce of self-control Norrie could muster to keep from running for the door.

Kade stared after her for a moment. Of all the women he had known, she was the first one to blush at seeing a man's naked chest. It amused the hell out of him. And then he frowned. She was nothing like the women he'd known.

He needed to remember that.

Norrie refused to meet Kade's eyes when she brought him his dinner. Keeping her gaze carefully averted, she placed the tray on the bedside table and quickly left the room.

Kade had just finished eating when the old man stepped inside and closed the door behind him.

"Did you give any thought to what I said?"

"Some."

"Well?"

"I'll stick around for a few days."

"Why's the law after you?"

"I killed a man. It was a clear-cut case of self-defense, lots of witnesses. But he was white. And I'm not." He felt the bitterness wash through him again because not a single witness would come forward and tell the truth of what had happened.

"That the only man you ever killed?"

"No. A few years back, I killed the man who shot my brother."

The old man shrugged. "I can live with that. My name's Connor McDonald. I reckon I don't have to tell you to keep your hands off my daughter."

"Because I'm a wanted man?" Kade asked, a note of resentment in his tone. "Or because I'm an Indian?"

"Both."

Kade grinned, amused by McDonald's honesty. "I'll need a few more days to rest up."

"Reckon so. Remember what I said."

Surprised to find himself liking the old man, Kade watched McDonald shuffle out of the room. Fathers with daughters, he thought, with a wry grin. They were all the same.

CHAPTER TWO

"Why don't you sit with me for a while?"

Norrie stared at Kade. He wore the shirt she had washed, mended, and ironed for him. He sat on the bed, his back propped against the wall, a clean sheet covering him from the waist down. Unable to think of a practical excuse, she sat on the small rocking chair in the corner, her hands clasped in her lap, the tray at her feet. "Is there something you need?"

"I could use some company besides my own."

She glanced around the room while she tried to think of a logical reason to leave.

Kade regarded her through narrowed eyes. "You're afraid of me, aren't you?"

"Why should I be afraid in my own house?"

"I don't know. You tell me."

"My father said you've killed two men."

And more. But he didn't tell her that. "That's right. One in self-defense and one because he shot my brother in the back."

"Is that why they're after you?"

"No."

She thought about asking what else he'd done, but decided she didn't want to know. Instead, she murmured, "I'm sorry about your brother. How did it happen?"

"It happened about five years ago. We were at the trading post, doing some business. Matozi was standing at the counter where he'd just traded his furs for a new Winchester when a buffalo hunter came in and told him to put the rifle down. My brother didn't speak English and when he didn't react, the hunter pulled his gun and aimed it at Matzoi's back. When he curled his finger around the trigger, I shot the hunter but I was a fraction of a second too late. He lived just long enough to pull the trigger. They hit the floor at the same time."

Norrie stared at him.

"The guy who ran the trading post saw what happened, but he refused to admit it. A couple of drunken soldiers who came in after I pulled the trigger tried me on the spot and found me guilty. They were dragging me outside to hang me when I grabbed my rifle from the soldier who'd taken it and told them I'd kill the first man who moved. I guess they believed me. I stole the nearest horse and high-tailed it out of there. They were a piss-poor bunch of shots," he said with a wry grin. "They didn't even hit the horse." He lifted one brow. "Nothing to say, Miss McDonald?"

Norrie shook her head, too stunned to speak.

"You think what I did was wrong?"

"I don't know." Brow furrowed thoughtfully, she picked up the breakfast tray she'd brought earlier and left the room.

Connor looked up from the kitchen table. "You okay, daughter? You look a mite pale."

"I was talking to Kade. He told me what happened to his brother."

Connor lifted one brow. "You disapprove?"

"I feel like I should, but I can't help wondering how I'd feel if someone killed Seth like that." Her brother had finally come home late last night. He hadn't been happy to learn there was a stranger in his bed and declared he was going back to Truvy's until Kade was gone. Her father had put a stop to that idea.

"I'd be surprised if he hasn't killed more men than the ones he mentioned," Connor said matter-of-factly. He pushed away from the table at the sound of hoofbeats. Glancing out the window, he muttered, "We've got company coming. Looks like the law. Better tell your patient to high-tail it out the back door and go hide in the barn."

Once Kade was safely hidden in the loft, Norrie grabbed a rake and started mucking out one of the stalls. She could hear her father talking to Sheriff Lyman Dawson, assuring him that they hadn't seen hide nor hair of a stranger. "What's this fella look like?"

"We don't really know," Dawson said.

"Got a name?"

"Nope. The flyer we got was pretty vague."

"Then how do you expect to find him?"

"That's a good question," the sheriff acknowledged with a laugh. "All we know is that he's got black hair and might be Mexican or Indian or both, and he's greased lightning with a hogleg."

"Needle in a haystack," Connor said. "We got mixed bloods everywhere in this part of the country. You know that."

"That I do," Dawson agreed. "Mind if we take a look around?"

Connor shrugged. "If you feel it's necessary."

Dawson chuckled. "Probably a waste of time. No one's mentioned seeing any strangers in town." Dawson glanced at his deputy. "Bradshaw, why don't you go check the barn while I take a look around out here. That way I'll feel like we're earning our keep."

With a nod, the deputy sauntered toward the barn.

When Norrie heard footsteps coming her way, she quickly climbed the ladder to the loft and started forking hay into the stall below.

"Afternoon, Miss Norrie," Elias Bradshaw said, his smile stretching ear-to-ear.

"Good afternoon, Mr. Bradshaw. What brings you out here today?"

"We're lookin' for an escaped convict."

"I can assure you he isn't up here." She grinned as she stabbed the pitchfork into a pile of hay. "I'd know if he was." She laughed softly as she held up the pitchfork. "And he'd know it, too."

Elias laughed with her and then glanced around the barn. "Sorry to bother you," he said, with a tip of his hat.

"No bother," she said. "I hope you catch him."

He started to turn away, then paused. "There's a dance at the Grange two weeks from Saturday. I'd sure like to take you."

"I'd like that." Elias was a tall, good-looking man, with sandy blond hair and brown eyes. He had been sweet on her for over a year. His sister, Naomi, said he was hoping Norrie would marry him, as soon as he got up the nerve to ask. Norrie hoped that day would never come. She liked Elias well enough, but not enough to marry him.

With a grin and a wave, he sauntered out of the barn.

Norrie stared after Elias until she saw him ride away with Sheriff Dawson and the rest of the posse. "You can come out now."

Gaining his feet, Kade shook the hay out of his hair. "Obliged."

With a shrug, she set the pitchfork against the wall, then scooted down the ladder.

Kade followed her, grimacing as pain splintered through his side.

"You're bleeding," Norrie remarked when he reached the bottom rung.

Kade swore under his breath when he glanced at his side. In his haste to scramble up to the loft earlier, he'd apparently opened the wound again.

"Come on," she said, "I'll have to rebandage that."

Kade sat on the edge of the bed while Norrie washed the wound, patted it dry, applied a thick yellow salve and put a new dressing on it. "Sorry to be so much trouble."

"Why didn't your brother speak English?" she asked, unable to restrain her curiosity. "You do."

"He was a full-blood Lakota. We had the same mother, different fathers. My old man spoke English and insisted that I learn."

"My father thinks you've killed more than two men."

"Is that right?"

She hesitated a moment before asking, "Why are they after you now?"

"Does it matter?"

"I don't know. Maybe."

"I broke out of jail in Cheyenne. Man claimed I was cheating at cards and had me arrested."

"Were you?"

"Not that time."

Unable to help herself, Norrie grinned. She should be appalled by his behavior and his attitude. Why wasn't she? A flush warmed her cheeks when he smiled back at her.

"Thanks for patching me up again."

Gathering up the bloody bandages, she murmured, "You're welcome," as she left the room.

In the kitchen, Norrie found Seth sitting at the table, a large slice of apple pie in front of him, a sour expression on his face.

"How long's that guy gonna be here?" he asked around a mouthful of pie.

"I don't know. Dad asked him to stay on."

"What? Why?"

"Why do you think? We've only got four cowhands left since Burdett chased the rest of them off."

Seth grunted. "What we need is a gunfighter, not some 'breed."

"That's why Pa hired him."

"He's a gunfighter? What's his name?"

"Kade."

"Damn. I've heard that name. If he's the same guy, he's wanted in three counties in Texas alone."

Norrie stared at her brother. "Three? What for?"

Seth looked at her as if she wasn't too bright. "What do you think?"

Norrie sank into the chair across from her brother. Her father had said he'd be surprised if Kade had only killed two men. Looked like he'd been right. They were harboring a fugitive, a murderer. The thought sent a chill skittering down her spine.

She flinched when she heard footsteps coming down the hall. She rose quickly, hoping to leave before Kade got there, but she wasn't fast enough.

He loomed in the kitchen doorway, his brow furrowing when he saw Seth.

"Did you want something?" Norrie asked, her voice coming out in a high-pitched squeak.

"I was wondering if I could get a cup of coffee."

"Of course. Sit down." Not meeting his gaze, she filled a blue-speckled mug. "Do you take cream or sugar?" she asked, setting the cup down in front of him.

"No. This is fine."

"I ... I have laundry to fold," she murmured, and fled the room.

"You must be Norrie's brother," Kade said, taking one of the empty chairs. Seth McDonald was a lanky, good-looking kid, with a shock of wavy brown hair and mild brown eyes. His left shirt sleeve was pinned up at the elbow, where his arm ended, leaving Kade to wonder if he'd lost his arm in an accident or if it was an accident of birth.

"Yeah. I hear my Pa asked you to stay on."

Kade sat back in his chair, arms folded over his chest. "You got a problem with that?"

"Not if Pa doesn't."

"Sorry to put you out of your room. I'll find somewhere else to bed down tonight."

"I'll bunk with the hands until you're on your feet," Seth said. "We've got lots of room in the bunkhouse since most of our hands run off."

"Your old man said someone's fouling your water and running off your stock."

"Yeah. My money's on Lyle Burdett. He owns the ranch next to ours. He's got the biggest spread in the valley. That would be enough for most men, but not for Burdett. He wants it all."

"Some men are like that. Never satisfied. Any proof that it's him?"

"No. I'm pretty sure that's why Pa hired you."

"I'll ride out in a few days and have a look around. See what I can find."

Kade spent the remainder of the day resting. His side ached like the devil but he'd been hurt worse and survived. He dozed most of the time, his dreams haunted by visions of his past, of men he'd killed, of women he'd left behind.

He woke with a start, his hand automatically reaching for the gun that wasn't there when someone opened the bedroom door.

It was Norrie.

"Sorry to wake you," she said. "I thought you might be hungry since you slept through supper."

"Thanks." Sitting up, he lit the bedside lamp.

Not quite meeting his eyes, Norrie handed him the tray. "Can I get you anything else?"

"A smile might be nice."

Stifling a grin, she managed to keep her expression impassive as she said, "I'll be back later for the tray."

Kade watched her leave the room, mildly amused by her attitude. Most white women were uncomfortable around him, and given his heritage and his questionable status with the law, it wasn't surprising. But she had been friendly enough earlier and he couldn't help wondering what had changed.

CHAPTER THREE

Kade sat in the rocker on the verandah. His wound was healing, although his side was still a mite sore. He had spent a lot of time on the porch in the last ten days. It was a good place to view life on the ranch. By his count, there were only four hired hands on the place—Old Tom, Noah Singleterry, Lee Jackson, and Pete Walsh. As far as he could tell, Norrie's brother wasn't around often and wasn't much help when he was.

And then there was Norrie. She didn't like him. She didn't trust him. And yet, he didn't miss the sidelong glances she frequently sent in his direction when she thought he wasn't looking. He spent far too much time thinking about her, but, damn, she was easy on the eyes. He could hear her now, singing in the kitchen while she prepared the mid-day meal.

A shout from the corral drew his at attention. The old man was down at the corral along with the hired hands, watching Jackson trying to work the kinks out of a buckskin mare, although the cowboy wasn't having much luck. Seth perched on the top rail of the corral, shoulders hunched.

There were some whoops and hollers as the cowboy went flying over the mustang's head, followed by some shouts of encouragement as Singleterry swung into the saddle. He didn't have any more success than Jackson.

Pete Walsh was about to give it a try when Norrie rang the dinner bell.

Supper was over and the family had settled down for the night when Kade stepped outside. He had taken to walking around the ranch every night. He wasn't used to sitting around all day with nothing to do.

He strolled down to the corral. Inside, the buckskin mare paced back and forth, head high. The mustang snorted, nostrils flaring, at his approach. "Easy, girl," he murmured.

Ears twitching at the sound of his voice, the mare backed away. She stood there a moment, then sidled up to the fence.

Kade's gaze ran over the mare. She was a pretty thing, with good conformation and a little quarter horse blood somewhere down the line. He had always been partial to buckskins and this one was a beaut. Over fifteen hands high, her coat was a dark gold, her mane, tail, and stockings as black as ebony. Holding out one hand, he crooned, "Come here, darlin'."

The mare eyed him warily for several moments, then took a step forward and nosed his hand.

Kade spoke to her in Lakota as he stroked her neck and scratched her ears, stilled when he sensed someone coming up behind him. He relaxed when he realized it was Norrie. "You're up late," he remarked, glancing over his shoulder.

She shrugged. "I couldn't sleep. The men have been trying to break that mare for over a week. Dad's thinking of turning her loose."

"I'd like to buy her."

"We could sure use the money," Norrie muttered, then clapped her hand over her mouth, mortified by what she'd let slip.

"Yeah, I figured that."

She frowned at him. "How could you know?"

Kade made a broad gesture with one hand. "House needs painting. Barn needs a new roof, the doors are sagging." He shrugged. "No shame in being broke."

"It's not Dad's fault," she said, quietly. "We've lost a hundred head in the last few months due to one thing or another. But that's not the worst of it. Another five hundred have been stolen, fifty or sixty head at a time. Our payment on the mortgage is due in a few weeks and..." She blew out a sigh.

"How much do you owe?"

"Just over a thousand dollars. Dad took out a loan on the place when my mother took sick four years ago. Doc Williams couldn't help her so Dad sent her to a specialist back East. She got better for a little while and then..." Norrie cleared her throat. "Mr. Perkins at the bank was a good friend of Pa's and he let the payment slide the first year, and then agreed to let us pay just the interest. But Mr. Perkins isn't there anymore and the new man said we have to pay half the amount of the loan or they're going to foreclose on us. We're going to lose the ranch if we can't come up with the five hundred dollar minimum."

"I'm sorry to hear that. Seems like a nice place."

"I don't know what we'll do if we lose it."

Kade crossed his arms on the top rail. "I told your old man I'd see if I could find out who's been rustling your stock."

"Even if you do, it won't get our cattle back. They've probably been sold by now."

"Yeah." If it was Burdett, as Seth seemed to think, the man couldn't keep stolen stock on his property. Unless they were using a running iron to change the brand. "I'll ride out tomorrow and see what I can find. What happened to your brother's arm?"

"We were attacked by Indians soon after Seth turned sixteen. He was badly hurt. There was no doctor in the valley then. The wound festered. In hopes of saving his life, Pa amputated his arm. Seth's never really forgiven him for that. He's been angry and bitter ever since. I know he feels guilty because he can't help out more around the ranch. He does what he can, but…" She shrugged. "He feels useless here."

"That's rough."

"Sometimes I wish…" Her voice trailed off as she gazed into the distance.

"What do you wish, Norrie?"

It was the first time he'd said her name. It warmed her cheeks and did odd things in the pit of her stomach. "I wish we had stayed back east."

"How long have you been out here?"

"Almost twenty years. I don't remember much of our life in Boston except that we had a nice house and my mother smiled a lot. She was never happy after we moved out here, although she tried not to let my father know. And now we might lose the ranch. I love the land, but I can't help thinking my mother might still be alive and Seth would still have his arm if we had just stayed in Boston."

"I guess you'll never know."

"I guess not." She shivered as her gaze met his. "I'd better go."

Resisting the urge to take her in his arms, Kade nodded. "Good night, Norrie."

He stared after her until she was lost in the dark. "You won't lose this place," he murmured. "Not if I can help it."

Kade borrowed a horse from Pete Walsh and left the ranch before breakfast the next morning. The land stretched before him, shallow valleys and rolling green hills dotted with trees and cattle. A winding river shaded by cottonwoods meandered through the flatlands. He followed it for several miles until he came to a section of barbed wire. In the distance, he saw a large, two-story house flanked by a bunkhouse on one side and an over-sized barn on the other. While he watched, a dozen or so cowboys emerged from the bunkhouse and saddled up.

He watched another few minutes before heading back to the McDonald place.

Norrie glanced over her shoulder at the sound of footsteps. "There you are," she said as Kade sauntered into the kitchen. "We missed you at breakfast."

"I went out to have a look around."

"Did you find anything?"

He shrugged. "That spread to the south. Is that Burdett's place?"

"Yes."

"I'll be needing my Colt."

She stared at him, her eyes widening.

"Now."

She hesitated a moment, then left the room only to return moments later carrying his gunbelt.

He took it from her without a word, winced as he buckled it on with the ease of long practice. His fingers were quick as he lifted the Colt from the holster, checked to make sure it was loaded, and eased it back into the leather. He wore it as if it was a part of him.

And perhaps it was, Norrie thought. He had always looked dangerous. Now he looked deadly.

"Any chance I could get some breakfast?"

She gave him a curt nod. "I'll call you when it's ready."

She obviously didn't want his company. He regarded her silently for a moment then turned on his heel and left the room.

Norrie breathed a sigh of relief. She just didn't know how to feel about Kade anymore. She couldn't deny the attraction she felt for him, but he frightened her. He seemed so cold, so callous. And yet she sensed there was more to him than that. Or maybe she just hoped there was.

Norrie was still thinking about Kade later that morning as she ironed the clothes she had washed the day before. A glance out the kitchen window showed Kade and her father standing near the corral, talking.

Setting the iron aside, she moved closer to the window. She couldn't hear what they were saying, but it was obvious they were discussing the mustang. After several moments, her father nodded and the two men shook hands. So, Kade had bought the mare. As he came in the back door, she couldn't help wondering if he always got what he wanted.

"Your old man asked me to go into town and pick up some harness he left to be repaired. He said you might want to go along and do some shopping."

"Do you think you should be going into town when the Sheriff is looking for you?"

"I heard his description. Black hair, maybe Mexican or Indian. Hell, that could be half the people in the territory."

"I guess so," she said dubiously.

"Well, make up your mind. I'll be leaving as soon as I hitch up the team. Meet me at the barn if you want to go along."

She nodded, her desire to go into town overcoming her reluctance to spend time alone with Kade.

Thirty minutes later, Norrie settled on the buckboard's hard wooden seat next to Kade, her hands folded primly in her lap, a bonnet shading her face. She was all too aware of the man beside her, especially whenever the buckboard hit a rut and his thigh brushed hers. His hands were large and capable as they handled the reins. She searched her mind for something to say to break the taut silence between them, but couldn't think of a single thing.

Troubled and ill-at-ease, she fidgeted with the ribbons on her bonnet while she glanced at the passing country-side. She loved spring, when wildflowers bloomed on the distant hills and everything was green and new. A red-tailed hawk soared overhead, wings spread wide as it rode the air currents. It let out a piercing shriek as it suddenly folded its wings and arrowed toward the ground, no doubt having spied a rabbit or a squirrel. Whatever the prey was, she hoped it got away.

"You're awfully quiet," Kade remarked after a time. "Sorry you came along?"

Norrie worried her lower lip for a moment, not sure how to answer.

"Can you handle the reins?" he asked. "I can sit in the back if it'll make you more comfortable."

"That's not necessary."

"What is it about me that makes you so nervous? The fact that I'm Indian? Or that I've killed a few people?"

"The latter."

"Would it make a difference if I told you I've never killed a man in cold blood?"

"I don't know," she replied honestly. "Maybe."

"Life and death. It's what living is all about, especially here in the west where there are towns that don't have any law."

He was right, she thought. When they had first come here, Clayton's Corner had been little more than a wide spot in the road with only a saloon and a three-room hotel. There had been no law to speak of, and no one to enforce it anyway. Her father had administered justice on the ranch on his own terms on more than one occasion.

"You sweet on that deputy?" Kade asked.

Taken aback, Norrie stared at him. "Excuse me?"

"I saw the way he looked at you."

"I'm sure I don't know what you mean. And even if I did, what business is it of yours?"

He shrugged. "I was just curious. He seems ... young."

"What's wrong with that?"

Kade's gaze met hers squarely. "I'd think you'd rather have a man than a boy."

Norrie felt her cheeks grow hot. Was he implying that she would prefer a man like him?

Relief washed through her when Clayton's Corner came into view.

❧ ❧ ❧

"You can drop me off here," Norrie said, gesturing at Minton's Groceries and Dry Goods. "The blacksmith shop is the next block over."

With a nod, Kade reined the team to a halt. He grinned when she hopped to the ground before he could offer to help her.

Norrie stared after him for several moments before entering Minton's. Inside, she took a deep breath. She loved wandering through the store with its myriad smells—everything from candle wax to tobacco, lamp oil and lavender hand soap.

She nodded at Mrs. Minton as she picked up a handbasket and strolled to the grocery section in the back of the store. Humming softly, she picked up some canned goods and baking soda, a can of lard, three bars of lavender soap, a box of cigars for her father, a bag of hard candy for Seth.

She was trying on a pretty white bonnet adorned with pink straw flowers when she sensed someone behind her. She knew it was Kade before she turned around.

"Looks good on you," he said.

Embarrassed, she replaced it on the shelf.

"You should buy it."

"No. We don't have any money for fripperies."

"Let me buy it for you."

"No! No. I couldn't let you do that. It isn't seemly."

"I need to pick up some new clothes," Kade remarked, glancing at the south side of the store where the menswear was located.

"Very well," she said. "I'll wait for you outside."

"It won't take me long."

Norrie sent a last, longing look at the bonnet, then hurried toward the front of the shop.

Kade stared after her, a faint smile curving his lips as he sauntered toward a stack of shirts piled on a shelf. It didn't take long to pick out a couple of shirts and two pairs of pants. It took a little longer to find a new black Stetson to replace the one he'd lost.

He made one more stop before going to the front to pay for his purchases.

Kade found Norrie waiting for him on the buckboard. In addition to the other things she'd bought, he saw a twenty-pound sack of flour and a ten-pound bag of sugar. She had loaded her purchases in the back and he dropped his packages besides hers—all but one. Swinging up on the seat beside her, he handed it to her.

"What's this?" she asked.

"Open it and see."

Curious, she removed the wrappings, let out a gasp of surprise when she saw the bonnet. "You shouldn't have," she said, trailing the bright pink ribbons through her fingers. "I told you, it isn't seemly for a man to buy apparel for a woman."

"Nonsense. You saved my life. It's the least I can do. Besides," he said, with a wink. "It looked right pretty on you."

She murmured her thanks and then, not quite meeting his eyes, she said, "Your new hat looks good on you, too."

Chapter Four

After dropping Norrie off at the house, Kade unhitched the team. He dropped off the harness he'd picked up from the blacksmith, then saddled one of the ranch horses and rode back to town.

Dismounting in front of the Three Queens Saloon, he dropped the reins over the hitch rack and ambled inside. He had spotted Norrie's brother in there earlier. A quick glance around showed Seth was deep in a poker game. And losing badly.

Kade watched for the next twenty minutes, then strolled over to the table and stood behind an empty chair. "Mind if I sit in?"

Three of the men looked up at him. One, wearing a brown slouch hat, said, "We'll be happy to take your money, stranger."

"You're welcome to try," Kade remarked, pulling the chair away from the table.

Seth stared at him when he sat down. "My pa send you?"

"No."

For the next half hour or so, there was little conversation. Seth lost four hands in a row. Kade won three, which didn't go unnoticed or unremarked.

A cowboy wearing a fancy vest said, "I'd hate to think you were cheatin', mister."

Kade shrugged. "No need. You're the worst poker player I've ever seen."

Red-faced, the man snarled, "Why you dirty, stinkin' Injun…"

The man closed his mouth with a snap when he found himself looking down the barrel of Kade's Colt.

A sudden silence fell over the table as the other players exchanged nervous glances.

"Go on," Kade said, his voice silky-soft with menace. "Let's hear the rest of it."

Fancy Vest swallowed hard. "I didn't mean nothin'."

"Uh-huh. You've been dealing from the bottom of the deck. By my reckoning, you cheated the kid here out of a hundred bucks."

Fancy Vest started to deny it but one look into Kade's narrowed eyes changed his mind. Hands shaking, he counted out a hundred dollars and slid the cash across the table toward Seth.

Kade stood. "Let's go, kid."

Seth started to argue but thought better of it. Pushing out of his chair, he scooped up the greenbacks and headed for the door.

Kade's gaze swept over the card players. "Guns on the table," he said quietly. "All of you."

He waited until they complied before picking up his winnings with his free hand. "Don't try to follow us," he warned as he backed toward the door.

Seth was waiting for him outside.

"Let's get the hell out of here," Kade said as he took up his horse's reins and swung into the saddle, quietly damning himself for drawing attention to himself. All he needed was for someone to tell the Sheriff about the trouble that some half-breed stranger had caused in the saloon.

Seth hauled himself into the saddle and drummed his heels into his mount's sides. The gelding took off at a gallop, with Kade close on its heels.

They didn't slow down until the town was far behind them.

"Did Norrie send you after me?" Seth asked, his expression sullen.

"No. I saw you in there earlier."

"In the future, mind your own damn business."

"I get the feeling your old man's got some money troubles. Do you really think you should be gambling with what little you've got?"

"My luck could have changed," Seth muttered sullenly. "I might have won."

Kade snorted his contempt. "No way. All three of them were cheating."

"Takes one to know one, I guess."

"That's right." Kade pulled a wad of cash out of his pocket and handed it to Norrie's brother. "When we get to the ranch, give that to your old man. I won two hundred and forty dollars. With the hundred you've got, that over half of the payment that's due."

Seth stared at the greenbacks and then at Kade. "What the hell! Were *you* cheating, too?"

"Does it matter?"

"No. I guess not."

"Do you want your room back?"

The kid shoved the greenbacks into his shirt pocket. "Nah. I like sacking out in the bunkhouse. Keeps Norrie from nagging me."

Kade grinned at him. "Don't tell your old man where that money came from. Let him think you won it all."

Norrie was sweeping the front porch when Kade rode up to the house.

"Was that Seth I saw with you?" she asked, shading her eyes against the setting sun.

"Yeah. He's gone down to the bunkhouse."

She lifted one brow, waiting for an explanation, but none was forthcoming. "I offered to move out of his room, but…"

Kade shrugged. "He said he was happy bedding down with the hands."

"Of course he is," she said with a knowing grin. "You might want to get washed up. Supper's almost ready."

Norrie sighed as she stacked the dishes in the cupboard. What were they going to do about Seth? She had been surprised at dinner when he thrust a handful of cash into her father's hand and said he'd won it playing poker. She was happy about the money, of course. Adding the money Seth had won to the cash they'd managed to save would be enough to make the first half of the mortgage payment. On the other hand, she didn't like knowing her brother was hanging out in one of the saloons in town. She didn't know how much money Seth had started out with, but he could just as easily have lost it all as won.

And then there was Kade. He had been quiet at supper, but she'd felt her cheeks grow warm with embarrassment every time he looked her way. What was wrong with her?

Removing her apron, she dropped it over the back of a chair and went out on the verandah for a breath of fresh air.

"Beautiful night."

She whirled around, a frisson of excitement unfurling deep within her at the sound of Kade's voice. There was a creak as he rose from the swing, the soft sound of footsteps as he came to stand beside her.

"Yes," she said. "Yes, it is." He was close, so close. Even though she couldn't see him clearly in the faint light of the moon, she could feel his gaze on her face. It was exciting and a little unnerving, being alone with him in the dark of the night. She told herself there was nothing to fear. Her father and brother were having a game of chess in the house. They would come running if she called.

But she didn't. She waited. Shivered when she felt his fingers thread through her hair.

"Norrie?"

Just her name, softly spoken, his breath warm against her cheek. She looked up at him, wishing she could see his face, but he was bending down, blocking what little moonlight there was. And then he was kissing her, his lips firm against her own, one arm sliding around her waist to draw her body against his.

And it was too late to call for help. She closed her eyes, her body all atremble as he kissed her again, and yet again. She had only been kissed a few times before. Once behind the barn when she was thirteen. More recently by Elias Bradshaw. But they faded into distant memory as Kade deepened the kiss.

"You out here, daughter?"

Before she could answer, Kade was gone.

CHAPTER FIVE

Saturday morning dawned bright and clear. Norrie looked up in surprise when Seth strolled into the kitchen. "What happened?" she asked. "Did Truvy throw you out?"

Seth snorted. "Hardly. I came home for a bath and a change of clothes. I'm taking her to the dance tonight. I hear you're going with Elias."

"Do you have a problem with that?" She filled a plate with bacon and eggs and handed it to him.

Seth poured himself a cup of coffee, then pulled out a chair and sat down. "It's nothing to me who you go out with."

"I thought you liked him."

Seth shrugged. "Where's Kade?"

"I don't know. I haven't seen him this morning."

"Do you think he's as bad as he makes out?"

"Who's bad?" Connor asked striding into the room.

"Kade."

Connor glanced around the kitchen. "Where is he?"

"Still asleep, I guess."

Connor grunted as he reached for the coffee pot. "I'm going out on the south range to look around after breakfast," he said as he filled his cup before taking the chair across from Seth's. "I want the both of you to stay close to home. Seth, tell Jackson to ride out and check the waterhole and send Pete and Noah to mend that broken stretch of fence to the north."

"Something going on, Pa?" Norrie asked, setting a plate in front of him.

"I'm not sure. I just want to go have a look around. "

"Don't forget about the Grange dance tonight," Norrie said. "I'm sure the Widow Brown is looking forward to seeing you."

Connor groaned. "Don't remind me."

"You know you're sweet on her," Seth said with a grin. "Heck, everybody knows."

Connor made a dismissive wave with his hand.

Norrie's heart skipped a beat when Kade entered the kitchen. She felt a rush of heat warm her cheeks when his gaze met hers. Was he remembering last night and the kisses they had shared? Had the memory kept him up until the wee hours of the morning?

"Sorry I'm late," he drawled. Leaving his hat on the rack, he took a place at the long oak table.

"I want you to stick close to the house today," Connor told him. "Keep an eye on things."

"Sure," Kade said, still watching Norrie. "No problem."

Connor pushed away from the table and reached for his Stetson. "I'll be back in time for supper."

"Be careful, Pa," Norrie called as he headed out the door.

"Where's he going?" Kade asked.

"He wants to take a look at the south range," Norrie said, handing him a plate piled high.

Kade grunted softly as he tucked into his breakfast. He hadn't eaten this good in years.

"I'll be down at the bunkhouse if you need me," Seth said, pushing away from the table. "See ya later at the dance."

Norrie filled a plate for herself and sat across from Kade, her gaze lowered as the memory of the kisses they had shared last night again jumped to the forefront of her mind.

He didn't say anything for a few moments, then asked, "Are you going to look at me this morning?"

"Why wouldn't I?"

"I don't know. You tell me."

She felt herself blushing as she lifted her gaze to his.

"That's better. So, what's this I hear about a dance?"

"At the grange tonight," she said. "Seth is taking Truvy."

"Who's taking you?"

"Deputy Bradshaw."

He grunted softly. "I didn't know you were spoken for."

"I'm not!" she exclaimed. "If I was, I certainly wouldn't have … I'm not."

"That's good to know. I'd hate to think I was fishing in another man's stream," he said, and grinned as the pink in her cheeks turned red.

Glaring at him, she lurched to her feet and grabbed his plate. "I'm sure you have work to do somewhere," she said with asperity. "Maybe you should get to it."

Stifling the urge to laugh, Kade pushed away from the table, winked at her, and sauntered out of the kitchen.

Angry enough to spit, she threw his plate against the door, wishing she could swear like her Pa and Seth.

With nothing else to do, Kade strolled down to the corral and ducked inside. The mare shied away from him, trotting to the far side of the pen where she regarded him warily, her fox-like ears twitching back and forth.

"Hey, girl, we're friends, remember," he crooned as he walked slowly toward her, one hand outstretched. "You've got no reason to be afraid of me."

The buckskin huffed a breath, tossed her head, and sniffed his hand.

"That's my girl." He ran his hands down the length of her neck, over her withers and across her back, murmuring to her in Lakota the whole time. Moving to the other side, he repeated the process, stroking his hands over her neck and back, and down her legs.

Reaching into his jeans, he pulled out a cube of sugar that he'd taken from the table and offered it to her. She sniffed it once and took it from his hand and nosed his pocket, looking for more.

"Next time," he promised. Draping his arm over the mare's neck, he took a step forward, pleased when she moved with him. He walked the buckskin around the corral like that, first one way and then the other, talking to the mare all the time.

Norrie watched Kade from the kitchen window, the dishes in the sink forgotten. She had never seen anyone win a horse's trust in that fashion. Was it some sort of Indian way of gentling horses? She shivered as she watched him run his hands—those big brown hands—over the mare. What would it be like to feel those hands…?

She thrust her wicked thoughts aside, blushed from head to foot when he turned to look up at the house. Lord have mercy, had he seen her staring?

She quickly ducked out of sight, ran up to her room, and shut the door. How would she ever face him again?

She remained in her room until suppertime, pretending she was mending her dress and using any other excuse she could think of to keep from going downstairs until she couldn't put it off any longer.

Determined to ignore Kade, she made her way into the kitchen to start supper.

Fully aware of Norrie's embarrassment, Kade spent the day down at the barn. He helped Seth curry the horses and muck the stalls, and then sat in the shade cleaning his Colt while Seth took a nap.

Norrie's earlier reaction amused him. He had spent little time in the company of decent women and he was a little confused by her discomfort. He had kissed her a few times and caught her watching him while he gentled the mare. It hardly seemed worth fretting over, but what did he know?

After missing the mid-day meal, he wasn't in the mood to go without supper, as well. He waited until he knew Connor and Seth were in the house before he entered the kitchen. He nodded at both men before taking a seat at the table.

"Everything all right out on the south range?" Seth asked.

Connor nodded. "Near as I can tell. I found a dead cow, but it looks like a pack of wolves brought her down."

Kade sat back, listening idly as the men discussed ranch affairs. Norrie ignored him completely.

"Appreciate your helping out down at the barn today, Kade," the old man said.

"Happy to do it."

"I saw you working with that mustang," Seth remarked. "You've got a way with horses."

"A little petting, a little sweet talk, and they'll eat out of your hand every time."

"That works with Truvy, too," Seth said with a grin.

Connor snorted. "You're still wet behind the ears, boy. I don't know about Kade, but you've still got a lot to learn."

The tips of Seth's ears turned red. "I know what I'm doing."

Connor stared at him. "You're not thinking about getting married, are you?"

"Maybe."

McDonald snorted. "You're barely twenty years old, with no job. How the hell are you gonna support a wife?"

"I'll find a way," Seth replied sullenly.

"Well, I need to go upstairs and get dressed," Norrie said, rising. "Seth, you can do the dishes tonight."

"What? Me?"

"Yes. You." Without waiting for further argument, she hurried out of the kitchen.

"I need to get ready, too," Connor said, pushing away from the table.

"Pa…"

"You heard what she said, boy. I'll see you later, in town."

Seth slammed his hand on the table top, hard enough to make the silverware dance. "He treats me like a kid," he muttered, his voice bitter.

"Then stop acting like one," Kade said. "Where's this dance?"

"At the Grange Hall in town." Seth glared at the dirty dishes. "Guess I'd better get those dishes washed up," he muttered. "Women's work."

Stifling the urge to laugh at the boy's sullen expression, Kade went down the hall to his room. He regarded the new shirts and pants he'd bought. They weren't fancy but he figured they were good enough for a country dance, if he was of a mind to go. Was he? Probably a bad idea, what with being wanted by the law. Still, no one in town knew who he was or where he'd come from, or anything else about him. With a shake of his head, he changed clothes, then went outside and sat on the porch.

Half an hour later, a buggy pulled into the yard driven by a tall, lanky man with short, sandy blond hair. He wore a white shirt, a black string tie, and a pair of brown whipcord britches. Bradshaw, no doubt. He reined the horse to a stop in front of the porch and hopped down from the seat.

The deputy frowned when he saw Kade. "Who might you be?"

"Name's Kade. I work here. And you are?"

"Elias Bradshaw. I've come to fetch Miss Norrie."

"I'm here," Norrie called as she stepped out on the porch, a covered plate in her hand.

Kade felt his breath catch in his throat when he saw her. Pretty as a spring day in the high country, she was, clad in a pale yellow dress, her hair pulled back at her nape and tied with a white ribbon.

Norrie hesitated when she saw Kade., felt her cheeks flush when his gaze met hers. Clearing her throat, she said, "Mr. Bradshaw, this is Kade."

"We've met," Elias said curtly. "Are you ready, Miss Norrie?"

"Yes." Bradshaw helped her with her coat, followed her down the steps, and handed her up on the seat before swinging up beside her.

Norrie didn't look back as they drove out of the yard.

Kade grunted softly. What did Norrie see in that guy? The deputy looked like he'd turn tail and run at the first sign of trouble. He sat there a few more minutes, then strode down to the barn and threw a saddle on one of the horses.

Norrie glanced around as Elias went to hang up her coat. The Grange had been decorated with colorful streamers, the long tables covered with white cloths. She left the cake she had made on the refreshment table, nodded to the sheriff and his wife.

Harry Lawson and his brother, Deke, were tuning up their fiddles while Alma Tripp ran her fingers over the piano keys.

"It looks like the whole town turned out," Elias remarked, coming up beside her.

"I know. I think our last get-together was last November." She waved to Seth, who had just arrived with Truvy Owens in tow. Truvy was a pretty young woman, with curly blonde hair, blue eyes, and rosy cheeks. Seth didn't seem to mind that she was three years older than he was.

"Hey, sis," he said. "Big crowd tonight."

"Yes." Norrie smiled at Truvy. "It's good to see you again."

"It's been a while," Truvy replied.

"How are things at the boardinghouse?"

Truvy shrugged. "It's hard, but Seth's a big help. I don't know what I'd do without him."

"It's always nice to have willing help," Norrie agreed, an edge in her voice as she recalled all the times Seth had made excuses to avoid doing any work around the ranch.

Seth flushed under her accusing stare.

A few minutes later, Harry Lawson stepped up to the front of the makeshift stage, fiddle in hand. "All right, gents, find your favorite gal for the Ten Step Polka."

Norrie loved to dance and even though she had come with Elias, she danced with several of the other men, which was not unusual, since the men outnumbered the women two to one.

She was waltzing with old Mr. Watson when Kade cut in. Norrie gaped at him as he took her in his arms. "What are you doing here?"

"Dancing with the prettiest girl on the floor."

"But…you're a wanted man," she whispered, mindful of the other couples around them. "The sheriff and Elias are both here."

He shrugged one shoulder. "No one knows who I am. They don't have much of a description."

"But…"

"Stop worrying, Norrie. I can take care of myself."

"It's not you I'm worried about," she retorted.

Kade glanced around. "The only man armed is the sheriff and he's got no cause to come after me."

She glanced down, surprised and relieved to see that Kade wasn't wearing his Colt.

Elias came to claim her when the band announced they were taking a break.

Kade moved to the sidelines. Standing in the shadows, he watched Norrie. He could see she was well-liked in the community by men and women alike. When dancing resumed, she was never without a partner. He couldn't take his eyes off her. Her cheeks were flushed, her eyes bright with excitement as she followed the intricate steps of a square dance.

The thought of her marrying Bradshaw left a bad taste in his mouth. He told himself it was none of his business.

He was just passing through. But the thought rankled just the same.

He was about to go out for some fresh air when he saw the sheriff headed his way.

Best not to duck out and make the man think he had something to hide, he thought. "Evening, Sheriff."

"Lyman Dawson. I don't think we've met."

"No, we haven't." Dawson was a tall, raw-boned man with dark brown hair and a penetrating gaze. Kade had the feeling he didn't miss much.

"Have you been in town long?" the sheriff asked.

"No."

"Are you planning to stay?"

"I'm not sure." Kade jerked his chin toward Norrie's father, who was smiling at a pretty woman with gray hair. "Connor McDonald said he was short-handed and asked me to stay on through the winter." It was mostly true.

"I see. Where are you from?"

"The Dakotas, originally."

The sheriff grunted. "Indian country."

Kade nodded.

"If I took a look through the Wanted posters in my office, would I find you there?"

"No, sir."

"Keep it that way."

"I intend to."

The Sheriff studied him a long moment. Then, with a curt nod, he turned away.

Kade grunted softly as Dawson paused to talk to McDonald, no doubt checking his story.

The party was about over when there was a ruckus outside, which drew everyone's attention. Kade followed the crowd out of the hall. Four men were fighting in the street while a saloon girl looked on.

Hollering for Elias, Dawson plowed into the fray to break it up. It didn't take long. All four men were drunk. The crowd applauded as the two lawmen escorted the troublemakers down the street to the jail.

Kade drifted over to where Norrie stood with her father, Seth, and Truvy.

"Looks like you'll need a ride home, daughter," McDonald said. "I reckon Elias will be busy for a while. Seth…?"

"I'm spending the night at Truvy's. Why can't you take her, Pa?"

McDonald flushed a bright red.

"I can take Norrie home," Kade offered.

Seth and his father stared at each other.

McDonald cleared his throat. "You can take the buggy Elias rented. I'll make it right with him later."

"Thank you, Kade," Norrie said with exaggerated politeness. "Just let me get my coat."

CHAPTER SIX

Kade tied his horse to the back of the buggy before set-tling onto the seat beside Norrie. Taking up the reins, he clucked to the gelding and it took off at a brisk trot.

Norrie was keenly aware of Kade's hard-muscled thigh brushing against hers every time the buggy hit a rut in the road. They rode in awkward silence for several minutes.

"Are you gonna marry that deputy?" Kade asked abruptly.

"What?"

"The deputy. He's sweet on you."

"That's really none of your business."

Kade shrugged. "From what I saw tonight, it doesn't seem like you've got a lot of choices other than Bradshaw, that skinny farmer with the freckles, or the old man."

Norrie glared at him. And then she sighed. Her choices weren't quite that limited, but she didn't find any of the men her age the least bit appealing—unlike Kade, who attracted her far more than she wanted to admit. Just looking at him made her heart skip a beat. He was tall and ruggedly hand-some. A man in every sense of the word, unlike Elias, who seemed like a callow youth when compared to Kade.

"You've got a lot of scars," she blurted, then slapped her hand over her mouth. What on earth had made her say such a thing?

"A few."

"I guess it's not surprising. I mean…" Her voice trailed off.

"I know what you mean," he said, his voice harsh.

"Kade…"

"No, you're right. I've lived a violent life and I've got the scars to prove it. Gunfights, knife fights. I can take off my shirt and show you the ones on my back."

"Kade, stop it."

He looked at her, his eyes narrowed.

"I'm sorry," she said, forcing herself to meet his gaze. "I shouldn't judge you. I don't know anything about you or the kind of life you've lived."

"No, you don't."

A heavy silence fell between.

At home, Norrie jumped from the seat and hurried into the house. After a moment, she peered out the front window.

Kade was still there, looking pensive. She watched him until he clucked to the horse and headed down to the barn.

With a sigh, she turned away from the window. She lit one of the lamps, took off her coat and dropped it on a chair. Dropping down on the sofa, she removed her shoes and stockings and wiggled her toes. It wasn't often she was home alone at night and she'd never liked it. The silence closed in around her.

She tensed when the door opened and Kade entered the house.

He was a wanted man, on the run for murder and who knew what else. And they were alone.

He lifted one brow, lips twitching in a wry grin. "Relax," he drawled.

"I don't know what you mean," she retorted. "I'm perfectly relaxed."

"Honey, if you were wound up any tighter, you'd go spinning around the room."

She opened her mouth to protest and closed it just as quickly.

"Mind if I sit down?"

She shook her head, relieved when he took the beat-up old easy chair instead of sitting on the sofa.

He stretched his long legs out in front of him, his elbows resting on the arms as he regarded her. "I get the feeling you'd like to ask about my past but don't have the nerve."

Meeting his gaze head on, she said, "You're right."

"I was born in the Black Hills. My old man was a trapper. My mother was Lakota, like I told you. They met quite by accident. She didn't speak English, but he spoke a little Lakota. I guess it was love at first sight because he followed her home. The Lakota made him welcome and after a year or so, they married."

"What about your brother?"

"My mother was a widow when she met my father. Matozi was five or six by the time I came along."

"And he never learned English?"

Kade shook his head. "My old man wanted to teach him, but Matozi hated the *wasichu* and refused to learn."

"The wasi-chu?"

"It's Lakota for white man."

"So, you never went back to your mother's people after your brother died?"

"No."

"How old were you?"

"Seventeen."

"Where did you go? What did you do?"

"I hid out in the Badlands for a while and then I lit out for Montana. I drifted from town to town for a couple of years. And then one night I won a Colt in a card game…"

"Where did you learn to play cards?"

"My old man. He said there might come a day when I'd want to see what civilization looked like, so he taught me how to shoot, how to fight, and how to hold my liquor. And how to play every kind of poker there is."

"A well-rounded education," she said dryly. "Did he teach you how to read and write, too?"

"No." Kade smiled faintly at the memory. "A pretty little red-headed schoolteacher in Deadwood taught me one summer."

Seeing the way he smiled made her wonder what else the red-headed schoolmarm had taught him. "Are your parents still living?"

"I don't know." He stared off into the distance for a moment, his expression thoughtful. "Like I said, I've never gone back home."

"Have you ever been married?"

"Not even close. Anything else you need to know?"

She fidgeted, thinking he was clearly amused by her questions. "Sorry. I…I guess I'm just curious. Well, I think I'll go up to bed."

He stood when she did. For a timeless moment, their gazes met. Anticipation unfurled deep within her when his arm curled around her waist, drawing her close. She closed her eyes when he bent his head toward hers. His lips were warm and firm and she leaned into him, wanting to be closer. His hand stroked up and down her back and she lost all track of time, forgot everything but his mouth on hers, the strength of his arms around her, the press of his hard-muscled body against the softness of her own.

Her lips felt bereft when, with a muttered oath, he thrust her away from him.

"You'd better go to bed," he growled. "I won't be responsible for what happens if you stay."

It took her a moment to grasp his meaning. And then she turned and fled the room.

Kade unleashed a string of oaths as he listened to her footsteps as she ran up the stairs to her room and slammed the door behind her.

When Kade rose in the morning, Norrie still hadn't come downstairs. He had just poured himself a second cup of coffee when her brother and her old man sauntered into the kitchen.

"Where's Norrie?" McDonald asked as he pulled a mug from the cupboard.

Kade shrugged. "She hasn't come down yet."

Seth and McDonald exchanged glances.

"Is she all right?" Seth asked.

"She was fine last I saw her."

"And when was that?" McDonald asked.

"When she went up to bed last night."

McDonald's eyes narrowed suspiciously. "Did she go alone?"

A muscle twitched in Kade's jaw. "I don't think I like what you're implying."

"It was a simple question."

"She went alone." Kade glanced over his shoulder at the sound of footsteps coming down the stairs. "If you don't believe me, ask her yourself."

Norrie paused in the kitchen doorway as three pairs of eyes swung her way. The tension in the kitchen was palpable. "Is something wrong?"

"I don't know, " McDonald said. "You tell me."

Norrie frowned. "I don't understand."

"Your old man wants to know if you spent the night alone," Kade said, his voice flat.

Cheeks flaming, she stared at her father, then turned and ran out the back door.

"Now you've done it, Pa," Seth muttered. "We're gonna have to fix our own breakfast."

Kade glanced from one man to the other, shook his head, and followed Norrie out the back door. He stood there a few minutes, giving her time to cool down, before trailing her across the yard.

He found her in the barn, tightening the saddle cinch on a pretty little bay mare.

"Don't talk to me." Face set in a determined line, she swung onto the mare's back, and galloped out of the yard.

Kade stood there a moment, weighing her need for privacy against the danger of letting her ride out alone. It didn't take long to make up his mind. He threw a bridle on one of the other horses, swung onto its bare back, and hightailed it out after her.

Respecting her need to be alone, he kept his distance. She rode like she'd been born to the saddle, her hair streaming behind her.

Kade blew out a sigh. It felt good to be riding across open prairie with nobody chasing him. He loved the feel of the wind in his face, the pulsing power of the horse as it effortlessly jumped a narrow ribbon of water. The sky was vast and blue, the distant hills covered with trees. A red-tailed hawk soared high overhead. It was almost like being home, he thought as he crested a hill. *Home.* He rarely let himself think of it, but Norrie's questions the night before had reminded him of how much he had loved it. And how much he missed it.

He slowed when Norrie did, trotted up beside her when she stopped alongside a shallow brook.

She flashed him an angry glance. "What are you doing here?"

He shrugged. "I didn't like the idea of you riding off alone."

"I can take care of myself."

"Uh-huh."

With a toss of her head, she dismounted. Sitting at the stream's edge, she removed her boots and stockings and dangled her feet in the water.

After a moment, he joined her, but not too close.

"What right do either of them have to ask me such a question?" Norrie muttered irritably. "Seth spends the night at Truvy's all the time. And Pa…" She shook her head. "The whole town knows he spends the night at the Widow Brown's house from time to time. Why is it all right for them and not for me?"

"I don't know, darlin'," he said. "But it's always been that way."

Her shoulders sagged as she let out a sigh. "Sometimes I wish I was a man."

"I'm almighty glad you're not."

She sent him a sideways glance, but there was no anger in it. "I guess you've made love to a lot of women."

Kade stared at her in astonishment, and then he threw back his head and laughed.

"What's so funny?"

"I've known a lot of women, and they've asked a lot of questions, but never that one."

She turned her head to the side, but not before he saw the blush that climbed into her cheeks. Damn, but she was prettier than a rose in a field of dandelions. And he wanted her, wanted to lay her down in the soft grass along the edge of the water and discover what lay beneath her plaid shirt and jeans.

Norrie bit down on her lower lip when she felt him staring at her. Slowly, she turned to face him, felt her cheeks burn hotter when she saw the way he was looking at her. His gaze moved to her lips and lingered there for a long moment.

Her heart thundered in her ears as he closed the distance between them. For stretched seconds, he just looked at her—and then he reached for her. It never occurred to her to pull away. He was going to kiss her. His hand cupped the back of her head as his mouth slanted over hers. And she was lost. No one had ever kissed her like this. Elias had kissed her a couple of times, chaste little pecks that stirred nothing inside her, but Kade . . . she clung to him as he kissed her again, and yet again, each more intense, more intimate, than the last.

He lifted his hand, his fingers threading through her hair. "Damn, girl," he murmured, and kissed her again as he fell back on the grass, pulling her down with him so that they lay side by side, their bodies pressed so close together she didn't know where his ended and hers began. And she didn't care. All she wanted was his mouth on hers, his arms around her.

He sat up abruptly, his gaze sweeping the area. "Get up, Norrie. Get on your horse and ride like hell for home."

"What is it? What's wrong?" Lordy, had her father found them?

"Norrie! Get the hell out of here."

She let out a cry of alarm when she saw riders in the distance. Indians! Spurred by the urgency of Kade's tone, she grabbed the reins, swung into the saddle, and kicked the mare into a gallop.

CHAPTER SEVEN

Kade cursed softly as he gained his feet and swung onto his horse's back. Dammit, he'd left his gun at home.

He saw the riders clearly now, six of them mounted on paint ponies, feathers tied into their long black hair. They were armed with a couple of rifles, bows and arrows. The lead rider had a deer carcass slung over the withers of his horse.

Hunters, he thought, and breathed a sigh of relief.

He lifted his hand in greeting as the warriors drew rein in a loose circle around him. "*Hau, tahunsa.*"

The lead warrior stared at him. "You speak our tongue?"

"I am *Tahatan Wakina,* of the Lakota nation."

"I am *Mila Sapa.*"

"What brings my brothers to my land?"

The warrior gestured at the deer carcass.

Kade nodded. "May the hunting always be good for my brothers."

"*Ai.* And for you. Why did the woman run away?"

"It seemed wise, until I learned who you were."

Mila Sapa's lips twitched in a half-smile.

Kade swept his arm in broad gesture that encompassed the land around them. "If game grows scarce this winter, my brother is welcome to take whatever he needs from my herd."

"*Pilamaya, kola.*" With a wave of his hand, Mila Sapa turned his horse back the way he had come. The other warriors fell in behind him.

Kade stayed where he was until they were out of sight. He hadn't missed the long blond scalps braided into the manes of two of the Lakota horses.

Norrie paced back and forth on the front porch, her gaze scanning the distance. What was taking Kade so long to get back to the ranch? Was he all right? What if the Indians had captured him? Or worse?

Seth and her father had both been gone when she arrived. The coffee pot was still warm, the sink full of dirty dishes, so they hadn't been gone long.

Her pulse quickened when she saw dust in the distance. And then Kade came into view and she released the breath she hadn't realized she'd been holding. Relief washed through her when he reached the house. Sliding from the back of the horse, he tossed the reins over the hitch rack.

"What happened back there?" she asked anxiously.

"Nothing."

"Nothing?"

He shrugged. "Half a dozen Indians came riding up."

Her face paled as she gripped the porch rail.

"Hunters," he explained. "They weren't looking for a fight."

Her breath whooshed out of her in a sigh of relief. "Thank goodness. We haven't had any trouble with the Indians for years."

"I hope it stays that way. What are you doing out here? Were you worried about me?"

She started to deny it, then nodded. "Of course. Just like I would have been worried about Noah or Jackson."

His smile said he knew she was lying.

"Any chance I could talk you into making me a late breakfast?" he asked.

"Yes, but only because I haven't eaten either."

He followed her into the house, sat at the kitchen table while she fried up a mess of ham and eggs and filled two cups with hot coffee.

Feeling self-conscious, Norrie put the plates, silverware and cups on the table before taking the chair across from his. The silence between them made her uncomfortable. Was he thinking about the kisses they had shared? Or did men just kiss and forget? Abruptly, she said, "Do you think we're in any danger from the Indians?"

"No. Things have been quiet in this part of the country for a long time now."

"Did you know any of them?"

He shook his head. "They were Brule. I'm Oglala. Different tribes of the same nation."

"I thought they were all the same."

"No. There are seven tribes in the Lakota nation."

"Do you miss living with the Indians?"

"Yeah. It's a good way to live."

She fell silent.

Kade grinned inwardly. He could see the questions already forming in that curious mind of hers. But she didn't ask them.

As soon as the meal was over, she rose and began clearing the table. Sensing that she wanted to be alone, he left the house. Taking up the reins of the horse he'd ridden, he made his way down to the barn. Inside, he gave the horse a good brushing, led the gelding into a stall, and forked it some hay.

Leaving the stable, he sauntered over to the corral. The mustang snorted when she saw him.

"About time we got better acquainted," Kade drawled. Returning to the barn, he found a saddle blanket and a saddle and carried them into the corral. Plucking a rope from a post, he lassoed the mustang and braced his heels as she backed away. "Easy, girl," he murmured. "No one's going to hurt you."

He stood in the middle of the corral, letting her get used to the feel of the rope around her neck. When she stopped fighting it, he walked toward her, his hand outstretched. She nosed his palm, then blew softly.

Kade snubbed her to a post, then picked up the blanket. The mustang eyed it warily as he walked toward her. "Just relax," he crooned. He let her smell the blanket before he ran it over her neck, her shoulder, her back, and down her legs, talking softly to her all while.

Finally, he placed the blanket on her back and left it there. "See? Nothing to be afraid of," he said as he scratched her ears.

He stood there for twenty minutes or so, just talking to her, letting her get used to the weight of blanket. Next, he picked up the saddle. "Easy, now," he said as she backed away. "This won't hurt at all."

Her ears twitched back and forth as he set the saddle in place and tightened the cinch, just enough so that the saddle wouldn't slip sideways. Taking hold of the rope, he walked her around the corral. She crow-hopped a couple of times then settled down.

He walked her one way and then the other and then stopped. "That's enough for one day." He removed the saddle and the blanket and set them on the top rail of the corral.

Lifting the rope from around her neck, he stroked her neck and scratched her ears for several minutes before ducking out of the corral and heading back up to the house.

Norrie stepped away from the kitchen window, awed by what she'd seen. She had watched cowboys break horses most of her life, but she had never seen anything like that. The cowboys usually snubbed the horse to a post, cinched the saddle in place, climbed aboard, and let her rip.

Norrie smiled faintly as she realized Kade didn't want to break the horse's spirit. Instead, he wanted to gain the mare's trust. Was he that gentle, that patient, with women, too, she wondered, as she imagined what it would be like to feel those strong, brown hands moving over her, gentling her to his touch.

Muttering, "Stop it!" she turned away from the window, gasped, "Kade," when she saw him standing behind her. She had been so lost in her wayward thoughts, she hadn't even noticed that he had left the corral. Merciful heavens, had he seen her staring again?

Before either of them spoke, her father stomped into the house.

"Norrie?"

"In the kitchen, Pa."

"Where the hell did you go in such a huff this morning?"

"Nowhere. Just out." She glared at him, her anger rising all over again.

McDonald cleared his throat. "Kade, I'd like to speak to my daughter alone."

With a curt nod, Kade went out the back door.

McDonald pulled a chair from the table. "Sit down, Norrie." When she was seated, he took the chair across from her. "I want to know what's going on between you and that gunfighter."

"Nothing is going on," she said, bristling at his tone.

"He followed you outside this morning. Where did you go?"

"Nowhere. I just rode for a while."

"Did he go with you?"

"He followed me. And it's a good thing he did," she snapped.

"Yeah? Why is that?"

"Because we ran into some Indians, that's why. Kade sent me away while he confronted them."

"Indians?" McDonald swore. "How many?"

"I think he said six."

"Did he say anything about what happened?"

"Just that they were hunters."

McDonald scrubbed a hand over his jaw. It had been a while since they'd had any Indian trouble. "I'm sorry for this morning," he said gruffly. "I spoke out of turn. But you stay away from him, hear?"

"I'm a big girl, Pa. I'm older than Seth, but I don't hear you telling him who he can and can't see."

"It's different with boys," her father said, not meeting her eyes. Pushing away from the table, he said, "Call me when dinner's ready."

Norrie glared at his back as he hurried out the door. Seth could smoke and drink and carouse until the cows came home because he was a man and it was expected.

Muttering under her breath about the unfairness of it all, she gathered the ingredients for beef stew, berating the entire male sex the whole time.

❧ ❧ ❧

Kade looked up from the bridle he was mending when he saw McDonald striding toward him. Here it comes, he thought. The third degree.

"Norrie tells me you run across some Indians this afternoon."

"That's right."

McDonald grunted softly. "We haven't seen any Indian sign for more than three years."

"They weren't looking for trouble, just game."

"Did you palaver with them?"

"Yeah. I told them if they got hungry they could take a couple of your cows."

"You what?"

"I didn't think you'd mind. Better for them to take a few head with your permission than fight you for them."

Connor's brow furrowed as he thought that over. And then he nodded. "I reckon so. I've seen how Norrie looks at you," he said, his voice hard. "I'm telling you flat out to keep your hands off my girl. She's got no experience with men. Especially men like you."

A muscle twitched in Kade's jaw. "Put your mind at rest, McDonald. I've got no intention of hurting her."

"Just as long as we understand each other."

"Oh, we do," Kade muttered darkly.

He understood all too well.

CHAPTER EIGHT

The next morning after breakfast, Kade threw a saddle on the buckskin mare. He led the mustang around the corral for a few minutes before he stepped into the leather. She looked back at him, as though surprised to see him there, then took off around the corral, bucking and crow-hopping, but it was half-hearted at best. When she settled down, he opened the corral gate and rode away from the house, headed east.

The mare had a smooth, easy canter and he rode for several miles, his mind empty of everything but the vast sea of grass around him and the bold blue sky overhead. It reminded him of home... of the buffalo hunts in the fall and the spring, the Sun Dance in the summer, winters spent in the Black Hills, where tall buttes and spires reached toward the sky. He had a sudden longing to see the Hills again, to explore the Badlands.

He slowed when he saw smoke rising from a line shack off to his left. Curious, he reined the mare in that direction. A chestnut gelding wearing the McDonald brand stood at the hitching post, its ears twitching as he rode up.

Dismounting, Kade tethered the mare, a prickle of unease running down his spine when he noticed the door was open. He saw the body as soon as he stepped inside. The man had been shot once, in the chest, at close range.

There was no sign of a struggle. Flies swarmed over the dried blood.

Moving closer, Kade recognized Pete Walsh, one of McDonald's hired hands.

Pulling a blanket from the cot, Kade wrapped it around the body, then carried it outside and dumped it face-down over the chestnut's saddle.

He went back into the shack for a last look around, but saw nothing that might indicate who the shooter had been.

Outside again, he checked the ground for sign, but it hadn't rained recently and the dirt was rock-hard. After closing the door to the shack, he swung onto the mustang's back, took up the chestnut's reins and headed back to the ranch.

The cowhand known as Old Tom was sitting on the front porch when Kade rode up to the house.

Pushing to his feet, the old man hobbled down the stairs. "That's Pete's horse, ain't it? Is he …?"

Kade nodded. "Afraid so. I found him at the line shack."

Old Tom shook his head ruefully.

"Where's McDonald?"

"He rode in a short while ago. Reckon he's still down at the barn."

Kade found McDonald rubbing down his horse.

Connor looked up, brows rushing together when he saw the body. "What happened?"

"I don't know." Dismounting, Kade hitched the mustang to a post. "I found him at the east line shack. Shot once in the chest. Looks like he's been dead for a day or two."

McDonald swore. "Damn Burdett. I'd bet every dollar I own he's responsible for this." He blew out a harsh breath.

"Pete's mother lives in town. I sure hate to take her news like this." He paused. "Thanks for bringing Pete back," he said as he saddled his horse again. "I'll drop him off at the undertaker's on my way to see his mother. Tell Norrie where I've gone, will ya?"

With a nod, Kade unsaddled the mustang, then turned her loose in the corral, where she immediately dropped down and rolled onto her back.

Grinning, Kade sauntered up to the house. He found Norrie in the kitchen, peeling apples.

"I saw you ride in," she said, her gaze searching his. "Was that Pete?"

"Yeah."

"What happened to him?"

"He was shot, up at the line shack."

"When?"

"Probably sometime yesterday, maybe the day before."

Her brows shot up. "We were near there yesterday. If only we'd stopped by..."

"Don't go there," Kade said quietly. "He died instantly. Nothing you could have done would have made any difference. Your old man's taking the body into town."

"Poor Mrs. Walsh. Pete was her only child."

"That's rough."

She stared off into the distance a moment, took a deep breath, and sighed. "Do you know who did it?"

"No. Your dad thinks it was Burdett."

"I'm sure he's right."

Hoping to take her mind off Pete's death, Kade jerked his chin toward the half-peeled apple in her hand. "Any chance you're making an apple pie?"

"What?" She looked at him blankly for a moment, then glanced down. "Oh, yes."

Kade winked at her. "It's my favorite."

Talk at the dinner table was subdued that night. Seth reminisced about some of the wild times he and Pete had had in town, then fell silent.

"How did Mrs. Walsh take the news?" Norrie asked.

"Hard," her father said. "Real hard. Times are gonna be rough for her without him. He always gave her half of his pay, you know. I, uh, told her I'd send her Pete's things, and a few dollars every month to make up for it."

"We can't afford that," Seth said. "We can barely make the payroll now."

"We'll get by." McDonald glanced at Kade. Changing the subject, he said, "I see you broke the mustang."

Kade sat out on the front porch step later that night, after everyone had gone to bed. Overhead, a million stars glittered against the black velvet sky. According to Lakota legend, every baby born was given a *wanagi*, a sort of sky spirit. When a person died, his *wanagi* returned to the stars.

His thoughts turned to Norrie. Being around her had made him realize how long it had been since he'd held a woman he cared for, and care for her he did. Far more than he should. McDonald had warned him to leave his daughter alone and Kade had agreed simply to avoid an argument. But Connor McDonald had more important things to worry about now, like who had killed Walsh. And why.

Tomorrow, he'd ride back to the line shack and take another look around, though he doubted he'd find anything. Whoever the killer was, he'd been careful not to leave any sign behind.

He was thinking about turning in the for night when the front door opened. He knew it was Norrie before she sat on the step beside him.

"Pete's death keeping you awake?" he asked.

"Yes. I feel so bad for his mother. She never wanted to come out here because she was afraid something like this would happen. And now it has."

"Life's a gamble, no matter where you live."

"What's keeping you awake?"

Turning to face her, he said, "You are."

"Oh."

"Your father told me to stay away from you. Is that what you want?"

"No," she whispered. "I don't want that."

When he slid his arm around her waist, she scooted closer, until her thigh rested against his. Holding her gaze, Kade kissed her lightly. When she leaned into him, he deepened the kiss, his tongue stroking hers.

Norrie let out a little gasp of pleasure as desire unfolded deep within her, as warm and welcome as summer sunshine. No one had ever kissed her like that, she thought, and wished he would never stop.

"It's getting late," Kade murmured against her lips. "You should get some rest."

"Kiss me good night?"

He cupped her face in his palms and pressed his mouth to hers. "Sweet dreams, Norrie."

"Good night, Kade."

He gave her time to get inside and go up the stairs before he made his way to Seth's room.

Sleep was a long time coming.

❧ ❧ ❧

When Norrie woke in the morning, her first thought was for Kade and the kisses they had shared the night before. She told herself she couldn't be falling in love with him. They had just met. She hardly knew anything about him. He was wanted by the law. But none of that seemed to matter.

She dressed with care, brushed out her hair and tied it at her nape with a red ribbon, pinched her cheeks and then hurried downstairs.

The men were already at the table. One of them had made coffee. She flushed when she caught Kade watching her while she fried bacon, scrambled a dozen eggs, and mixed batter for flapjacks.

She was so aware of Kade's presence, she scarcely paid attention to the conversation at the table until Kade said he was riding up to the line shack to have another look around. He was watching her when he said it. Was he asking her to go along?

"We'll be gone until late," her father said. "I'm riding out to look at the herd in the south pasture. I'm taking Seth and Old Tom with me. Jackson's staying close to the house today. I advise you to do the same, Norrie. Let's go, Seth. The day's not getting any younger."

Kade stood and poured himself another cup of coffee while Norrie filled the sink with hot water.

"What do you think you'll find up there?" she asked, plunging her hands into the soapy water.

Kade shrugged. "Probably nothing, but it's worth a second look." He took his Stetson from the rack and settled it on his head. "Stay close to the house."

"I'm coming with you."

"Your old man told you to stay here."

"I'm a big girl now."

His gaze moved over her, lingering a moment on her breasts. "I can't argue with that. I'll saddle your horse while you get ready."

Riding alongside Kade, Norrie searched for something to break the silence between them but nothing came to mind. All she could think about was the way he had looked at her earlier, the way the heat in his eyes had warmed her from head to foot. She told herself that the kisses they had shared had nothing to do with why she'd wanted to go with him this morning, but it was a lie. Her being here now had everything to do with the fire in his eyes and the kisses they had shared last night.

She had a feeling he knew it, too.

He confirmed it minutes later when he pulled up in the shade of a pine tree. Dismounting, he lifted her from the back of her horse and kissed her, a long slow kiss that sent heat lightning humming along every nerve and fiber in her body.

Wrapping her arms around his neck, she closed her eyes and leaned into him. His tongue teased hers as his hands skimmed up and down her back.

Still holding her close, he drew her down on the grass until they lay side by side, their bodies intimately pressed together. Norrie clung to him, lost in his touch. No other man had ever held her like this, kissed her like this, or made her feel the way she did now, alive and trembling with need. It was exciting. It was frightening.

She let out a soft cry of protest when he lifted his head. "What's wrong?"

"Have you ever been with a man before?"

She blinked at him. What kind of question was that to ask at such a time, she wondered, and then felt her cheeks grow hot. He was asking if she was still a maiden!

Filled with righteous indignation, she scrambled to her feet.

Kade sat up. "Norrie, I…"

"Don't speak to me! How dare you think that I…that I've ever… Oh!"

Getting to his feet, he pulled her back into his arms. "I didn't mean to imply you were a loose woman…"

"No?" She glared at him, her eyes flashing fire. "Just what did you mean, then?"

He swore under his breath, wishing he'd kept his mouth shut. "I'm sorry. I forget how young you are."

"I'm not young!" she exclaimed indignantly. "I'm twenty-two!"

And innocent as a newborn babe, he thought. And yet she responded to his kisses with a passion he had rarely known. Not the practiced kind the whores used, but that of a woman only now discovering the pleasures to be had between a man and a woman. And he yearned to teach her, but, dammit, she was untouched. And although he'd done a lot of despicable things in his time, he had never deflowered a virgin, or taken a woman by force. He grinned inwardly, because there was no doubt in his mind that Norrie was his for the taking.

Putting his hands around her waist, he lifted her onto the back of the bay. "We're supposed to be looking for some sign of who killed Walsh, remember?"

Feeling that her humiliation was complete, Norrie took up the reins and kicked her horse into a gallop.

Kade stared after her a moment, bemused by his feelings, before he vaulted into the saddle, settled his hat on his head, and lit out after her.

He caught up with Norrie outside the line shack. "You gonna stay mad at me all day?" he asked, dismounting.

She shrugged, waited a moment, then slid from the saddle. "What are we looking for?"

So it was going to be like that, Kade mused, and wondered how long it would take to smooth her ruffled feathers.

"Anything that looks out of place. A hoof print. A shell casing. Anything. Why don't you look inside and I'll check out here."

With a curt nod, she pushed the door of the shack open and stepped inside.

Muttering, "Oh, hell," Kade tethered the horses, then made a slow circle of the cabin, his gaze sweeping back and forth in ever-widening circles. He found a partial hoofprint but not enough to tell him anything.

When he returned to the shack, he found Norrie waiting for him outside.

"Anything?" he asked.

She shook her head. "You?"

"No."

Norrie ran her hands up and down her arms as the tension grew between them.

He reached for her then, slowly drawing her into his embrace. "I'm sorry," he said quietly. "I didn't mean to offend you. I just don't want to hurt you. Or take advantage of you."

She wanted to stay mad at him, but how could she when it felt so good to be in his arms?

"Come on," he said, kissing her brow, "I'd better get you back home before your old man comes gunning for me."

CHAPTER NINE

"Married?" Seth stared at Truvy, completely taken aback by the sudden change of topic. They had been talking about replacing the curtains in the front parlor of the boardinghouse when she'd suddenly mentioned marriage. "I can't afford a wife."

"It wouldn't be much different than it is now." Truvy snuggled closer to him on the bed. "Except that you could share my room openly instead of pretending you're renting one."

Seth ran his fingers through his hair. "I know, but married…"

"I thought you loved me," she said, her voice subdued.

"I do, honey. You know I do."

"And you could work here, with me. I don't think I can run the place without you."

Rising, Seth paced the bedroom floor. Everything she said was true. His dad didn't really need him out at the ranch. They both knew he wasn't much help. Ranching required a man with a strong back and two good hands. Someone like Kade, he thought, dropping down on the edge of the bed.

"Seth?"

"Sorry, what?"

"If you don't want to marry me … well … maybe it's time I find someone who does."

"No! Truvy, you know I love you! It's just that I…" He stared at the floor, all his old feelings of being less than a man welling up inside him.

"Seth, I love you just the way you are." Leaning down, she kissed him, let out a squeal when he pulled her down into his lap.

"And I love you." Taking a deep breath, he said, "Truvy Owens, will you marry me?"

"Oh, Seth!" she said, laughing and crying at the same time. "You know I will!"

CHAPTER TEN

Norrie sensed an underlying tension at the table during breakfast the next morning. Was it only guilt she felt for sneaking off with Kade, or was there something else going on that she wasn't aware of?

Seth had left for town yesterday as soon as he returned to the ranch and they hadn't seen him since.

They were half-way through breakfast when her father said, "We're mighty short-handed without Pete. And who knows when Seth will come home, so, Kade, I'll need you to ride out and check the southern fence line today."

"All right by me."

"Norrie, I want you to take Old Tom and go out and check the waterholes and the river."

"Where will you be, Pa?"

"I'm going to go ride the eastern boundary between our land and Burdett's."

"Do you think you should go alone?"

"I'm taking Noah with me. Jackson's gonna stay here and keep an eye on things." McDonald ate in silence for a few moments. "Where'd you go yesterday, Norrie? Jackson said you were gone a good long time."

Norrie felt the tension at the table increase as she risked a glance in Kade's direction.

He lifted one shoulder and let it fall.

"I rode out to the line shack with Kade to see if we could find any sign of who killed Pete."

"I see." McDonald fixed his gaze on Kade. "Since no one said anything to me about it, I'm guessing you didn't find anything."

"Part of a hoof print," Kade said. "That was all."

Norrie's hand tightened on her coffee cup as the two men stared at each other.

McDonald grunted softly, then drained the last of his coffee and pushed away from the table. "Keep a sharp eye out, you two," he said, plucking his hat from the rack. "Be home before dark."

"What was that all about?" Norrie asked when they were alone.

"Just your old man's way of reminding me to keep my hands off you."

"Oh." Norrie bit down on her lower lip. Surely her father didn't think anything had happened between them?

"Practically the first thing he ever said to me."

"I thought he trusted me," Norrie muttered.

"It's me he doesn't trust, not you. He's your father, Norrie. You can't blame him for worrying about you." Getting up from the table, he said, "I'll see you tonight."

"Aren't you going to kiss me?"

Knowing it was wrong, but unable to resist, he leaned down, cupped her face in his palms and kissed her. He had intended it to be a quick touch of his lips to hers, but she was so sweet, so eager, he lifted her to her feet, his hands spanning her waist to draw her closer. With a little sigh, she pressed against him, her breasts soft and warm against his chest. One kiss melted into two, and then three.

He might have swung her into his arms and carried her to bed if Seth hadn't chosen that moment to clomp into the house.

"What the hell!" he exclaimed.

Norrie scooted out of Kade's embrace as if someone had lit a fire under her feet. Cheeks awash with embarrassment, she stared at her brother.

"Does Pa know you're carrying on like this?" Seth asked.

"Of course not! And you aren't going to tell him."

"No?"

"No. Or I'm going to tell him about that bottle of whiskey you keep in the bottom drawer of your dresser, and maybe let it slip that the Sheriff arrested you a couple of weeks ago for being drunk and disorderly."

"How'd you hear about that?"

"None of your business."

Seth glanced at Kade, his brow furrowed. "You sweet on my sister, or just looking for…" His voice trailed off as Kade's eyes narrowed ominously.

"You'd best not say anything unkind about your sister in my hearing," Kade warned. "She's a fine woman. And she hasn't done a damn thing wrong. You got that?"

Seth's head bobbed up and down, his face suddenly pale.

"I'm glad we understand each other."

Seth nodded again.

Kade glanced at Norrie, then grabbed his hat and left the house.

"Norrie, what the hell are you thinking?" Seth exclaimed. "He's an outlaw! Probably a gunfighter. Don't get me wrong, I like him, but he's no fit company for you."

"Why don't you take Old Tom and go check the waterholes and the river?"

"Where's Pa?"

"He's riding the eastern fence line with Noah."

"And what are you gonna do?"

"Clean the house. Unless you'd rather do it?"

Seth frowned at her. "What makes me think you're supposed to go check the waterholes with Old Tom?"

Norrie felt a rush of telltale heat rise in her cheeks. "I was, but now you're here, so you can do it."

"Where was Kade going?"

"Pa told him to check the southern fence line."

"Why do I think you'll be headed in that direction as soon as I'm gone?"

Norrie glared at him. "Never mind what I'm doing. Go find Old Tom."

"Pa won't like it," Seth muttered as he turned and headed for the back door.

Norrie stared after him. Seth was right. Pa wouldn't like it. But she'd deal with that later.

She quickly washed the dishes, left them on the counter to dry, and hurried down to the barn to saddle her horse.

Kade drew the mustang to a halt as a rider crested a low hill behind him. He knew immediately that it was Norrie, though he had no idea how she had found him. Still, he couldn't deny the rush of pleasure he felt at seeing her.

He smiled as she rode up beside him, her cheeks flushed, her eyes sparkling. "Weren't you supposed to be checking the waterholes with Old Tom?"

She shrugged. "I sent Seth in my place. Do you mind?"

"Not a bit. Happy for the company."

He clucked to the mustang and she moved out. Norrie rode beside him.

"Have you found anything?" she asked.

"No. The fence looks fine. I found a dead calf. Looks like a wolf kill."

"It happens," she said with a shrug.

They rode in silence for a time. Norrie couldn't stop looking at Kade. His profile was sharp and clean, his jaw firm and square. She had never seen a more handsome man, not that she'd seen that many men. Clayton's Corner was a small town in the middle of nowhere. She blushed when he caught her staring.

"Something wrong?" he asked.

"No."

She was so young, he thought, not for the first time. So innocent in the ways of men and women. He was far too old for her. It had nothing to do with age, but with experience.

They had ridden for several miles when Kade reined the mustang to a halt in the shade of a tree and dismounted. "Let's sit for a while," he suggested.

Nodding, Norrie lifted her canteen from the horn and slid out of the saddle. "It's so pretty here," she remarked. "It's one of my favorite places. I often come here when I want to be alone."

She sank down on a patch of grass shaded by a willow tree.

After a moment, Kade hunkered down beside her. "I can see why." A narrow stream meandered a few feet away. Wildflowers grew in scattered clumps along the shore. Birds twittered in the branches overhead.

Norrie smiled as she reached for a bright yellow flower, only to freeze when she heard an ominous rattle. Afraid to move, she looked at Kade in time to see him draw and fire before the snake could strike. Blue-gray smoke curled from the barrel of his Colt.

She stared at him, her heart pounding in her ears as she realized the outcome might have been far different. She had never been so close to a rattler before. Sure, she'd seen them from a distance, but this...

She blew out a shaky breath as he reached behind her, picked up the rattler and tossed it aside. It was the biggest snake she had ever seen.

"You all right?" he asked as he ejected the spent shell, replaced it, and then slid his Colt back into the holster.

"Y...yes. I've never seen anyone draw that fast."

"Yeah, well, I've had a lot of practice."

She glanced around. "Do you think there are any more?"

"I doubt it. I don't suppose you brought any food along?"

"There are apples and sugar cookies in my saddlebag."

Rising, he looked in her saddlebags and found two apples and several cookies wrapped in a white towel. Sitting again, he offered her one of the apples.

She took it with a hand that trembled slightly. "I've never been that close to a rattlesnake before."

"He probably wouldn't have bit you," Kade said, "but I didn't want to take that chance."

"Thank you."

They sat in companionable silence for a while. Kade offered their apple cores to the horses, who quickly gobbled them down.

"My mare likes cookies, too," Norrie remarked.

"Yeah, a lot of horses have a sweet tooth," he said, his gaze meeting hers. "I've got one myself."

He wasn't talking about cookies, she thought, and felt a shiver of pleasure.

"You're a good cook."

"Thank you. Not as good as my mom, though."

"I guess you miss her."

"Every day. It's hard to be the only woman on the ranch. Sometimes Pa treats me like one of the hired hands. Especially since Seth lost his arm."

"That's rough." His gaze moved over her from head to foot. "I can't imagine anyone mistaking you for one of the boys."

Norrie's whole being grew warm, inside and out, as he looked at her. Without conscious thought, she leaned forward, felt a prickle of anticipation as his arm curled around her waist, drawing her close as his mouth covered hers in a long, searing kiss that left her breathless.

"Damn, girl," he muttered as he put her away from him. "Who taught you to kiss like that?"

Stifling a grin, she murmured, "You did."

Kade stared at her and then laughed. "I'm a hell of a teacher," he said, and reached for her again.

The sound of hoofbeats brought Kade to his feet, his hand resting on the butt of his Colt.

"Who is it?" Norrie asked.

"It's Seth."

"Seth?" Shading her eyes, she stared toward the oncoming rider. "What's he doing out here, I wonder?"

"Reckon we'll find out."

"Norrie!" Seth hollered as he drew rein beside her. "Pa's been shot!"

"Shot!" She scrambled to her feet. "Is he all right?"

Tears welled in her brother's eyes as he dismounted. "He's dead."

"No!" Norrie shook her head in denial. "No, he can't be. How...Who...?"

"What does it matter who did it?" Seth asked, his voice choked with unshed tears as he wrapped his arm around her. "He's gone."

They stood together for a few moments, only the sound of their shared tears breaking the silence.

"We should get back," Norrie said. "We need to notify the sheriff and … and look after Pa."

With a nod, Seth mounted his horse.

Wiping her eyes, Norrie glanced at Kade.

He longed to take her in his arms and offer what comfort he could. Instead, he lifted her into the saddle. "Go on. I'll be right behind you."

When they reached the house, Seth and Norrie hurried inside.

Kade took their horses down to the barn. Dismounting, he unsaddled all three animals and forked them some hay.

A short time later, he saw Noah Singleterry leave the house. The cowboy looked badly shaken, which was to be expected, Kade thought. He was lucky to be alive.

"What happened?" Kade asked as Singleterry neared the barn, then dropped down on a bale of hay.

"We were ambushed on our way home," Noah said. "My horse bolted at the sound of gunfire. By the time I got back to the boss, he was dead, plugged clean through the heart."

"Any chance you got a look who shot him?"

"No."

"Trail sign? Hoof prints?"

"No. The ground was too soft to hold a print."

"Are the other hands up at the house with the family?"

"Yeah. I couldn't stay. I couldn't face his kids." Singleterry raked his fingers through his hair. "Well, hell! I should have done something."

"If your horse hadn't bolted, you'd probably be dead now, too."

"Yeah." Singleterry looked at Kade through guilt-filled eyes. "But it doesn't make me feel any better."

Norrie sat on the edge of her bed, staring into the darkness. The sheriff and the doctor had come and gone though she had no memory of what they had said or done. Nothing seemed real. She couldn't believe her father was dead. He had always been there, strong and dependable. Jackson and Old Tom had comforted her and Seth as best as they could, but their words had fallen on deaf ears. Her father was gone and all the words in the world wouldn't bring him back.

Unable to sleep, she went downstairs for a glass of water.

"I guess you couldn't sleep, either."

"Seth. I didn't see you." Finding a match, she lit a lamp, her need for a drink forgotten as she sat at the kitchen table across from her brother. "What are we going to do now?"

He shrugged. "I don't know. Sell the ranch and move into town, I guess."

"You'd sell this place?"

"We can't run it on our own," he said. "I'll be surprised if Noah is still here after the funeral. So that really just leaves us with Jackson and Old Tom, and you know Tom ain't much help. Hell, neither am I."

"We have Kade," Norrie said.

"I doubt if he'll stick around." Seth took a deep breath and expelled it in a rush. "I meant to tell you this earlier, you and Pa ... I asked Truvy to marry me the other night and she said yes. She wants me to live in town and help her run the boardinghouse."

Norrie stared at her brother in disbelief. "You want to sell the ranch and move into town, just like that?"

"You know I'm useless around here. Burdett will give us a good price for the land…"

"Burdett! How can you even think of selling to that man when he's likely the one who killed Pa?"

"You don't know that. If we sell, you can use your half to move into town, buy a place of your own. And I'll be able to help Truvy fix up the boardinghouse, maybe add a few rooms."

"I don't want to live in town." Blinking back her tears, Norrie pushed away from the table. "I'm not selling," she cried, and ran out the back door.

And straight into Kade's arms.

"Whoa, girl," he murmured. "Where do you think you're going in the middle of the night?" His gaze moved over her. "In your nightgown."

She looked up at him, tears swimming in her eyes.

"Norrie?"

"I was… I was hoping to find you."

"I'm here." Drawing her into his arms, he stroked her hair, her back. "I'm sorry about your old man."

"Seth wants to sell the ranch. To Burdett!"

"And you don't."

"No. Pa wouldn't sell. I think Burdett killed him."

Kade wiped the tears from her cheeks with the pads of his thumbs. "You shouldn't be making decisions right now. Wait a while."

"Seth's getting married. He's already made plans for his half of the money."

"I'm sorry, darlin'."

"You won't leave me… I mean, leave us… will you?"

His gaze searched hers. And then he shook his head. "I'm not going anywhere."

CHAPTER ELEVEN

They held the funeral the following afternoon. It was a simple affair, conducted at the family plot on a small hill behind the barn. Kade noted there were two headstones already in place, one for Norrie's mother, and one for Daniel McDonald, who had died shortly after being born.

Norrie and Seth stood side by side, holding hands. Truvy stood on Seth's other side, with Lee Jackson, Noah Singleterry and Old Tom behind them. Several of the townspeople, including Sheriff Dawson and Elias Bradshaw, fanned out behind the family, heads bowed, as the town minister prayed over the coffin.

Kade lingered near the edge of the crowd, all too conscious of the fact that he was still a wanted man and that there was always a chance the Sheriff's Office had received a flyer carrying more than the color of his hair and his ethnicity.

When the service was over, he ducked out of sight but stayed close enough to keep an eye on Norrie.

"Your father was a good man," Mr. Oatman said. "He helped me out more than once."

"Thank you," Norrie said. Hal Oatman lived east of the ranch. His wife had recently passed away.

"So sorry to hear of your loss," Marvene Saunders said, taking Norrie's hand in hers. "If there's anything me and Floyd can do, we'd be happy to help."

Norrie nodded and forced a smile as her neighbors came forward to offer her and Seth condolences. Many of the women had brought food, as was customary. Cakes and casseroles, a pot of beef stew, a loaf of freshly baked bread.

"We'll find the man who did this," Sheriff Dawson assured her. "And we'll make him pay."

"We know who did it," she said flatly. "It was Burdett."

"We need proof," Dawson said, not unkindly. "Not just your suspicions."

"He's fouled our water. He's stolen our cattle. He's…"

The Sheriff held up his hand. "I know what you think. And I reckon you might be right. But I can't prove it. And I can't arrest him until I can." He looked at Seth. "If you find anything, anything at all, you let me know."

"I will," Seth said. "Thanks for coming."

With a tip of his hat, Dawson went to get his horse.

"I'm right sorry, Miss Norrie," Elias Bradshaw said, hat in hand. "I hope, when your mourning period is over, I might call on you again."

"Mr. Bradshaw, this really isn't a good time."

"I know. I just…I mean…" Red-faced, he jammed his Stetson on his head and hurried after Dawson.

"I'm glad that's over," Seth said as he watched the two lawmen ride away. "Pa's lawyer took me aside before the funeral. We need to go into town on Monday for the reading of the Will."

"I don't even want to think about that now," Norrie said.

Seth laid a hand on her shoulder. "We can order a headstone for Pa while we're there."

Norrie nodded as she took a last look at the grave, then headed for the house. Where was Kade? She had expected him to be at the grave side, but then, the presence of Sheriff

Dawson and his deputy had likely kept him away. Not that she could blame him.

Still, she couldn't help wondering if he had decided to ride on.

Norrie served one of the casseroles for dinner, though she had little appetite, and even less interest in chatting with Truvy, who had decided to stay and visit with them for a while.

"Did Seth tell you our good news?" Truvy asked brightly.

"Yes. Congratulations, both of you," Norrie said without much enthusiasm. "Have you set a date?"

"No, but it should be as soon as possible."

"Oh?"

Truvy's cheeks flushed bright pink when she glanced at Seth. "We're going to have a baby."

Seth blinked at her as if she had grown another head. "A...a baby? You? Us?"

"I didn't want to say anything until I knew you really wanted to marry me."

Seth swallowed hard. "When?"

"Near as I can figure, about five months from now."

He stood up, then sat down again, hard. "A...a baby? In five months?"

"You two should be alone," Norrie said. Lurching to her feet, she fled the house.

She didn't know whether to be happy for Seth or beat him with a stick. He would be no help at all to her now, what with a new bride and a baby on the way. How was she going to run the ranch without him? He would want to sell for sure now.

Blinking tears from her eyes, she almost plowed into Kade, who seemed to appear in front of her as if by magic.

"Easy, now," he exclaimed softly. "That's the second time you've come barreling into me."

"I'm sorry," she said, and burst into tears.

He held her close while she cried. She'd had a hell of a day. When her tears subsided, he led her toward the old swing in the backyard and pulled her down beside him. "I don't think all those tears are for your old man," he said quietly. "What else is bothering you?"

"Truvy...she's...she's in a family way. Seth's going to be twice as eager to sell the ranch now. And how can I refuse when he'll have a wife and a baby to support?"

"That's his responsibility. Not yours."

"I know, but...but he's my brother."

"He shouldn't expect you to give up the ranch because of his decisions. This is your home."

"But it's half his."

"Maybe you could buy him out."

"I can't even meet the next mortgage payment. How am I going to give him half of what the place is worth?"

"I could rob the bank."

Norrie stared at him, wide-eyed with shock.

"It was just an idea," Kade said, grinning.

"Well, it's a terrible one."

"I know. I wasn't serious." He slipped his arm around her shoulders. "Don't think about it now. You're got plenty of time to decide what to do."

"We have to go into town tomorrow and talk to Pa's lawyer. Will you go with us?"

"Sure, darlin', if you want me to."

The way he caressed the word *darlin'* made her heart skip a beat. "Thank you, Kade. I don't know what I'd … we'd … do without you."

They met with the lawyer at two o'clock the following afternoon. Norrie sat beside her brother, curiosity mingling with her grief as she waited for Mr. Thompson to read the Will. She had no idea what to expect. Kade stood behind her chair, one hand resting lightly on her shoulder. Seth's face was grim.

Connor McDonald's Last Will and Testament was short and to the point. He left everything he had to his children, to be split equally, with two stipulations—both parties had to agree to any sale. If only one party wanted to sell the ranch, their right to it was forfeit. In such a case, the sibling who wished to sell would be entitled to five thousand dollars when he or she reached the age of twenty-five. Until then, the money would be held in trust.

Seth stormed out of the lawyer's office after the reading of the Will.

"Thank you, Mr. Thompson," Norrie said, shaking the lawyer's hand.

After clearing his throat, the lawyer said, "I hesitate to tell you this under the circumstances, but I talked to your father the day before he was killed. He was going to change his Will. I wrote up a rough draft and he was coming in tomorrow morning to look it over before it was finalized. He was going to use part of that five thousand to pay off the mortgage."

Norrie felt as if she had been punched in the stomach. All this could have been so easily avoided if her father had just acted a few days sooner. Now, according to the terms of the Will, Seth would be entitled to the money if he wanted to sell, but not until he was twenty-five, and even then, it wouldn't do her any good.

She nodded at Mr. Thompson, glanced at Kade, then walked out of the office.

Kade trailed behind her. "Are you going to go look for Seth?"

"I'm sure he's in the nearest saloon."

"Reckon so. Do you want me to go after him?"

"No." She gathered her horse's reins and put her foot in the stirrup, then glanced over her shoulder. "Are you coming?"

"Yeah." Taking up the mustang's reins, he swung into the saddle and followed her out of town.

Old Tom was sitting on the porch when they got home. One look at his face and Kade knew he had bad news.

"Noah done quit 'bout an hour ago," Tom said. "Just saddled up his horse and lit out."

Norrie dismounted and tethered her horse. "Without his pay?"

Old Tom nodded.

"Didn't he say anything?"

"Just said he was sorry."

With a nod, she went up the stairs and into the house.

Kade grunted softly as he took up the reins to Norrie's horse and rode down to the barn.

He had a bad feeling about this.

Norrie dropped into one of the kitchen chairs, laid her head on her arms and wept.

Maybe selling the ranch was the right thing to do. She had two hired hands and no ready cash. She couldn't help wondering how long Jackson would stay. Old Tom wasn't much help around the ranch. Her father had kept him on the payroll because the old man had no family and nowhere else to go. She couldn't count on Kade to stick around indefinitely.

Seth would certainly want to leave now. Truvy wanted to get married as soon as possible, what with the baby and all. Seth had never liked the ranch, and since he'd lost his arm, he had felt useless.

What was she going to do?

Lifting her head, she wiped her eyes. There was no use in crying about it. She only had two options—sell the ranch to Burdett and move into town, or stay and fight.

"How can I sell this place, Pa?" she murmured. "How can I give up everything you worked so hard for and just ride away and leave you and Mama behind? How can I let Burdett win? How can I…? Her voice trailed off when she realized she was no longer alone. Sometime during her crying spell Kade had quietly entered the back door.

"You're not alone, Norrie," he said, drawing her into his arms. "I've got an idea. Not sure you'll like it, though."

"Right now I'm open to just about anything."

"I saw some Indian sign on the way home. What would you think about hiring some of my people?"

"Indians?" She looked up at him, eyes wide and a little scared. "Are you serious?"

"Yeah. You can pay them off in cattle instead of cash. Your herd is pretty small now. Why don't you keep a hundred head and sell the rest to one of your neighbors? That'll give you some money to help with the mortgage. We could round up a herd of mustangs, break them and sell them to the Army. They pay damn good money for a well-broke mount." And if that didn't work out, he could probably win a fair amount at the poker table, at least enough to hold off the bank for a while, and put groceries on the table.

"Sell the cattle," Norrie murmured, her brow furrowed. "That's not a bad idea. But hire Indians? I don't know."

"Trust me, they'll do a good job. And no one rides better."

"I'll have to discuss it with Seth."

"Do you want me to talk to him?"

"No. No, it's my responsibility. If he doesn't come home tonight, I'll ride in to town tomorrow afternoon. Thank you, Kade."

"Happy to help." Lowering his head, he kissed her lightly. "I'll ride out tomorrow and see if any of the Lakota are still in the area."

"You'll be careful, won't you?"

"Don't worry about me, darlin'. I'm always careful."

Her gaze searched his. "Are you?"

"Don't you believe me?"

"I know we haven't known each other very long," she said. "And you don't owe me anything, but…I can't lose you, too."

"Here, now," he said. "I told you, I'm not going anywhere."

Seth came home that night. Norrie was relieved that he was alone and sober.

"Truvy wants to get married right away," he said, not meeting her eyes. "I know it's soon, what with losing Pa and everything, but the baby…well, that changes things, you know?"

"I know."

"We're gonna have Reverend Carmichael marry us. Nothing fancy, just family and a few of Truvy's friends. Day after tomorrow."

"I understand."

"I'm gonna sign my half of the ranch over to you." He held up his hand to silence the protest he saw rising in her eyes. "I'm about to become a husband and a father, Norrie. I could sure use that money now, but I can't touch it until I'm twenty-five." He grimaced. "I got the feeling Pa knew I wouldn't stick around if anything happened to him."

Norrie shrugged. She'd had the same feeling, but she thought her father had been wise in his decision not to release the money until she and Seth were older. If Seth was able to get his hands on that money now, she was afraid that, wife or no wife, he'd gamble it away. If only her father had changed his will just a few days earlier, it would have made all the difference in the world. If she owned the ranch free and clear, she might have been able to take out a small loan for Seth using the ranch as collateral. But wishing wouldn't make it so.

"Me and Truvy are gonna be a little strapped for cash," Seth was saying, "so besides helping out at the boarding house, I'm plannin' to get a regular job. Maybe clerking at Minton's or bartending at the saloon."

"If that's what you want," Norrie said quietly.

"You'll come to the weddin', won't you?"

"Of course. You're my brother. I love you."

"One o'clock at the church."

"I'll be there."

Seth hugged her quickly, then left the house. But not before she saw the tears in his eyes.

CHAPTER TWELVE

Kade left the ranch first thing in the morning before Norrie was up. He rode east, toward the mountains, hoping to find the hunters he had met before.

He crossed their trail a few miles later and followed it to a shallow valley. He paused at the top of the hill that overlooked the camp. A dozen hide lodges were scattered in the valley below. Horses grazed on the short grass. Two young women knelt side by side skinning a deer which made him think it was a hunting camp, since women rarely went on raiding parties, although women warriors were not unknown to his people.

Clucking to the mustang, he rode down the hill, careful to keep his hand away from his Colt. He was immediately surrounded by half a dozen men, including Mila Sapa.

Kade lifted his hand in greeting. "Ho, brother."

Mila Sapa stepped forward. "Why are you here?"

"I work on a ranch. We are looking for men to round up and break a herd of horses. We can pay you in white man's money or cattle or both."

The warrior grunted softly. "Come, let us go to my lodge."

With a nod, Kade dismounted and followed the warrior into a lodge located near the center of the village. Memories of home flashed through his mind as he stepped inside— the scent of smoke and sage and roast venison, the curly buffalo hide on the floor, the fire pit in the center of the lodge, the willow backrests on either side.

Mila Sapa invited him to sit.

A tall, slender woman handed Mila Sapa a bowl and then offered one to Kade.

Beef stew. Kade murmured, *"Pilamaya,"* as he accepted the bowl of soup, wondering, as he did so, if he was eating beef stolen from Connor McDonald's herd.

The woman flashed a shy smile and ducked out of the lodge.

They ate in silence.

When they were done, Mila Sapa asked, "How many of my warriors will you need?"

"I was thinking of three or four."

"For how long?"

"I'm not sure. Several weeks at least, maybe longer."

The warrior's gaze pierced Kade's for several long moments. And then he nodded. "We will be there in two days' time."

"You know where it is?"

"Ai." The warrior's lips twitched in a smile as he glanced at the bowl in his hands. "We have eaten your beef from time to time."

Grinning, Kade rose. "Good talk."

"Ai."

Kade found Norrie out back, hanging a load of wash, when he returned to the ranch. She looked up when Kade rode into the yard. "Did you find any of your friends?"

"Yeah." Dismounting, he dropped the mustang's reins. "They'll be here in a couple of days. You doing all right?"

Norrie made a vague gesture with her hand. "I guess so. Seth's getting married tomorrow afternoon." Shoulders sagging, she said, "He's going to sign his half of the ranch over to me."

"It'll be all right. You'll see."

"I just have a terrible feeling that I'm going to lose everything."

"Here, now," he said, taking her into his arms. "I won't let that happen."

"Do you really think selling mustangs to the army is going to save us?"

"I can't guarantee it, but it's worth a try. You can't just give up."

Norrie rested her head on his chest, wondering what she would do if Kade left. She couldn't run the ranch on her own. The only bright spot was that Lyle Burdett might leave them alone once the cattle were gone. If only they could find a way to prove he had killed her father, but they had no evidence, no proof of any kind.

She looked up at Kade. "You'll come to the wedding, won't you?"

"If you want me to."

She smiled faintly. She didn't know how it had happened, but she was afraid she might be falling in love with him. And equally afraid that her heart would shatter into a million pieces when he moved on.

Seth's wedding day bloomed bright and clear, but it did nothing to chase the gloom from Norrie's heart. It seemed her life was changing every day, growing more complicated, more hopeless.

At noon, Norrie went upstairs to get ready. After donning her best dress, she brushed out her hair and pinned the sides back with a pair of tortoiseshell combs that had belonged to her mother. Glancing in the mirror, she wished she didn't feel so depressed. She should be happy. Happy for her brother and Truvy. But it was hard to be happy when she felt as if her whole world was slowly falling apart.

Sighing, she went downstairs.

Kade was waiting for her in the parlor. He smiled when he saw her. "You look right pretty," he said. And she did, he thought, except for the sadness in her eyes.

"Thank you." Just seeing him made Norrie's heart feel a little lighter. He looked so handsome in his dark-blue shirt and black trousers, his Stetson shading his eyes. Tall and broad-shouldered, with an easy air of self-confidence and strength, she could almost believe that with Kade on her side, everything really would work out.

Seth and his best man, Aaron, were already at the church when Norrie and Kade arrived. Mrs. Trent, the church organist, was in place at the organ. Truvy's mother, Ada, sat in the front pew. Norrie wondered if Mr. and Mrs. Owens were aware of their daughter's pregnancy.

Three young women sat behind Ada Owens, whispering in excited voices. Undoubtedly friends of the bride.

Norrie smiled at Truvy's mother as she slid into the pew on the opposite side of the aisle. Mrs. Owens looked proud and happy, which made Norrie think Truvy hadn't yet told her parents about the baby.

Reverend Carmichael entered the church a few minutes later and took his place in front of the altar. He nodded at Mrs. Trent and she began to play.

Truvy's maid of honor, Helen Miller, walked slowly down the aisle and took her place beside the minister.

Truly followed. She looked radiant, her eyes bright with happiness as her father escorted her down the aisle and placed her hand in Seth's.

Norrie blinked back tears as Truvy and Seth exchanged their wedding vows. Her little brother was a married man now, soon to be a father, with a responsibility to his own family.

There were hugs and congratulations all around when the ceremony was over.

Outside, Norrie hugged her brother. "I hope you'll be very happy," she said, her throat tight with unshed tears.

"I'm already happy," Seth replied, smiling down at her. "We'll come visit often, I promise. And we'll expect you to come see us." He grinned as he whispered, "Aunt Norrie."

"Her parents don't know about the baby, do they?"

"Not yet. They're giving us a reception at their house. You'll come, won't you? Kade, too."

"Of course."

Kade glanced at Norrie. She had been unusually quiet since they'd left the wedding reception. Not that he could blame her. She was carrying a heavy load now that Seth had left the ranch. He couldn't fault the boy for moving to town. Branding, roping, forking hay, mucking stalls, and calving required a man with two good arms and two good hands.

Still, it left Norrie with more responsibility than one young woman should have to bear.

When they reached home, Kade pulled the buckboard up in front of the house. Norrie hopped down without a word and hurried inside. He stared after her a moment before heading for the barn. He hated to see her looking so down, but he supposed it was normal. She had lost her father only days ago. Pete had been killed not long ago. Noah had quit. And now her brother had moved out. He wondered how long Jackson and Old Tom would stick around.

Swearing under his breath, Kade unhitched the gelding, led the horse into the barn, and forked it some hay. He spent a few minutes at the corral scratching the mustang's ears, and then sauntered up to the house, wondering what he could possibly say to Norrie to cheer her up.

Heavy-hearted, Norrie made her way upstairs. After changing out of her dress and into a shirt, pants, and boots, she slipped out the back door and headed for the barn, only to come to an abrupt halt when she saw Kade striding toward her.

"Were you looking for me?" he asked as he drew closer.

"No. I thought I'd go for a ride and try to clear my head."

"It'll be dark soon. I don't think you should be riding alone."

"I'll be all right."

"Maybe. But I'm going with you."

Norrie saddled her favorite mount, a pretty little Appaloosa mare, while Kade saddled the mustang. Ten minutes later, the ranch was behind them.

Norrie felt a sense of peace as they rode. The sky was clear and beautiful, the horizon awash with splashes of red and pink and lavender as the sun made its slow descent. There was something about riding across the range that touched her spirit and calmed her soul. Troubles came and went but the land was forever. She was aware of Kade riding silently beside her. He seemed to know she wasn't in the mood to make conversation.

When they reached the stream, she reined the Appy to a halt.

Kade pulled up beside her and dismounted, then lifted her out of the saddle and into his arms.

Norrie gazed up at him and in the depths of his eyes, she saw everything she had ever wanted.

There was no need for words. Her eyelids fluttered down as his mouth covered hers, the warmth of his kiss chasing away the numbing cold that had been with her ever since her father's funeral.

Norrie slid her arms around Kade's neck as he deepened the kiss, her body molding to his, her breasts crushed against the hard wall of his chest. Still locked in each other's arms, they slowly sank to the ground. He rained kisses on her brow, her cheeks, the tip of her nose, before returning to her mouth.

She moaned softly as his hands stroked her back, her thigh, the curve of her breast, until everything faded from her mind but Kade, the gentle touch of his hands, his mouth on hers, the heat of his muscular body pressed intimately against hers.

"Norrie." Her name was a groan on his lips. "Tell me to stop."

"No." She cupped his face in her hands. "Don't ever stop."

Seconds stretched into eternity as Kade's gaze searched hers. He wanted her as he had never wanted another woman. But she was young, hurting from the death of her father. How could he take advantage of her now, when she was feeling vulnerable and alone? How could he let her go?

When she kissed him again, her body sliding invitingly against his, he was lost.

Norrie sighed as she rested her head on Kade's shoulder. She had never made love before. It was nothing like she had expected and more wonderful than anything she had ever imagined. He had made love to her tenderly, every touch, every kiss, filling her with pleasure, arousing her in ways she had never dreamed possible. She had reveled in the weight of his body bearing down on hers, the incredible explosion of desire that had engulfed her as his body melded with hers, making the two of them one in the most intimate and elemental way. She was bound to him now, heart and soul, she thought, a part of him.

"Norrie?"

"Hmm?"

"Did I hurt you?"

"No." She smiled at him, felt her heart melt at the look of love and concern in his dark eyes. "I love you, Kade."

His knuckles brushed her cheek as he returned her smile. "No more than I love you."

Easing up on his elbows, he kissed the tip of her nose. "I must be getting heavy," he remarked. But when he started to roll to the side, she held him tight.

"Don't. Not yet."

He nuzzled the side of her neck, rained kisses on her brow and her cheeks. "Come on, darlin'," he said. "It's getting dark. We should head for home."

She clung to him, thinking she had never felt anything as wonderful as being close to Kade with nothing between them. She felt bereft when he rolled to his side.

"It'll be even better in a bed," he promised with a wink as he took both of her hands in his and pulled her to her feet.

Norrie found herself smiling all the way home.

CHAPTER THIRTEEN

Norrie let out a startled cry when she stepped out the back door the next morning and saw four Indian men milling around the barn. At first, she thought they'd come to burn the place down, but then she saw Kade emerge from the barn and she realized they were Kade's friends. Still, it took several minutes for her heart to stop pounding.

She smiled when Kade waved and then strode toward her.

"They showed up late last night," he said. "They made camp in the hollow behind the barn."

"Oh."

"They gave Jackson quite a scare."

"Really? I can't imagine why."

Kade laughed. "You can't, huh? I saw the look on your face before you saw me."

"Can you blame me??

"No, I guess not. We're going to ride out and see if we can round up any mustangs. Mila Sapa saw a herd over near the box canyon. If we can drive them inside, they'll be easy to round up."

"How long will you be gone?"

"Most of the day, I reckon. Jackson and Old Tom will be here to look after the ranch."

"I'll miss you."

"I'll miss you, too."

"What should I fix your friends for dinner?"

"Don't worry about them. A couple of the men brought their wives along. They'll do the cooking."

"All right," she said, casting a dubious eye at the Indians. 'Be careful."

"Always." Drawing her into his arms, he kissed her, long and slow. "Stay close to home, Norrie."

"I will. Hurry back."

With a nod, he set off toward the barn.

Norrie stood there, arms crossed over her breasts as she watched Kade and the Indians mount up. She hoped his idea of selling mustangs to the Army was a success because it seemed to be her only hope of keeping the ranch.

Kade had been gone close to two hours when Lyle Burdett came calling. Norrie could hardly believe her eyes when she opened the door.

"What do you want?" she asked, unable to believe he had the nerve to show up on her doorstep.

"Why, I've come to pay my condolences," he said, removing his hat. "With all the bad blood between your family and mine, I felt it best to stay away from the funeral."

Norrie stared at him. The gall of the man! "We all know you killed him," she said, fighting back her tears.

"Why, Miss Norrie, I…"

"Shut up! Just shut your mouth and get off of my property. I can't stand to look at you, or listen to your lies!"

"See here, you've got no call to speak to me like that, missy," he growled, shaking his finger in her face. "I came here to make you an offer on your place. A right good offer.

I know you're struggling and that your brother moved out. But now I'll just sit back and wait until your next mortgage payment comes due and then I'll buy the place out from under you for half of what it's worth!"

With a wordless cry, Norrie slammed the door in his face.

Then sank down on the floor and buried her face in her hands, tears of anger and grief coursing down her cheeks.

It was dusk when Kade returned to the ranch. Hot and dusty and tired, he unsaddled his horse and fed the stock before going up to the house. He was looking forward to a hot bath and a hot meal in that order when he stepped through the back door into the kitchen.

And forgot both when he saw Norrie sitting at the table looking as if she'd lost her best friend. "What is it?" he asked. "What's wrong?"

"Burdett was here."

A muscle twitched in his jaw. "I guess I know what he wanted."

She nodded. "He's threatened to buy the ranch out from under me when the mortgage comes due. Not that it came as any surprise."

"Well, he can go to hell." Kade pulled out a chair and sank into it. "We rounded up twenty-eight mustangs today, herded them into a canyon and blocked the entrance. Tomorrow, Mila Sapa and a couple of his warriors are going to bring half of them here for me to break, while he and his men work the others. When they're ready, I'll ride over to the fort and let them know we've got some prime stock that's saddle broke and ready to ride. Last I heard, the Army was paying forty dollars a head. That's over a thousand dollars, more than enough to pay off the mortgage. You might even have a little left over."

"You make it sound so easy."

"No sense looking for problems."

"I guess not. You must be hungry."

"I could eat. But first," he said, slapping his hands on his knees, "I need to wash up."

When Kade returned to the kitchen half an hour later, Norrie had dinner ready. Jackson and Old Tom had taken to eating with them, now that the other hands were gone.

Kade told the men about their plans to break the mustangs and Jackson thought it was a fine idea. Old Tom would take care of the chores around the ranch while Kade and Jackson worked with the horses. They'd start first thing in the morning.

Old Tom and Jackson took their leave as soon as the meal was over.

Norrie poured Kade a second cup of coffee, then cleared the table.

Kade sat back, watching her, thinking that his life had taken quite a turn since Norrie saved his life. He hadn't stayed in any one place this long in years, but he had no desire to move on.

No desire to leave Norrie.

Ever.

CHAPTER FOURTEEN

Mila Sapa and two of his warriors showed up with fifteen mustangs about an hour after breakfast. At Kade's direction, they herded the animals into the largest corral and stayed long enough for coffee before heading back to the canyon.

Kade sat on the top rail of the corral fence and looked over the stock. All mares. All healthy and full of vinegar. He lifted a rope from the corral post and caught up a rawboned bay. Once the horse stopped bucking, he led it into the small corral and gave the animal its first lesson—the rope always wins.

Norrie paused in front of the kitchen window, felt herself smile as she watched Kade work one of the mustangs. Unlike some men, he had endless patience with the mare. He never raised his voice, never used a crop. Slow and easy, he won the horse's trust before he ever stepped into the leather.

She thought about what Kade had said last night and for the first time, she felt a flicker of hope. All they had to do was sell the mustangs and the cattle. It sounded so easy. But what if none of her neighbors wanted her cattle? What if the Army didn't need any remounts…?

She thrust her doubts away. Like Kade said, there was no point in looking for problems.

Norrie glanced at the basket of laundry waiting to be ironed, then looked out the window again. She told herself the ironing could wait a few more minutes, but as she watched Kade work the mare, the minutes stretched into an hour and the next thing she knew, it was time to start thinking about the mid-day meal.

Kade was pleased with the mare's progress when he led her back into the larger corral. He glanced at one of the other pens where Jackson was mounted on a chestnut that was bucking for all it was worth.

He grinned as Jackson sailed over the mustang's head. Ain't a horse that can't be rode, he mused, or a cowboy that can't be throwed. He had to admit Jackson had grit as he picked himself up and vaulted into the saddle for another go-round.

Still grinning, Kade headed up to the house, eager to spend a little time with Norrie before he got back to work. He found her in the kitchen putting dinner on the table—fried chicken and potato salad and corn on the cob. "Smells good," he said.

She smiled at him over her shoulder. "There's a pan of hot water on the back porch."

"Yes, ma'am." Stepping outside, he washed his hands and face, slicked back his hair. He'd just returned to the kitchen when Old Tom and Jackson entered the room. A short time later, they were all sitting at the table reminiscing about days past.

Norrie paid little attention to the men as they traded stories about headstrong horses and loco broncs. She found herself constantly glancing at Kade, pleased to discover that he was paying more attention to her than to the conversation. She felt her heart melt when he winked at her.

All too soon, the men were grabbing their hats and heading out the door.

Kade was the last one to leave. He paused long enough to take her in his arms and give her a quick, heated kiss before hurrying after Jackson and Old Tom.

For the rest of the day, Norrie smiled every time she thought about that kiss.

It wasn't until after sunset that they had a chance to be alone. Sitting beside Norrie on the porch swing, Kade blew out a sigh. He was getting soft, he thought as he gazed into the distance. Sleeping in a bed every night. Eating three meals a day. Spending time with a beautiful woman. He slid a sideways glance at Norrie. He had never expected to settle down. Or fall in love. Ever since leaving his people, he had been a wanderer, a gambler. He hadn't depended on anyone else and no one had depended on him. He had lived life on his own terms and to hell with the rest of the world.

Meeting Norrie had changed all that. For the first time since leaving the Lakota, he found himself thinking about settling down in one place.

With one woman.

The next few days were busy ones. By the end of the week, Kade and Jackson had eleven horses saddle broke. Mila Sapa and his warriors had twelve more ready to go. Norrie's neighbor, Roy Clifford, heard she wanted to sell off some of her cattle and offered to buy them for a decent price. He sent a couple of his cowhands over to drive them to his place.

Norrie felt a twinge of regret as she signed a bill of sale for the cattle. What would her father think? The herd had been his pride and joy. He had started with one good bull and fifty cows. And now that was all she had left. But she needed the money more than the cattle. Now, everything depended on selling the horses to the Army.

She smiled as she glanced out the window. Kade was working another bronc. He stuck to the saddle like a cocklebur as the mare bucked and crow-hopped around the corral. He had removed his shirt. Sweat glistened on his copper-hued skin. He wore a bandana around his forehead to keep the perspiration from his eyes. He looked as wild and unbroken as the horse he rode.

The last few days had been hard. She missed her father and Seth. Nightly, she thanked heaven for Kade. She didn't know what she would do without him. He worked tirelessly and refused to accept any payment in return. Jackson and Old Tom treated Kade as if he was the foreman, even though they had both been on the ranch longer. He seemed to be a natural leader.

What would she do if he suddenly decided to ride on? He had made her believe she could make a go of the ranch, cheered her up when she was down.

She put the thought out of her mind. He was here now and that was all that mattered.

It was after seven when Jackson and Old Tom thanked Norrie for dinner and left the house. As usual, Kade stayed behind.

Norrie wondered what Old Tom and Jackson thought about Kade living in the house with her. She knew it was unseemly, could only imagine what her neighbors would say if they knew. But she didn't really care. It wasn't as if they shared a room. She had asked him to stay because she couldn't bear the thought of living in the house alone. It was easier to face the nights knowing he was there. It wasn't that she was afraid of the dark, but she liked knowing she wasn't alone.

And there was no denying she liked being with Kade, or that she looked forward to the few moments they spent together on the sofa each night, a fire in the hearth, while they talked about the day's events. Inevitably, she found herself in his arms, his mouth on hers.

"I need to go into town tomorrow," Norrie remarked. "We're running low on just about everything. And with the money I made on the cattle, I'll be able to pay off my bill at the mercantile," she said with a smile. "And pay cash for whatever I need."

"Is Old Tom going with you?"

"No. He's been feeling poorly lately. I told him to stay home and rest. I'm worried about him."

Kade grunted softly. Tom had to be seventy if he was a day.

"I wanted him to go with me and go see Doc Williams, but..." She shrugged. "He refused."

Kade ran his knuckles along her cheek. "I don't want you going alone."

"It won't be the first time," Norrie said. "I thought I'd go visit Seth while I'm there."

"Good idea. But I'm still going with you."

Norrie grinned inwardly. Stubborn man. But she didn't mind. There was nothing she would rather do than spend time with Kade.

And then he was drawing her closer, raining feather-light kisses on her cheeks, her brow, the tip of her nose, before slanting his mouth over hers.

And there was no more time for thought.

In the morning at breakfast, Kade asked Jackson to keep working the roan mare. Norrie told Old Tom to rest until she got back. While Norrie did the dishes and cleaned up the kitchen, Kade went down to the barn to get the buckboard.

It was nearly nine before they were on their way.

Norrie hummed softly as the buckboard bounced along. It was a beautiful day, the sky a bright, clear blue. Wildflowers bloomed here and there alongside the road. A gentle breeze played hide and seek in the leaves of the trees. And a handsome man sat beside her. Who could ask for more?

They were about halfway to town when Norrie saw two riders coming toward them. She frowned as they drew closer. She didn't recognize either one of them, which was odd. This stretch of road led to the McDonald ranch before veering off toward the Burdett place about a mile further down.

"Something wrong?" Kade asked, noting the worry furrowing her brow.

"Probably not. It's just unusual to see strangers on this road."

Kade frowned as the men drew closer. Norrie might not recognize them. But he did. They were brothers. Bounty hunters. How the hell had they found him, he wondered, and then swore under his breath. Had Burdett sent for them?

"We're looking for the Burdett spread," Dirk Crowley said as they drew rein side by side in front of the buckboard, blocking the road.

Kade swore again as Dirk Crowley confirmed his suspicions.

"Stay on this road until it veers to the right," Norrie said.

"Obliged, ma'am."

Kade held his breath, waiting, hoping they wouldn't make their play with Norrie sitting there beside him.

"Dirk, hang on a minute." The other Crowley brother's eyes narrowed as he jerked a thumb in Kade's direction. "Don't you recognize him?"

Kade tensed as Dirk Crowley glanced his way. "Looks like our lucky day, Jake."

"We can do this easy or hard," Jake said. "Easy and no one gets hurt. Hard?" He shrugged.

Norrie slid a sideways glance at Kade. Jaw clenched, he stared at the two men.

"Hard." The word still hung in the air as Kade pulled his Colt and fired two shots that came so close together, it sounded like one, long report.

Norrie watched in horror as blood spread across the shirtfronts of the two men before they toppled from their horses and hit the ground.

She stared at Kade, one hand pressed to her heart. "What have you done?"

"They're hired guns," he said brusquely. "It was me or them."

"But…"

"I've seen them before, in the Dakotas," he said, holstering his Colt. "They never bring their quarry in alive. I think Burdett hired them." Kade handed her the reins before hopping down from the buckboard. He lifted the bodies one by one and draped them over the backs of their horses, then secured the reins to the back of the buckboard before climbing back up beside her.

"What are you doing?" Norrie asked as he took the reins from her hand and turned the horse around.

"We're going back to the ranch."

"Why?"

"What do you want me to do? Take the bodies into town?"

"Of course."

He shook his head. "I can't do that. There's already paper out on me. No jury in the world is gonna believe it was self-defense. And from the look on your face, you don't believe it, either."

"Kade…how do you know they were going to draw on you?"

"Years of experience in reading men," he said flatly. "If you want to take them into town, I won't stop you. But I'm not going with you. I can't. As soon as the sheriff finds out what happened, he'll be coming out to question me."

"What are you going to do?"

"That depends on you. We can go back to the ranch. I'll bury the two of them and turn their horses loose. Or you can take them into town, and I'll be gone when you get back home."

Norrie clasped her hands in her lap as he reined the horse to a stop. How was she supposed to make a decision like that? He had killed two men, seemingly in cold blood. Had they made a move toward their guns? If so, she hadn't seen it. Her attention had been focused on Kade.

"What do you want to do?" he asked.

"I don't know. I can't think."

With a nod, he handed her the reins. "You do what you think best." His gaze moved over her, then he dropped lightly to the ground.

Blinking back her tears, Norrie turned the horse toward town.

CHAPTER FIFTEEN

Kade ran effortlessly, tirelessly, toward the ranch. It reminded him of his early training to be a warrior. He had run for miles day after day to build strength and stamina, spent hours learning to hunt and trap game, to read trail sign and distinguish between the tracks of wolf and coyote, bear, mountain lion and bobcat, elk and moose and buffalo. He had learned the subtle differences between the moccasin tracks of Arapaho, Crow, and Cheyenne. And still more hours had been spent practicing with bow and arrow, learning how to throw a knife and an axe, how to skin game—though the latter was generally considered women's work.

Try as he might, he couldn't keep his thoughts from turning to Norrie. Dammit!

He never should have let himself care for her, should have known that sooner or later fate would step in. Not that he blamed Norrie. She was a good woman, a decent woman. She couldn't be expected to turn a blind eye to killing, even if it had been self-defense, though there was no way to prove it. But he had been watching the brothers. He'd seen them shift in the saddle, the shared glance, the subtle change in their eyes when the decision was made to slap leather.

Only he did it first. And faster.

But like he'd told Norrie, no jury of twelve white men was going to deliver any verdict but murder.

Shit! Of all the bad luck, he thought. What were the odds of running into the Crowleys? Damn Burdett. Kade had no doubt the rancher had hired them to gun him down and bully Norrie into selling the Lazy Double D.

Jackson was walking the roan when Kade reached the barn. The cowboy frowned when he saw him. "Where's Norrie?"

"She went to town."

"I thought…" Jackson's brow furrowed. "What happened?"

Kade shook his head. "It doesn't matter. I'm leaving." He grabbed a blanket and saddle from a sawhorse and went into the small corral. The mustang blew softly as she trotted up to him. In minutes, the mare was saddled and bridled.

Kade led the buckskin out of the corral and swung into the saddle just as Norrie drove into the yard. When she saw Kade, she pulled the horse to a stop and jumped from the seat. Running toward him, she cried, "Kade, don't go!"

"Norrie!" Swinging out of the saddle, he caught her in his arms. "What changed your mind?"

"I thought about what you said. I didn't see either man reach for a gun, but if you say you did, I believe you." She glanced over her shoulder as Jackson hurried toward her. He jerked a thumb at the bodies. "What the hell happened?"

Norrie looked at Kade, a question in her eyes.

"Tell him."

"We met them on the road. They were bounty hunters."

Understanding dawned in Jackson's eyes. "Well, damn!" he exclaimed, grinning from ear to ear. "You took them both? I'd like to have seen that." And then he frowned. "Does that mean...?"

"Yeah," Kade said, his voice harsh. "If Burdett reports them missing, the law is sure to come here looking for me."

"We can bury the bodies out behind the spring house," Jackson suggested. "The ground's soft there."

Norrie stared at Jackson, and then, feeling guilty for agreeing, she nodded.

"I'll do it," Kade said.

"What about their horses?" Norrie asked, liking what they were doing less and less.

"I can take them into town and drop them off at the livery," Jackson said.

Kade shook his head. "The sheriff's likely to come around here sooner or later asking questions. Drive the buckboard to the springhouse. While I bury the bodies, I want you to burn their saddles, then take their horses out to where the mustangs run and turn them loose."

With a nod, Jackson climbed into the buckboard and clucked to the horse.

Kade waited until Jackson was on his way before he said, "I'm sorry I got you involved in this, Norrie."

"Maybe Burdett will just think they never showed up."

"Maybe."

"What if Sheriff Dawson shows up asking questions?"

"Let's cross that road when we come to it." His gaze searched hers. "It might be best if I move on."

"No!"

"If the truth comes out, you're liable to end up in jail, too, as an accessory."

Eyes wide, she stared at him. She hadn't thought about that. But he was probably right. With a sigh, she rested her cheek against his chest. Right or wrong, she couldn't let him be arrested. Though she hated to admit it, she knew he was right—he would never get a fair trial in Clayton's Corner. She had heard how the men in town talked about Indians, their hatred and mistrust of all of them. How many times had she heard one of them mutter that the only good Injun was a dead one? Not that she could blame them. Although the tribes hadn't been on the warpath lately, every rancher she knew had had trouble with the Indians at one time or another. Kade would never get a fair trial.

If he got a trial at all.

CHAPTER SIXTEEN

Late that night, Kade sat on the front porch staring into the distance. The peace of mind he'd felt only days ago was gone. As much as he cared for Norrie, as much as he liked being on the ranch, he knew the best thing he could do for her was ride one. For all he knew, the brothers had wired Burdett that they were on their way. When they didn't show up, Burdett would start wondering why. He'd go to the sheriff with his suspicions and sooner or later, Dawson and Bradshaw would come sniffing around.

Kade swore softly. He needed to be long gone before that happened. He didn't want Norrie mixed up in his troubles, didn't want her to lie for him. No matter what she'd said about believing him, he knew that what he'd done bothered her more than she let on. But that was to be expected. She was a good, decent woman, and she deserved far better than a man like him—a man who was wanted for more than one killing. Sooner or later, his past would catch up with him. Not that he was sorry he'd shot the man who killed his brother. Or gunned the Crowley brothers. Hell, he'd do it all again.

Gaining his feet, he strolled down to the corral. The buckskin nickered softly as he approached.

"Looks like we'll be moving on," he murmured as he scratched her ears. "Maybe we'll go home."

"This is your home, Kade."

He turned at the sound of Norrie's voice. "What are you doing up so late?"

"I could ask you the same question. Please don't go."

"It's for the best."

"For who?"

His knuckles caressed her cheek. "For you, darlin'. I'll ride out in the morning and talk to Mila Sapa. He can bring the mustangs in when they're saddle broke. Jackson can ride to the fort and make a deal. You'll be able to pay off the mortgage and get on with your life."

"I don't want a life without you in it," she murmured, her voice thick with unshed tears.

"Ah, Norrie." Drawing her into his arms, he held her close. He had never loved anyone the way he loved her. How was he going to leave her? How could he not?

"Stay the night with me."

He arched one brow. "Excuse me?"

"Please, Kade."

"Norrie…"

Taking his hand in hers, she led the way into the house and up the stairs to her room. After removing her robe, she slid under the covers. She didn't light the lamp on the bedside table.

With a sigh, Kade undressed down to his underwear and crawled in beside her.

She snuggled against him, her head pillowed on his shoulder. "I love you, Kade," she whispered.

"I know." His fingers stroked up and down her back. "I love you, too."

She shivered with pleasure at his touch. Rising up on her elbow, she kissed him with all the love in her heart.

An ache rose deep inside him as he drew her closer, his hand slipping under her nightgown to glide up and down her thigh, his tongue teasing hers.

Norrie moaned softly as his kisses deepened. She didn't protest when he lifted her nightgown over her head and tossed it on the floor. His underwear followed. And then his hands were caressing her, arousing her, until she ached for him. He murmured her name as he rose over her. She surrendered to him gladly, her arms holding him tight, her hips lifting to receive him.

Knowing he had to leave her, he made love to her as tenderly as he could, hoping she would know how much he loved her even as he wondered how he would ever find the courage to leave her now.

Kade held her close as she shuddered beneath him. A moment later, his own release came. His heart ached with regret and longing as tears dripped down her cheeks. "Don't cry, darlin'," he murmured. "Please don't cry."

"Promise me," she said in a voice that trembled. "Promise me you won't leave without saying goodbye."

Whispering, "I promise," he rolled onto his side, carrying her with him so they lay face to face, bodies still entwined.

She relaxed against him then, one arm draped across his waist. Moments later, she was asleep.

Kade held her all through the night, determined to leave her before she woke in the morning in spite of his promise.

Kade woke with a start at dawn, not certain what had roused him. He glanced at Norrie, sleeping soundly beside him, tempted to forget his intention to leave and make love to her instead—until he smelled smoke.

Throwing the blankets aside, he darted to the window, swore a vile oath when he glanced at the barn and heard the frantic neighing of the horses inside.

Pulling on his pants, he ran barefooted down the stairs and sprinted toward the barn. Flames licked at the roof and one wall. The double doors were open.

Jackson came out a moment later, leading one of the horses.

Kade darted inside, threw a rope around the Appy's neck, covered her eyes with a burlap bag and led her outside. In the corrals, the mustangs ran back and forth, panicked by the smell of smoke and the scent of the fire. One of the mares jumped the fence and the rest followed in a rush.

Kade tied the Appy to a post, grabbed a bridle, and ducked into the small corral. The buckskin paced back and forth, nostrils flared, eyes wide. He spoke to her quietly as he walked up to her and slipped a hackamore over her head, then secured her to one of the posts.

By then, Jackson had led the last of the horses out of the barn.

Kade stood beside him, eyes narrowed. There was nothing to do but watch it burn.

"Where's Old Tom?" Kade asked.

"In the bunkhouse. I think he's dead."

"What?"

"I tried to rouse him, but…" Jackson shrugged. "I think he died in the night. He hasn't been feeling well."

"Yeah." Kade stared at the empty corral. Of all the bad luck…or was it bad luck? Had Burdett decided to burn Norrie out?

He turned at the sound of footsteps and saw Norrie running toward him, her robe flapping behind her. "What happened?" she asked breathlessly.

"I'm not sure.," Kade said. "We got the horses out of the barn, but the mustangs took off."

Shoulders sagging, she leaned against him. For a time, they simply stared at the flames.

After a few minutes, Norrie asked, "Where's Tom?"

Kade slipped his arm around her shoulders. "He's gone."

"Gone?"

"He passed away in the night, Miss Norrie," Jackson said. "I think he went right peaceful like."

Norrie nodded. She had known the old man most of her life. Was she going to lose everyone close to her?

They poked through the rubble late that afternoon, but there was nothing left worth salvaging.

Jackson dressed Tom in his Sunday best. The old man had no kin, but Norrie wanted to do everything by the book, so Jackson laid the old cowboy out in the back of the buckboard and covered him with a blanket.

"Seems like a waste of time," Kade remarked as they walked back to the house. "Taking him into town so the doc can pronounce him dead, and then bring him back out here to bury him."

"Maybe," Norrie said. "But I don't want anyone thinking I've got anything to hide."

Kade snorted. "You mean besides the two bounty hunters? And the fact that you're harboring a wanted man?"

She glared at him, then ran up the stairs to her room and slammed the door.

Shit! He'd put his foot in it that time, he thought as he went into Seth's room to wash up and get dressed.

"Maybe you shouldn't go with me," Norrie said as Kade helped her up onto the high seat of the buckboard. "I mean, what if there are more bounty hunters in town?"

He supposed it was a possibility. The bigger worry was that a new wanted poster had showed up with a better description on it, or worse, his name.

"Maybe you're right," he allowed. Probably best if I lay low. Keep your eyes and ears open while you're there."

Nodding, she took up the reins. "You'll still be here when I get back?"

"I'll be here."

With a faint smile, she clucked to the gelding.

Kade blew out a sigh as he watched her pull onto the road. He had a feeling this wasn't going to end well.

Norrie had no sooner pulled up in front of the doctor's office than Sheriff Dawson strolled up. "Miss Norrie," he said, with a tip of his hat.

"Hello, Sheriff."

The lawman glanced into the bed of the buckboard. "What happened?"

"I think Old Tom had a heart attack last night. Jackson found him this morning." Descending from the seat, Norrie tethered the horse to the hitch rack and crossed the board-walk to the door. "If you'll excuse me," she said, and stepped into the doctor's office.

Norrie quickly explained what had happened to Doc Williams, who assured her that he'd deliver the body to the funeral parlor and arrange for a casket.

After expressing her thanks, she said, "There won't be a funeral. I'm going to take him back home and bury him there."

"I'll examine him tonight," Williams assured her. "When I'm done, I'll get in touch with Jurgensen over at the funeral home. You can pick up Old Tom tomorrow less something suspicious turns up."

With a nod, Norrie took her leave.

The Sheriff was waiting for her by the buckboard when she stepped outside.

"Is there something I can help you with?" she asked.

Dawson pulled a wrinkled sheet of paper out of his inside coat pocket and handed it to her.

Norrie's heart sank when she unfolded the paper. There was a rough pencil sketch of a dark-haired man, together with a description that fit Kade.

"Does he look familiar to you?"

She shrugged. "There are half a dozen men in town who fit that description."

"Perhaps. But I can't help thinking he looks a lot like that man who showed up at the dance at the Grange."

Norrie pretended to study the sketch again. "I guess there *is* a similarity."

"Do you know where he is?"

"I can't say as I do," she said, returning the wanted poster.

"Two men were in town the other day asking about him."

"Oh." Norrie swallowed hard. Her heart was pounding so loud, she wondered that Dawson couldn't hear it.

"Funny thing is, one of their horses drifted into town last night. Lee Bailey over at the livery recognized it."

"I'm sorry I can't help you, Sheriff. Is there anything else?"

His gaze bored into hers. "Are you going to be in town long?"

"No. I just came to order a casket for Old Tom." Shifting from one foot to the other, she said, "We're going to bury him at home."

Dawson nodded thoughtfully.

"Good day, Sheriff." Forcing a smile, she climbed onto the seat, took up the reins, and clucked to the gelding. She had thought to pay a quick visit to Seth and Truvy while she was in town, but it would have to wait for another day. Right now, she needed to get back to the ranch and warn Kade.

She could feel Dawson's gaze on her back as she turned the horse toward home.

She was passing the bank when Clive Simmons stepped onto the boardwalk and called her name.

Norrie reined the horse to a halt as Mr. Simmons approached her. " This is fortuitous," he said. "Mr. Burdett stopped in to see me early this morning."

"Oh?" A sense of dread engulfed Norrie at the mention of the rancher's name.

Mr. Simmons cleared his throat. "Mr. Burdett has purchased your mortgage from the bank. You have thirty days to vacate the property." He tugged at his shirt collar. "I'm sorry to be the bearer of bad news."

Unable to think of anything to say, Norrie urged the horse into a gallop, heedless of the way the buckboard bounced and swayed over the rutted road.

Just when she'd thought things couldn't get any worse, they did.

Kade was sitting on the porch steps when Norrie pulled up in front of the house. One look at her face and he was at her side, lifting her from the seat and into his arms. "What is it, darlin'?" he asked. "What's happened?"

"Burdett bought our mortgage from the bank. I have thirty days to move out."

Kade swore a vile oath.

"I guess he didn't burn down the barn, after all," she said, her voice flat.

"Yeah, I was gonna tell you I found some Comanche sign while you were gone, but I guess it doesn't matter now." If he'd had more time, if he'd known Burdett intended to buy her out, he might have been able to win what she needed to pay off the mortgage, but he'd thought they had more time ... Time, he thought. There was never enough.

"Nothing matters now," she said, her voice devoid of emotion. "Where's Jackson? I need to let him know. Maybe Burdett will hire him."

"Where will you go?"

"I don't know. Maybe I can work for Truvy at the boardinghouse."

"Norrie ..."

Blinking back tears, she murmured, "You'd better leave. The sheriff has a flyer with a sketch and your description on it. He asked me if I knew where you were. I said no, but I have a feeling he'll be out here again before nightfall. He said those brothers were asking after you in town."

Kade swore again. It never rained but it poured. Hell and damnation! How could he go off and leave her like this? But he couldn't stay. He wasn't afraid of much, but the thought of being locked up again filled him with dread. He had been born on the Plains, surrounded by open prairie and a vast blue sky. Being locked up in the white man's jail, confined to four walls in a six-by-eight cell, was worse than death. Not that he would likely be confined for long, he thought glumly. They'd probably just hang him.

Kade put Norrie away from him when he saw a cloud of dust rising in the distance. He had little doubt that it was the Sheriff. Judging by the dust being kicked up on the road, he figured Dawson had a half-dozen men with him.

"Norrie, I've got to go." He kissed her quickly, then sprinted for the corral. He didn't take time to saddle the mustang, just threw a bridle over the buckskin's head, vaulted onto her bare back and drummed his heels against her sides. She cleared the fence with room to spare.

Norrie stared after Kade, one hand pressed to her heart. "Be careful," she whispered.

Climbing the porch stairs, she wiped her eyes, and squared her shoulders, determined to face whatever happened next with her head held high.

CHAPTER SEVENTEEN

Grim-faced, Sheriff Dawson and Elias Bradshaw reined their horses to a halt in front of the McDonald house. The six-man posse fanned out behind them.

The Sheriff dismounted. "You know why I'm here. Miss Norrie." It wasn't a question but a statement of fact.

"I don't know where he is," Norrie said. "There's no one here except me and Jackson."

"Then you won't mind if we have a look around?"

"Not at all."

Dawson gestured to the posse and in minutes, eight men were swarming through the house, fanning out to search the barn and the grounds.

Norrie waited on the porch, arms folded across her breasts. She saw Elias Bradshaw questioning Jackson down by the corral and smiled inwardly when Jackson shook his head in answer to every query.

"He was here, wasn't he?" Dawson asked, stepping out onto the porch.

"Of course not."

"No? Then who belongs to those clothes in your brother's room?"

"Who do you think? They're in Seth's room, aren't they?"

Dawson grunted. "So he moved out and left his clothes behind?"

Norrie shrugged. "I don't see anything so unusual about that."

"Pants are a little long for him, aren't they?"

Norrie felt her cheeks flush.

"I should run you in for harboring a fugitive."

"No sign of him," Elias Bradshaw said, striding toward the porch. "We searched everywhere."

Dawson nodded. "Saddle up, men." Descending the stairs, he stepped into the saddle. He gave Norrie one last look of disgust before riding out of the yard. The posse trailed behind him.

Elias was the last to leave. "I'm right sorry about your troubles, Miss Norrie. If there's anything I can do…" He tipped his hat before setting out after the others.

Norrie blew out a sigh. The mustangs were gone. The barn was gone. Seth and Kade were gone. And now, so was the ranch.

Heavy-hearted, she went inside to begin packing.

Kade returned to the ranch several hours after dark. He had ridden out to see Mila Sapa and let him know his plans had changed. He thanked the warrior for his help, told him he was welcome to a couple head of cattle, as well as the mustangs.

Now, hidden in the shadows behind what was left of the barn, Kade stared at the lights in the house. He could see Norrie moving around upstairs. He longed to go see her but couldn't help wondering if it would be easier for both of them if he just rode on. He hated goodbyes. And as much as he wanted to stay with her, it was no longer possible. He figured she'd move into town and stay with Seth, but he couldn't do that. Not now, when the Sheriff was looking for him. He had nowhere to go, no home to offer her.

He swore softly when she moved to the window. He watched her wipe her eyes, knew she was crying. Dammit, he couldn't just ride out of her life without a word.

Norrie was in the kitchen when she heard the front door open. Her heart skipped a beat in anticipation even though she told herself it couldn't be Kade. Surely he wouldn't be foolish enough to come back here.

"Norrie?"

Turning away from the sink, she ran into his arms. "I was afraid I'd never see you again."

"I know." He held her close, one hand stroking her hair, her back. "I couldn't leave without seeing you one last time."

"Where will you go?"

"I don't know. I think, hell, I think I might just go home."

"Back to your people?" She looked up at him, worry in her eyes. "Is that safe?"

"It's been a long time since I've been back. I reckon most people thereabouts have forgotten about me."

"And if they haven't?"

He shrugged. "Did you talk to Jackson?"

"Yes. He left right after the Sheriff."

"Are you still thinking of moving to town?"

"I've got nowhere else to go."

Kade took a deep breath, let it out in a long, slow sigh. "You could go with me."

She stared up at him, wide-eyed. Live with the Lakota? It was beyond thinking about. She would be a stranger in a strange land. She would miss her brother, miss the birth of his baby. And yet she would be with Kade…

"It wouldn't be forever," he said. "Just a few days while I sort things out."

"And then what?"

"I guess that's up to you. We could find a place where no one knows me. Settle down." His gaze caressed her. "Get married?"

"Are you proposing?"

"Sure sounds like it."

"Then my answer is yes!"

"Norrie." Pulling her closer, he slanted his mouth over hers.

A moment later, his head snapped up.

"What is it?" Norrie asked.

Before he could answer, Sheriff Dawson appeared in the doorway, his Colt aimed at Kade. At the same time, the back door swung open and Elias Bradshaw and two other men stepped into the kitchen, their guns drawn.

"Get your hands up where I can see 'em," Dawson growled. "You're under arrest. Bradshaw, get his gun."

Kade backed away from Norrie. Every instinct for survival urged him to make a run for it, but he couldn't do that, not with Norrie in the room. He couldn't take a chance that one of the men would open fire and hit her by mistake. Unbuckling his gunbelt, he held it out to his side.

Looking hesitant to get near him, Bradshaw reached for the gunbelt. After handing it to Dawson, he cuffed Kade's hands behind his back and gave him a push toward the door. "Let's go."

Norrie followed them outside, mouth set in a thin line as she watched Bradshaw boost Kade onto the mustang's back. One of the men took the reins of Kade's horse. Bradshaw and the other deputy took up positions on either side of him.

"You should thank your lucky stars I don't run you in for harboring a fugitive," Dawson growled at Norrie as he climbed into the saddle. "And I damn well would if you weren't Connor's daughter, I can promise you that." After giving her one last baleful glance, he reined his horse around and fell in behind his deputies.

Norrie waited until they were out of sight, then ran down to the corral and saddled her Appy mare.

Kade scowled into the darkness as they rode toward town. He wondered again if they would waste time with a trial or just throw a rope over the nearest tree. Lynching was a bad way to go. He had seen too many hangings where something had gone wrong and instead of a quick death from a broken neck, the condemned man had slowly, painfully, strangled to death. Some Indians believed that when a man was hanged, his spirit couldn't escape and was forever trapped inside his body.

For a moment, he thought of making a break for it. A bullet in the back was a hell of a lot better than kicking and choking at the end of a rope.

As if reading his thoughts, the men surrounding him moved in closer.

The cell was small and square, the bars set close together. A barred window was set high in the back wall. A bare mattress sat on a narrow iron cot. There was a chamber pot under the bed. A thick, wooden door separated the cells from the main part of the jail. The other two were empty.

Dawson looked smug as he locked his prisoner inside the nearest cell before removing the handcuffs. When that was done, the sheriff closed the door and left him alone in the darkness.

Seth looked up from the oil lamp he'd been filling, surprise flickering in his eyes when his sister stepped through the door of the boardinghouse. "Norrie! What brings you to town at this time of the night?"

"They've arrested Kade!"

"Well, hell, I'm sorry to hear that," Seth said sympathetically. "But you knew he was a wanted man."

"I don't care. They'll hang him! I can't let that happen."

"I don't know how you can stop it."

She glanced up at the sound of footsteps.

"Seth, are you coming to bed soon?" Truvy called, coming down the stairs. "It's cold without you…" Her voice trailed off when she saw the expression on Norrie's face. "What's going on? Is something wrong?

"They've arrested Kade," Norrie said, and burst into tears.

"Oh, no! Come in and sit down and tell us all about it."

Norrie followed Seth and Truvy into the common room and sank down on the sofa. "That's not all," she said, sniffling.

Seth frowned as he handed her a handkerchief. "What do you mean?"

"The ranch is gone," she said, wiping her eyes. "Burdett bought the mortgage from the bank. I have thirty days to vacate."

"I'm so sorry," Truvy said. "You're welcome to move in here, if you like, for as long as necessary."

"Thank you." She'd have to go back to the ranch and pack her things, decide what to keep and what to sell, but none of that was important now. Burdett could have it all. It didn't matter. Nothing mattered but Kade.

"Can I get you anything?" Truvy asked.

"No." Norrie dabbed at her eyes again. "Is it all right if I stay here tonight? I don't feel like riding back home."

"Of course." Striding into the office, Seth retrieved a key and brought it out to her. "Take the first room at the top of the stairs. The bed's already made up." He gave her a quick hug when she stood. "I'm real sorry about Kade and the ranch. But like Truvy said, you're welcome to stay here as long as you've a mind to."

Blinking back a wave of fresh tears, Norrie nodded, her steps heavy as she climbed the stairs. The room was lovely. Lace curtains hung at the window, a patchwork quilt covered the brass bed. A highboy stood on the opposite wall, a white porcelain pitcher and bowl resting on top, together with several neatly folded towels.

Norrie undressed down to her underwear, crawled under the covers, and closed her eyes.

Tomorrow, she thought, she would think of some way to free Kade tomorrow.

CHAPTER EIGHTEEN

Kade paced the floor, his steps short and angry, his jaw clenched. He hated being locked up. For most of his life, he had been free to come and go as he pleased, with no one to answer to. He had hunted the buffalo with the Lakota, roamed the high hills and deep valleys of the *Paha Sapa*, explored the rocky terrain, the stark buttes and pinnacles of the Badlands known as *mako sica* to the Lakota.

Even when he'd left his people, he had lived life on his own terms. He had often shunned hotels, preferring to sleep outside under the moon and the stars.

He dropped down on the narrow, iron cot, only to get up and begin pacing again. He had to get the hell out of here.

His thoughts turned to Norrie. He hadn't even had a chance to tell her goodbye. Thank goodness Seth lived in town. Hopefully, her brother and Truvy would look after her.

Glancing up, he stared at the narrow swath of sky visible through the window, wondering if he would ever see the sacred hills of the *Paha Sapa* again.

Norrie woke after a long and restless night. Her dreams had been more like nightmares, with images of Kade being led to the gallows, a noose tight around his neck, his hands bound behind his back. She remembered what he'd told her—that no man this side of the Mississippi River would ever hang a white man for killing an Indian. She was afraid it was equally true that no jury would hesitate to string up an Indian accused of killing a white man. How could they arrest him without a warrant or a witness? Was suspicion enough? They had no proof other than that sketchy wanted poster. But maybe, when the suspect was an Indian, that was all they needed.

Fighting back her useless tears, she washed her face, dressed, and headed downstairs, wondering if Sheriff Dawson would allow her visit Kade.

Truvy smiled sympathetically when Norrie padded into the kitchen.

"You look like hell," her brother remarked.

"Seth!" Truvy scolded. "What a terrible thing to say. Sit down, Norrie, and I'll fix you some breakfast."

"I'm not hungry."

"At least have a cup of coffee and a muffin," Truvy urged. "They're blueberry and still warm from the oven."

"Thank you." Norrie slumped listlessly onto the chair across from Seth.

"What are you going to do now?" he asked.

"I don't know."

"If there's anything you need, anything we can do, you have only to ask," Truvy said. "Isn't that right, Seth?"

"Of course." Reaching across the table, he squeezed Norrie's hand. "We're family."

Norrie murmured her thanks, but her thoughts were on Kade. How was she going to get him out of jail? She couldn't afford a lawyer and even if she could, she would never be able to find one in this town who didn't have a grudge of one kind or another against the Indians. It seemed beyond hopeless.

Kade stopped in mid-stride when he heard a noise from the alley outside his cell. Head cocked, he frowned when he heard it again, smiled faintly when Norrie's face suddenly appeared at the window. Glancing outside, he saw that she was precariously balanced on a wooden crate. "You're gonna break your neck, darlin', but I'm sure glad to see you." Reaching through the bars, he caressed her cheek. "Are you all right?"

"I'm fine," she lied. "What about you?"

"I've been better," he muttered. "Dawson was in here earlier. He said the trial is set for tomorrow afternoon." A muscle clenched in his jaw. "The hanging is set for the day after."

Norrie clutched the bars as she felt the blood drain from her face.

"Hey, you're not going to faint on me, are you?" he asked, brow furrowed with concern.

"No." She took a deep breath, her gaze searching his. "What can I do?"

"I don't know what the hell it would be."

"There must be something."

He laughed bitterly as his knuckles caressed her cheek. "The lawyer appointed by the court told me to plead guilty and save everyone the cost of a lengthy trial."

"Oh, Kade," she murmured. Two days, she thought. Two days and he would be lost to her forever.

"Don't come to the trial," he said. "And for damn sure don't come to the hanging."

Fighting back tears, she bit down on her lower lip. How could she not go? It would be her last chance to see him.

"Promise me," he said. "I don't want you to remember me like that, twisting at the end of a rope." He glanced over his shoulder when he heard the sound of heavy footsteps outside the door. "You'd best get going."

"I love you!"

"I love you, too, darlin'. Now get."

Tears rolled down Norrie's cheeks as she hurried toward the boardinghouse. *Two days. Two days. Two days.* The words pounded in her mind over and over again. Two days. What was she to do?

She fretted over it the rest of the afternoon until her head was throbbing. In the evening after supper, she went to the jail. Elias Bradshaw was on duty when she arrived. There was no sign of the sheriff.

Bradshaw's face lit up when he saw her. "Miss Norrie! I'm right pleased to see you," he said. And then he frowned. "What brings you to town?"

Norrie stared at him for a moment. "I came to stay with Seth for a few days," she said with a smile, "and I thought I'd visit you while I was here. Seth and I have some business to discuss about the ranch."

He nodded. "I heard Mr. Burdett bought you out. I'm right sorry about that."

"It's for the best. The ranch has been losing money for some time, and I can't run the place alone. I'll probably be moving in with Seth and Truvy when Burdett takes possession of the ranch, and I thought, that is, I was hoping maybe we could..." She batted her eyelashes and looked away. Was she overdoing it?

"Could what?" he asked.

"I thought maybe we could...ah...renew our friendship."

"Why, Miss Norrie, I...that is..." His cheeks flushed bright red with embarrassment.

Moving closer to him, Norrie laid her hand on his arm. "I'm sorry I treated you so badly in the past."

"Ah, there's no need to apologize." He swallowed hard. "Maybe we could go to church services together on Sunday and..." He cleared his throat. "And maybe go for a picnic after."

"I was thinking maybe we could take a walk tomorrow evening."

"I'd surely like that, but I'll be on duty until ten."

"Maybe I could stop by for a few minutes."

"I don't know," he said, looking doubtful. "Sheriff don't allow visitors after seven. You shouldn't be here now. He ain't too happy with you, you know?"

Thinking hard, Norrie said, "I know, but I...uh, need to come by for a few minutes anyway."

"Oh?"

"Kade used to work for us, you know. My Pa liked him."

"I had the feeling you did, too."

She dismissed the notion with a wave of her hand. "I feel it's my Christian duty to see if he has any last requests or any kin who should be notified."

Bradshaw nodded slowly, his expression doubtful.

Feeling desperate, Norris said, "Truvy's baking pies tomorrow. Maybe I could bring one by."

"That would be mighty fine. She makes the best pies in town."

"Yes, indeed."

I guess it'll be all right, long as Sheriff Dawson doesn't see you and you don't stay too long."

"Until then," Norrie said.

"Until then," he agreed.

With a sigh of relief, Norrie hurried back to the boardinghouse, hoping Truvy would agree to make her a pie.

Kade stood at the window, staring out into the night. Somewhere in the distance, an owl hooted. It sent a shiver down his spine. The Indians believed the hoot of an owl outside a lodge meant death was near.

Turning away, he paced the floor. He had expected Norrie to visit him again. He told himself she likely had a good reason to stay away. Had he hurt her feelings by asking her not to attend the trial and the hanging? He shook his head. Surely she understood how he felt about that?

With a sigh, he dropped down on the cot and closed his eyes.

Two more days.

Seth looked up from the newspaper at the sound of Norrie's footsteps. "How's Kade?"

"I didn't see him."

"You didn't? Why not?"

"Something came up. They're going to hang him, Seth. I just know it."

Laying the paper aside, Seth said, "I wish there was something I could do to help."

"I know. Where's Truvy?"

"She's upstairs, resting. She's not feeling so good." His gaze ran over her face. "You're not lookin' so good, either."

"Can you blame me?"

"No, I reckon not."

"Kade asked me not to go to the trial. But you'll go, won't you?"

"Sure, if you want me to."

"Thanks, Seth." Blinking back her tears, she headed upstairs.

That night, she prayed as she had never prayed before, begging for mercy for Kade, that his lawyer would defend him honestly, for a sympathetic judge and jury that wouldn't convict him for killing the man who had shot his brother in the back.

It was hours before sleep came.

Staring out the window, Kade took a deep breath. His only real regret was leaving Norrie, he thought. She would be alone now, except for Seth and Truvy. She'd lost her father and soon the ranch. He had hoped ... Hell, it didn't matter what he'd hoped. The best he could look forward to now was a speedy trial and a quick hanging.

He lifted his hand to his neck. He hadn't feared much in life, but the thought of dying at the end of a rope sent an icy shiver down his spine. He had watched men climb the stairs to the gallows, heard them scream and cry for mercy, seen them wet their trousers as they felt the noose settle around their neck.

"*Wakan Tanka*," he murmured, "help me die with courage, as a warrior should."

CHAPTER NINETEEN

In the morning, Norrie packed a small bag with a change of clothes for herself and Kade and slipped it under the bed. After breakfast, she went to the stable and moved Kade's mustang and her Appy into the small corral behind the boardinghouse.

Later, she helped Truvy make several loaves of bread and an apple pie. No doubt sensing Norrie's distress, her sister-in-law said little.

While waiting for the bread to rise, Norrie excused herself and walked down the boardwalk toward the courthouse. She stood on the corner, out of sight, hoping for a glimpse of Kade. Luck was with her. A few minutes later, she saw him walking between the sheriff and Elias. Two other deputies trailed behind them, rifles at the ready. She wondered what they expected Kade to do when his hands and feet were shackled.

She ducked out of sight when Kade glanced in her direction.

When the crowd had gone inside, she made her way to Dunston's Gun shop where she bought a used .44 Colt and several boxes of ammunition.

"You expectin' trouble?" Mr. Dunston asked as he rang up her purchases.

"You never know," Norrie said with a wry smile. "My hired hands have all been killed or left. A girl has to be able to protect herself."

Mr. Dunston nodded. "I'm right sorry about your Pa's death. He was a good man. I guess trouble never comes by itself. Seth told me about you losing the ranch. If there's anything I can do…"

"Thank you," Norrie said as she put the Colt in the over-sized handbag she had brought with her. "I appreciate that."

"Give my best to your brother and his missus," Mr. Dunston said as he wrapped the ammunition and handed it to her.

"I will. Good day to you, sir."

Her next stop was the dry goods store where she bought a pair of men's trousers, a long-sleeved shirt and jacket, and a pair of boots. "For Seth," she explained to Mr. Minton, the shopkeeper. "It's his birthday."

"Looks a mite small for him," the proprietor remarked.

"He's lost some weight."

"Did he get shorter, too?" Mr. Minton asked dryly.

"Actually, the clothes are for me," Norrie said, lowering her voice. "Truvy hasn't been feeling well, being in the family way and all, and I've been helping out around the boardinghouse, you know, scrubbing floors and washing windows. And skirts and petticoats just get in the way."

"That's what my Margie says," Mr. Minton confided with a conspiratorial grin.

Taking up her packages, Norrie left the store. Outside, she took a deep breath. She paused when she saw the men piling out of the courthouse, laughing and slapping each other on the back. The trial couldn't be over already, she thought. She'd been shopping less than an hour.

Kade came out the door a few minutes later. Her heart sank when she saw his face.

Norrie bit down on her lower lip when Seth hurried toward her. "They found him guilty. The verdict was a foregone conclusion. The jury was out less than fifteen minutes. The vote was unanimous."

She nodded, unable to speak past the rising lump in her throat.

"He hangs in the morning. I'm sorry, Norrie." Seth jerked his chin toward the packages in her arms. "What have you got there?"

"What? Oh. A change of clothes. I didn't bring much with me when I left home."

"Tell Truvy I'll be home soon. I need to go order some supplies."

She nodded, her gaze following Kade until he disappeared inside the sheriff's office.

"Are you going to be all right?" Seth asked, his voice thick with concern. "Norrie?"

"Don't worry about me," she said.

"'Fraid I can't help it. You're my sister. It comes with the territory." Giving her arm a squeeze, he moved down the boardwalk.

Feeling numb inside, Norrie made her way back to the boardinghouse.

Later that evening, Norrie sat on the boardinghouse steps, her hands tightly clenched in her lap. Sure as clockwork, Sheriff Dawson passed by on his way to the restaurant for supper.

He gave her trousers a lingering look of disapproval. "Evenin'," Miss Norrie," he said, with a tip of his hat.

"Good evening, Sheriff," she replied, forcing a smile she was far from feeling.

She waited until he entered the restaurant, then picked up the dish beside her and walked briskly toward the jail. It was suppertime and there were only a few people on the street. Those she passed were mostly men conversing about tomorrow's hanging.

When she reached the jail, she peered into the front window, relieved to see that Elias was inside. Taking a deep breath, she knocked on the door.

"Who's there?"

"It's me. Norrie."

Her heart skipped a beat as he lifted the bar and opened the door.

"One apple pie," she said, offering it to him. "As promised."

"Come on in. Smells mighty good." Closing the door behind her, Elias set the pie on the desk. He frowned as he gestured at her clothes. "Why are you wearin' men's' britches?"

With a hand that shook, Norrie pulled the .44 from inside her jacket. If she hadn't been so nervous, she would have laughed at the stunned expression on his face.

"I need you to open the cell door," she said.

"Miss Norrie, what do you think you're doing?"

"I think I'm going to shoot you if you don't do as I say."

"Now, we both know you ain't gonna do that."

Eyes narrowed, she eared back the hammer. "Elias Bradshaw, don't you doubt it for a minute. Take off your gunbelt and put it on the desk."

"You'll never get away with this," he said as he reluctantly followed her instructions, then lifted a key ring from a hook on the wall.

"Open it!"

She stayed well behind him as he unlocked the door to the cellblock. Jerking the Colt toward an empty cell, she said, "Drop the keys on the floor, then get in there."

He must have seen the determination in her eyes, because this time he did as she asked without an argument.

Picking up the keys, she closed and locked the door behind Elias.

"Norrie!" Kade exclaimed. "What the hell do you think you're doing?"

"I think I'm getting you out of here," she said, unlocking his cell door. "Let's go. The horses are out back."

He didn't argue. In the office, he grabbed a rifle from the rack and checked to make sure it was loaded. He snatched Bradshaw's hat from the desk, jammed it on his head and pulled it down low. Taking the Colt from Norrie's hand, he shoved it into his waistband, then followed her out the back door.

Luck was with them. Dark clouds scudded across the sky, playing hide and seek with the moon. Kade boosted Norrie into the Appy's saddle, then vaulted onto the mustang's back. "Go slow," he said, keeping his head down. "We don't want to attract any attention."

Her nerves were humming like piano wires as they headed away from the saloons.

She jumped at every noise, every shadow, until they reached the town limits.

Just when she thought they'd make it without a hitch, the moon broke through the clouds.

Norrie froze when a familiar voice called, "Is that you, Bradshaw? Why the hell aren't you at the...?

Dawson's words trailed off when he recognized Norrie's horse. It took him a heartbeat too long to realize who her companion was. But by then, it was too late.

Kade slapped Norrie's horse on the rump, then jacked a round into the rifle and fired a shot over Dawson's head.

Dawson went ass over tea kettle when his gelding reared and took off after the other horses. Dawson rolled to his feet, drew his Colt and cranked off six rounds, cussing mightily all the while. But it was no use.

His prisoner had escaped.

Norrie had never been so afraid in her life. Afraid to look back, terrified that she'd be hit by mistake, she leaned over the Appy's neck, her heart thundering in her ears as they raced hellbent for leather out of town and into the darkness beyond.

After what seemed like hours, Kade drew rein under a rocky outcropping sheltered by a small stand of timber. "Are you all right?" he asked, his voice gruff.

Huffing a sigh, she brushed her hair away from her face. "I think so. Are you... oh, Lord, Kade, you're hurt!"

He glanced down at his side, muttered an oath when he saw the blood leaking down his right leg.

Norrie was off her horse in an instant, her eyes filled with worry as Kade slid from the back of the mustang and dropped heavily to the ground. Opening the bag tied behind her saddle, she pulled out the extra shirt she had packed for Kade and ripped several strips from the bottom edge. Kneeling beside him, she pulled his shirttail out of the waistband of his trousers, and grimaced when she saw the ugly wound low in his right side. Even in the faint light of the moon, she could see there was no exit wound.

Lifting her head, she met his gaze.

"You'll have to dig it out," he said between clenched teeth.

Just the thought made her stomach churn. But he was right. The bullet had to come out before it festered.

She stood, her legs trembling as she opened her other saddlebag. She had packed a loaf of bread, coffee and a pot, some hardtack and bacon, a few utensils, and several knives for cutting the bread and slicing the bacon.

Swallowing hard, she selected a knife with a slender blade and returned to Kade's side. "Are you ready?"

Jaw clenched, he nodded as he lay back on the ground and closed his eyes. "Just do it."

Willing her hands to stop shaking, Norrie wiped the blood from his side. What if the knife slipped and sliced into something vital? What if she passed out? What if the wound got infected?

Whispering, "Stop it!" she took a deep breath, said a quick prayer for strength and a steady hand, and probed the wound. It took a while to locate the slug. She knew every time she moved the knife caused Kade pain. Sweat beaded on his brow. His hands were tightly clenched at his sides. But he never made a sound.

At last, she managed to dislodge the slug. Such an ugly, misshapen little thing to cause so much pain, so much blood loss. She wrapped a thick strip of cloth around his middle and tied it in place.

She offered him a drink of water when she was done.

"What are you doing?" she asked when he sat up. "You need to rest."

"Not now. Give me your hand." He let out a low groan as she helped him to his feet. He stood there a moment, panting softly. Then, leaning heavily on her, he made his way to his horse. He grimaced as he climbed onto the mustang's bare back and took up the reins.

"Where are we going?" Norrie asked as she mounted her horse.

"To Mila Sapa's village. Dawson won't follow us there."

Norrie glanced anxiously at Kade. His face was pale, his brow damp with sweat. He rode slumped in the saddle, occasionally lifting his head long enough to look around and make sure they were headed in the right direction. She had no idea how he managed to stay upright.

She had insisted they stop from time to time to rest the horses, but it was Kade she was worried about. She insisted he drink from the canteen every time they stopped.

Norrie glanced at their back trail constantly, always expecting to see a posse coming after them, but there was no sign of anyone, or anything, just miles and miles of open country.

The sun had been up for two hours or so when they topped a rolling hill. Below, she saw dozens of hide lodges strung out in a loose circle alongside a slow-moving river. A horse herd grazed on the far side of the river. Smoke rose from several cookfires, carrying the faint scent of roasting meat. Children ran through the village, black hair tousled by a cool breeze. Men in breechclouts and moccasins and women in deerskin dresses moved through the camp. Babies cried. Dogs barked. Two women were skinning a deer, while a third looked on.

A glance at Kade told her they had arrived just in time. Another few miles and he wouldn't have made it.

There was a cry of alarm from the village when one of the men spotted them. In minutes, a dozen armed warriors brandishing rifles were riding toward them.

Norrie breathed a sigh of relief when she recognized Mila Sapa in the lead.

The warrior reined his horse in beside Kade's. He quickly assessed the situation, took the reins from Kade's hand, and led his horse down the hill toward a lodge near the center of the camp.

Norrie trailed behind, acutely aware of the stares— some curious, some hostile—sent her way.

When they reached the lodge. Mila Sapa helped Kade from his horse and led him inside. Norrie hesitated, then dismounted and followed them inside where she stood by the door.

Mila Sapa spoke to the woman kneeling beside a small fire—his wife? Norrie wondered. When they finished speaking, he lowered Kade onto a buffalo robe and left the lodge.

The woman paid little attention to Norrie as she set about adding sticks to the firepit in the center of the floor. When that was done, she removed the blood-stained cloth around Kade's middle and gently removed his shirt. After washing the wound, she dried it with a strip of calico cloth and then, chanting all the while, she sprinkled some kind of herbs over the affected area, then wrapped a clean length of cloth around his middle. When that was done, she offered Kade something to drink, then lit a small bundle of sticks and passed the smoke over Kade from head to foot. The scent of sage filled the air. When Norrie looked at Kade again, he seemed to have fallen asleep.

"He will be well," the woman remarked in stilted English. "Do you want to eat?"

"Yes, please," Norrie said, wondering where the woman had learned to speak English.

With a nod, the woman went outside. She returned moments later carrying a wooden bowl. She handed it to Norrie, along with a spoon made of what looked like buffalo horn, and gestured for her to sit.

"Thank you," Norrie murmured as she sat cross-legged on the robe beside Kade.

With a nod, the woman left the lodge.

Norrie glanced at her surroundings. The interior was quite large. Furs covered the floor. There were half-a-dozen buckskin bags and bundles on one side and what looked like a bedroll on the other. A few cookpots and utensils occupied a place beside the entrance, fat hide pouches hung from the lodgepoles. She wondered what was in them. The lining inside the lodge depicted a crudely drawn painting of a herd of buffalo being chased across the grasslands by several warriors on horseback.

Norrie took a tentative taste of the stew. She had heard the Indians sometimes ate their dogs—and their horses— and sincerely hoped this was venison or buffalo.

Whatever it was, she was too hungry to be picky.

She wondered how long they would stay here. And how safe it was for them to be here. And where they would go if they left. Kade had a price on his head. The best thing they could do would be to leave the territory. Tempting as that sounded, they had no money, nothing but their horses, a little food, and the change of clothes she had brought with them. She might be able to find a job as a maid in a hotel, but they would always be looking over their shoulders, afraid someone would recognize Kade. She frowned, thinking it highly unlikely that lawmen outside the Dakotas would have been notified.

Beset by doubts, and worried about Kade, she set the bowl aside, curled up on the floor beside him, and closed her eyes. Time enough to worry about tomorrow, she thought. It was enough that they were safe. For now.

CHAPTER TWENTY

Norrie sat in the shade of the lodge, trying to ignore the curious looks being sent her way by men, women, and children alike. She wondered if she was the first white woman they had ever seen. Kade had told her that the woman sharing her lodge with them was, indeed, Mila Sapa's wife. His second. Her name was Winter Leaf. His first wife and their eight-year-old son had been killed by soldiers two years earlier.

Kade had eaten earlier and gone back to sleep, leaving her at loose ends.

Glancing around, she saw men standing together, talking. Others seemed to be making weapons. An old man across the way dozed in the shade of his lodge. Little girls stayed close to their mothers. A couple of boys were playing some kind of game with a wooden hoop and a stick. There were dogs everywhere of every size and shape. On the far side of the camp circle, a woman knelt on the ground, scraping what looked like a deer hide.

Never had time passed so slowly. No one spoke to her. Her legs began to ache from sitting for so long. Rising, she stretched her back and shoulders, wondering if she dared walk down to the river and dip her feet in the water.

Deciding to take a chance, she strolled in that direction. No one stopped her.

Sitting at the water's edge, Norrie removed her boots and stuffed her stockings inside, then dangled her bare feet in the water. She gazed into the distance, wondering what the future held, wondering if she would ever see Seth and Truvy again.

Kade woke with a groan. He pressed his fingertips against his side, which was still tender, but when he removed the bandage, there was no sign of infection. He'd been lucky, he thought. Damn lucky.

Where was Norrie?

Pain skittered down his side as he sat up and tugged on his boots. Jaw clenched, he slowly gained his feet, stood still a moment waiting for the worst of it to pass.

When he could breathe again, he stepped out of the lodge, squinting against the sunlight.

He knew a moment of relief when he saw her sitting at the water's edge. Moving like an old man, he made his way toward her.

Norrie turned at the sound of footsteps, eyes widening when she saw Kade. He was shirtless, his skin the color of copper, his hair as black as ebony. Never had his Lakota heritage been more obvious than now. "What are you doing up?" she exclaimed.

"I needed some fresh air." Jaw clenched and moving carefully, he sat down beside her. "Are you all right?"

"I'm fine." He wasn't, she thought, noting the faint sheen of sweat on his brow, the tentative way he moved, the tight lines of pain that bracketed his mouth. "You should have stayed inside. You need your rest."

He shrugged off her concern. "Fresh air is the best medicine. Is Winter Leaf treating you all right?"

"Yes, but I feel strange, staying in their lodge. I mean, there's no privacy." How did parents with children ever have any privacy, when the whole family slept in the same lodge?

Kade grinned at the flush in her cheeks. He recalled hearing odd grunts and soft moans coming from his parents bed late at night. As a boy, he'd had no idea what was going on under the buffalo robes. By the time he was old enough to ask questions, he already knew the answer.

"How long are we going to stay here?" Norrie asked.

"I don't know. At least until my side heals up a little more. And then…" He shook his head. "I'm sorry I got you into this."

"You didn't. It was my choice to come. And I'd do it again." She longed to feel his arms around her but not here, in view of the camp. And there was no privacy in the lodge. She sighed heavily.

"Are you sure you're all right?" Kade asked.

"I just miss… never mind."

Moving slowly, he gained his feet. He stood there a moment, panting softly, then held out his hand. "Come on, let's go for a walk."

"Are you up to it?"

"Don't worry about me."

Ignoring his hand, she grabbed her boots and stood up.

When he reached for her hand again, she took it, and they walked along the shore and away from the village. The river curved after a while, and after another few yards, the camp was out of sight. The prairie stretched away, miles and miles of grassland as far as the eye could see. A red-tailed hawk soared overhead, making lazy circles in the sky. As they walked along, there was only the bubbling song of the river and the faint sigh of the wind ruffling the leaves of the cottonwoods.

Kade stopped beside a fallen tree and sat down. Tugging Norrie down beside him, he slipped his arm around her waist. "Is this better?"

"Much."

When he leaned closer, she lifted her face for his kiss. And suddenly the world was brighter and anything was possible. She slipped her arms around his neck, everything forgotten but the wonder of his touch. His hands moved restlessly up and down her spine as he deepened the kiss.

Kade's head jerked up at the sound of laughter. From across the river, two young boys clad in breechclouts and moccasins were staring at them, wide-eyed. With a shake of his head, he said, "Looks like we've been discovered."

"So it does."

Kade called something in Lakota and the boys turned and ran downriver. "Now, where were we?"

It was late afternoon when they returned to camp. Winter Leaf offered them bowls of venison stew and while they ate, Kade told Norrie something of the Indian way of life. "The Lakota don't have clocks, or schedules. They eat when they're hungry and sleep when they're tired. When they need meat, the men go hunting, sometimes a man goes alone, sometimes there are tribal hunts, usually in the spring and the summer. When the men are in camp, they seem like a lazy bunch to the whites, but a warrior's sole purpose is to provide meat for his lodge and protect the village. The women take care of everything else. They cook, skin hides, make moccasins, and raise the kids."

"I guess they don't go to church, or believe in God," Norrie remarked.

"Not the same God as the white man," Kade said. "The Lakota believe in *Wakan Tanka*, the Great Spirit. They have other spiritual entities—*Wi*, the sun, *Hanwi*, the moon, *skan*, the sky, *Inyan*, the rock. And *Wakinyan*, the thunder beings. They're creatures of power, like the Thunder Birds. The *Wakinyan* control rain and hail, thunder and lightning. They bring new life to the earth after the winter."

"That's a lot of gods," Norrie remarked thoughtfully.

"I suppose."

"Is that what you believe?"

Kade shrugged as he stared into the distance. "These days, I'm not sure what I believe."

Lying on her side beneath a buffalo robe, Norrie watched Kade sleep, his shape barely visible in the faint light filtering through the lodge's smoke hole. How long would they stay here? How were Seth and Truvy getting along? What were the chances of Kade clearing his name so they could go home? What if that never happened?

She rolled onto her back and stared up at the sliver of sky visible overhead. She loved Kade, but did she want to spend the rest of her life in this village? Even if she learned the language and had a lodge of her own, she would never be one of them. Even if they eventually accepted her, she would never fit in. She would always feel like an outsider. But what was the alternative? Going back to stay with Seth, when her heart and soul would be here?

Too restless to sleep, she slid out from under the buffalo robe and slipped out of the lodge. Millions of stars twinkled overhead like diamonds carelessly scattered across a black velvet sky. A baby's cry broke the stillness of the night and was quickly hushed. She could see the Lakota horse herd in the distance. Nearer at hand, a large dog lifted its head and began barking. A moment later, a chorus of growls and barks filled the air and suddenly warriors clad in only breechclouts—and some wearing nothing at all—poured from their lodges, weapons in hand.

"What's happening?" Norrie asked as Kade stepped out of the lodge.

"I'm not sure." His gaze swept the camp, and then he swore. "Get inside and stay there!"

"What…?"

But he was already gone, running toward the horse herd, his gun in hand, with a warrior close on his heels.

Norrie saw them then, mounted riders appearing like ghosts out of the dark, their sudden whoops spooking the herd, driving them across the river, while some of the Lakota men swung onto the backs of the horses tethered near their lodges and gave pursuit.

Women were coming outside now, some cradling babies in their arms. Fires were lit and in the faint glow of the flames, she saw their worried faces as the men rode off.

She glanced at Winter Leaf, standing beside her, hands clenched at her sides.

It was near dawn when the warriors returned. They had managed to capture a few of their horses, but the majority of the herd was gone. Norrie was relieved to see that her Appy and Kade's mustang were still tied close to the lodge. He'd told her that it was customary for warriors to tether their favorite mounts close by.

A high-pitched wail rose in the distance. Glancing that way, Norrie saw one of the women walking beside a horse bearing a dead warrior. A moment later, another wail echoed the first.

Suddenly anxious, Norrie went up on her tiptoes, her gaze searching for Kade.

Breathing hard, Kade hunkered down on his heels, his injured side on fire from the strain of lifting Mila Sapa onto the back of an abandoned Crow pony. The warrior had taken an arrow high in the back near his right shoulder. Kade had broken the shaft but left the arrowhead inside, since he had to way to stop the bleeding once it was removed.

When the pain in his side eased, Kade took up the reins and began the long walk back to the village. There would be war now between the Lakota and the Crow, which left him with two choices—stay and fight alongside his people, or take Norrie and hole up in one of the small towns that dotted South Dakota. The odds of anyone recognizing him were slim, but it was always a risk. Still, if anything happened to him, it would be safer for Norrie if it happened in a town rather than here, with the Lakota.

He'd talk to her about it tomorrow and see what she had to say.

CHAPTER TWENTY-ONE

"Leave?" Norrie stared at Kade. They were sitting by the river's edge after the morning meal. Unable to stand wearing her travel-stained pants and shirt any longer, she had changed into her dress after breakfast. It didn't make her feel any less out of place, but it felt good to be in her own clothes instead of a pair of men's pants and a shirt.

"The Lakota are preparing to go to war with the Crow for stealing our horses. I don't want to be here when that happens. I don't want to put you in danger."

"Where would we go?"

"We'll find a place. There's a little town east of here a'ways. If you agree, we'll leave today."

Norrie blew out a sigh. She didn't want to stay, but she didn't like the idea of going farther away from home, either. In the end, leaving seemed the better option. She didn't know what she would do if anything happened to Kade while they were here.

An hour later, they rode out of the village. Winter Leaf had packed them enough food to last a few days. Mila Sapa had given them two trade blankets, offered Kade a buckskin shirt, and a saddle for the mustang.

It was a lovely day, the sky a bright, clear blue, the air warm, fragrant with the scent of grass and sage. Norrie's mood lightened at the thought of living in a town again. Hopefully, they would be able to get a change of clothes, though how they would pay for them, she had no idea. With luck, they might be able to wash the ones they were wearing. And hopefully have a bath.

She glanced at Kade, riding silently beside her. She could tell his wound was still hurting him, but he never complained.

As the miles went by, she spied a doe with a couple of half-grown fawns, and, far off in the distance, a small herd of buffalo.

After a while, they reached a small stream. Kade drew rein alongside and slid from the back of his horse.

When he came to help her dismount, she shook her head. "I can do it."

He flashed a wry smile, knowing she was afraid that lifting her from the back of the horse would cause him pain.

They sat on the grass while the horses drank. In no hurry to get back in the saddle, Kade tethered the horses to a nearby willow tree and let the animals graze.

"It's beautiful out here," Norrie remarked. "No wonder the Indians are fighting so hard to keep it."

He nodded. He loved the wide open spaces, the sense of freedom, of being where he belonged.

He glanced at Norrie, wondering if she was homesick, if she was sorry she had followed him, how he was going to support her. All he knew was gambling and he was damn good at it. But he wasn't sure she wanted that kind of life. He'd been a wanderer for years. It wouldn't be easy, settling down in one place, maybe finding a job, but he would do it for her. He owed her that much.

Norrie sat with her back against a tree, watching Kade sleep. The horses stood head-to-tail, idly swishing flies. Bees buzzed around a straggly patch of flowers. A gray squirrel darted from one tree to another, scolding her the whole while.

It was so quiet, so peaceful. She imagined building a house here, planting a garden, raising a family. But it was just a dream. It would be foolish to build here, with warring tribes only a few miles away. The winters would be harsh. There would be no water if the stream ran dry. She wondered about their destination. They should be safe in a small town. News didn't travel very fast out here. What were the chances that anyone would have heard of him? Or that they would run into someone he knew?

Smiling, she plucked a blade of grass and twirled it between her thumb and forefinger, content to watch him sleep.

The sun was high in the sky when Kade awoke to find Norrie lying beside him, her head pillowed on her hand. For a moment, he simply watched her. Lying there, with the sun shining in her hair and pinking her cheeks, she looked like a fairy tale princess in disguise. Why she loved him, he had no idea.

Leaning down, he brushed a kiss across her lips. "Norrie?"

"Hmm?" Her eyelids fluttered open. She smiled when she saw him. "I was dreaming," she murmured. "We were married, living on my father's ranch, raising horses and children."

162

"It's a beautiful dream," he said, running his fingers through her hair. "I wish I could make it come true."

"We'll make another one," she said, and drawing his head down to hers, she kissed him.

The touch of her lips on his chased every thought, every hurt, from his mind as he pulled her close. She went into his arms willingly, her body molding itself to his as he kissed and caressed her.

When he groaned her name, she boldly undressed him before shedding her own clothes. The grass was cool beneath her bare skin, but she felt only Kade's lips on hers, his hands caressing her, the warmth of his breath in her ear as he whispered that he loved her...

Kade groaned softly as he kissed Norrie's cheek, then sat up.

She looked at him, a worried expression on her face. "Did I hurt you?"

He laughed softly as he pressed a hand to the cloth wrapped around his middle. "A little," he admitted with a wink. "But it was worth it."

Norrie felt her cheeks grow hot. She had never been so bold before, but he didn't seem to mind.

They rode until sunset, then made camp in a shallow draw. Kade unsaddled the horses while Norrie gathered wood for a fire. A short time later, they sat side by side as Kade roasted a chunk of venison, which they washed down with water from a rawhide container. It wasn't much of a meal, but it was better than nothing, and Kade was beside her.

When the fire died down, they snuggled together under a blanket of stars. Norrie drifted off with her head on Kade's shoulder while a wolf howled a lonely lament to the night.

Norrie was heartily sick of sleeping on the ground and eating jerky and pemmican three times a day by the time they reached their destination. A sign on the edge of the town read:

Welcome to Moses.
Population—Changes Day by Day

Riding down the dusty street, Norrie noticed that a number of houses were spread in a wide circle around the town. Some were large, some small, some a stone's throw from the main road, some further back. All were made of wood.

They passed a blacksmith shop, a livery, a combination barber shop and public bath, a jail made of stone, a two-story hotel, and a general store that also housed the post office. A hand-lettered sign in front of a white-washed house announced that Doctor A. P. Henley treated people and horses. There was also a saloon. And a restaurant that promised good home cooking. A small white-washed church and grave yard surrounded by a rickety wooden fence stood at the end of town

All the buildings looked like they'd been put up in a hurry and might be taken down the same way.

There were no boardwalks, just a wide, dusty street.

Kade drew rein in front of the hotel, amusingly named The Grand Palace.

Looking forward to taking a bath and sleeping in a bed, Norrie slid from the back of her horse and stretched her arms over her head.

Kade dismounted and tethered both horses to the hitch rack in front of the hotel.

He looked as weary as she felt, Norrie mused, as she followed him inside. The long ride hadn't done his injury any good, that was for sure.

The interior of the hotel wasn't grand, but it was clean. The walls were papered in a green-and-white stripe. A single, high-backed sofa stood against one wall flanked by a pair of side tables.

A middle-aged man in a starched white shirt and black string tie stood behind the counter. He smiled when he saw them. "Welcome, strangers," he said cheerfully. "How can I help you?"

"We need a room with a double bed and lots of hot water."

"Yes, sir." The desk clerk pulled a leather-bound book from under the counter and handed Kade a pen. "Just sign the register."

Kade hesitated a moment, then wrote *Mr. and Mrs. Smith.*

The clerk lifted a key from a board behind him. "That'll be one dollar, in advance."

Kade laid his Colt on the counter. "I'm a little short of cash right now. Will you take this as collateral until I sell my rifle?"

"Fall on hard times, did ya?"

"You could say that."

Brow furrowed, the man studied Kade for a long moment. "You're an Injun, aren't ya?"

A muscle ticked in Kade's jaw. And then he nodded curtly.

The man grunted thoughtfully as he looked at Norrie, who forced a smile.

"I reckon I can trust ya until tomorrow," the man decided, handing Kade the key. "Room 6, upstairs, second door on the left. I'll bring the water up as soon as it's hot."

"Much obliged," Kade said.

The room was small, furnished with a double bed and a badly scarred three-drawer dresser. There were a couple of hooks on the wall for clothes. A washstand held four less-than-white towels and a porcelain pitcher and bowl. A solitary, ladder-back chair sat in front of the room's single window. There was a chamber pot under the bed.

"Not very grand," Kade muttered as he closed the door behind them.

"But the bed's not bad," Norrie said, testing the mattress.

"Why don't you stay here and get cleaned up? I need to see if I can find someone to give me a few dollars for the Winchester, or we won't eat tonight."

Norrie nodded dubiously.

"You'll be okay," Kade assured her as he brushed a kiss across her lips. "Just lock the door after me."

Kade strolled down the street to the general store. A few women sent suspicious glances in his direction as he stepped up to the counter.

A rotund man with pink cheeks and slicked-back brown hair offered him a tentative smile. "Can I help you?"

"I'm looking to sell my rifle. Do you know anyone in town who might be interested?"

"Mind if I look at it?"

Kade laid the Winchester on the counter.

The desk clerk picked it up and turned it over in his hands, then lifted it to his shoulder and sighted down the barrel. "How much do you want for it?"

"They cost hundred dollars new."

166

The clerk stroked his chin thoughtfully. "Does it work?"

"I'd hardly be carrying it around if it didn't."

"I'll give you forty."

"Are you kidding me?"

"Fifty."

"Done. Any chance I can buy it back?"

"You just lookin' for a loan?"

"More or less."

"I'll hold onto it for a week. If you don't come up with the money by then, it's mine."

"Sounds fair."

After leaving the general store, Kade took the horses down to the livery. From there, he went to the saloon. The Lazy Ace was pretty much like every other saloon he'd ever seen— a painting of a barely clad buxom woman hung behind the bar that ran along the back wall. Tables were scattered around the sawdust-covered floor, a cheap chandelier hung from the ceiling. A man wearing a red vest over a white shirt plunked *Oh, Susannah* on an old, out-of-tune piano.

Kade made his way to one of the tables and jerked his thumb at an empty chair. "Mind if I sit in?"

The three men sitting there looked him up and down and one of them shrugged.

"We'll deal you in for the next hand."

Wishing she could soak in a tub of hot water, Norrie washed as best she could, grateful that there was at least soap and hot water and a bed to sleep in. She hated to put her dusty clothes back on. They hadn't been washed in days and they smelled of horse and sweat. Maybe, if Kade managed to sell his rifle, they could afford to buy a change of clothes.

She washed her hair as best she could, then sat by the open window to let it dry, only then remembering that she didn't have comb or brush.

She stared out the window, wondering where Kade was, how long they would stay here, how they would pay for the room and something to eat if he couldn't sell the rifle. She wondered how her brother and Truvy were getting along, if they were happy, if the boardinghouse was turning a profit. If she would ever see them again.

Two hours later, Kade left the saloon, four hundred dollars to the good. He'd been surprised at how rich the pots were, only to learn that some of the men had struck a rich vein of gold in the mountains and formed a sort of co-op with rotating shifts—a third of them worked during the day, a third of them slept, and a third of them took turns guarding the mine at night. He couldn't help wondering how long it would be before someone decided they wanted it all. But that was their worry, not his.

He made a stop at the general store to pick up a few things, including his Winchester and a box of ammunition, before he returned to the hotel. He paid for their room and retrieved his Colt before heading upstairs.

He found Norrie asleep in the chair by the window. "Hey, Norrie," he said, giving her shoulder a shake. "Wake up."

She blinked up at him, then smiled. "Did you sell the rifle?"

"Yep. And bought it back. Along with a few other things," he said, and dropped several packages wrapped in brown paper in her lap.

"What's all this?"

He shrugged. "A change of clothes and a nightgown for you, a hair brush." He tugged lightly on a lock of her hair. "And just in time, too."

Gathering the packages into her arms, Norrie dumped them on the bed and began to open them. "Oh, Kade," she exclaimed as she unwrapped a blue gingham dress, "I love it!"

Like a child at Christmas, she unwrapped her presents—a long, white nightgown that tied with a pink ribbon, a pair of stockings, two lacey handkerchiefs, a pair of combs for her hair, a ruffled skirt and pink shirtwaist.

Eyes shining with happiness, she threw her arms around his neck and kissed him. "Thank you! But, didn't you buy anything for yourself?"

He jerked his thumb at several packages stacked on the dresser, topped off by a black Stetson.

"What did you buy besides a hat?"

He shrugged one shoulder. "Pants, shirt, new boots. Nothing as pretty as that dress."

"I can't wait to wear it!"

"Well, you get dressed while I wash up, and I'll take you out to dinner."

"How can we afford it?"

"I played a little poker this afternoon."

"And you won?"

He winked at her. "Enough to last us awhile."

❖ ❖ ❖

An hour later, they left the hotel. Norrie felt like she'd been reborn. She was clean from head to foot. She had on a pretty new dress. All she needed was a new pair of shoes to replace her old ones, something Kade said he hadn't bought because he wasn't sure of her size. He'd done well enough guessing her dress size, though.

He looked handsome in a pair of black pants and a dark blue shirt. His .44 rode easily in the new holster on his right hip, his hat was tilted at a rakish angle.

A few men eyed him warily as they walked to the restaurant.

Inside, they found a table for two. Norrie glanced around. It was nothing fancy, but the tablecloth was spotless, the red-checked curtains added a cheerful note, and went well with the white-washed walls.

There were only three choices on the menu—steak, beef stew, or fried chicken.

She asked for chicken, Kade wanted a steak, rare.

Norrie leaned back in her chair, wondering what the future held for the two of them. Kade had asked her to marry him and she had said yes. She wondered if being married would change their relationship. Being a man, he probably wasn't in any itching hurry to tie the knot. Maybe he was happy with things the way they were. Still, after they had made love, she had assumed they'd be married right away. Now, here she was, living with him in a hotel like a kept woman, which, she supposed, was what she was. After all, he was paying for the room and her clothes, buying her dinner...

She felt a rush of color sweep into her cheeks. What would the people in town think if they knew?

Kade frowned as Norrie's cheeks turned a bright pink. "What's wrong?" he asked. "You feeling all right?"

"Yes. No."

"What is it?"

"We can't talk about it here."

"Norrie…"

"Not now," she hissed as the waitress served their dinner.

Damn, Kade thought, what the hell was wrong with her?

CHAPTER TWENTY-TWO

Norrie was silent as the grave as they made their way back to the hotel. In their room, she removed her shoes, then slumped into the chair by the window, her back to him.

"Norrie, what the hell's wrong?"

"Nothing."

Shit. Unbuckling his gunbelt, he dropped it on the dresser, huffed an impatient sigh as he stared at her back. He hadn't had a lot of experience with decent women and he was at a loss to know what do to. And then he frowned. *Decent women.* He swore under his breath as he crossed to the window and drew her into his arms.

She didn't resist, just stood there as stiff as dried leather, refusing to meet his eyes.

"Norrie, I'm sorry. I didn't mean to treat you with disrespect when I didn't let you have your own room. It's just that this is a strange town and I didn't want to leave you alone."

She shrugged one shoulder, but still wouldn't look at him.

Kade frowned. And then he knew what was bothering her. It wasn't just that they were sharing a room. They'd been sleeping together and they weren't married.

Damn! He'd proposed and she'd said yes, but with everything that had happened since then, it just hadn't been a priority. Nor had he stopped to think what being married to him would mean for her. Women would snub her for being married to a half-breed. Men would look at her differently. He needed to make sure she understood what she would be letting herself in for if they tied the knot.

Cupping her chin in his palm, he forced her to look at him. "I love you, Norrie, but I'm no fit husband for anyone. You must know that. Hell, your reputation is already in shreds just from being with me. I don't have anything to offer you. And if the day comes that I'm caught, or killed, I don't want you burdened by my name. Do you understand?"

"Do you think I care about any of that?"

"I don't know, darlin', but I do. It might not matter in a place like this, but in a decent, God-fearing town, folks will hold it against you that you married an Indian."

Kade drew her into his arms as tears filled her eyes. "I've got enough money to send you back home if that's what you want."

"Is that what *you* want? To send me away?"

"No, darlin', of course not." Cupping her face in his palms, he wiped away her tears with the pads of his thumbs.

"If you don't love me, why did you ask me to marry you?"

"Norrie, darlin', I love you more than my life. I just want what's best for you."

"You're the best thing for me," she said, sniffling. "I don't care if we stay here forever as long as we're together."

Murmuring, "Ah, Norrie," he rested his chin on the top of her head. "What am I going to do with you?"

"Love me, Kade," she whispered. "Just love me."

Kade stayed awake long after Norrie had fallen asleep, her legs tangled with his, her head resting on his shoulder. He was no good for her and he knew it. He never should have let things go this far, but how could he leave her now? She was the best thing that had ever happened to him.

This wasn't much of a town, but one of the houses was for sale. Another few good hands at the poker table and he'd be able to buy it. Maybe he could get a job dealing at the Lazy Ace. It wouldn't be much of a life, but they'd be together. Hell, he would gladly marry Norrie if it would make her happy. It would sure as hell make him happy, he thought, and fell asleep smiling.

In the morning, they went out to breakfast and then took a walk about the town. Kade stopped at the livery to make sure their horses were being cared for and to pay for a week's board in advance.

They were passing the general store when Norrie noticed a Help Wanted sign in the window. Tugging on Kade's arm to stop him, she gestured at the sign. "Maybe I could get a job."

"You want to go to work?"

"Well, we could use the money."

"It's up to you."

She worried her lower lip between her teeth, then straightened her shoulders. "Do you want to come in with me?"

"I think you'll do better on your own."

"Okay." Taking a deep breath, she opened the door and stepped inside. A bell over the door announced her arrival.

A man stepped out from behind the counter. "Can I help you, Miss?"

"I . . . I saw your sign in the window . . . and, I, that is . . ."

"You want the job?" he asked.

"Yes, very much."

"Do have any experience?"

"No. But I'm sure I could learn."

"All right. We'll try it out for a week and see how you do. I need someone to stock the shelves and to fill in behind the counter when I go to lunch. Things are slow in the evening and first thing in the morning, so I'll need you from ten to six. You can start tomorrow. Does that work for you?"

"Yes, sir! Thank you, Mister …?"

"Goodman. Matthew Goodman. What shall I call you?"

"Norrie will do. Or Miss McDonald, whichever you prefer."

"Norrie it is."

Smiling, she hurried outside to tell Kade the good news.

"Well, congratulations, working girl," he said.

"I'm excited and scared at the same time," she confessed. "I hope I do all right."

"You'll be fine."

"What will you do while I'm working?"

"I'll be working, too, in my own way."

"You mean gambling."

"It's what I'm good at. I'm hoping the saloon will hire me."

Norrie frowned as it occurred to her that she would be at the general store during the day and Kade would likely be at the saloon at night. "When will we see each other?"

"I can gamble any time of the day or night," he said. "We'll be together when you get home from work. With luck, we'll have a place of our own before long."

Norrie took a deep, calming breath as she stepped into the general store the next morning.

Mr. Goodman smiled at her from behind the counter. "Are you ready to go to work?" he asked, coming around the end of the counter.

"Yes, sir."

"Good." He handed her a white apron. "I got a new shipment of canned goods this morning," he said, gesturing for her to follow him. "I need you to stack them on the shelves."

"I can do that," she said, slipping the apron over her head.

She followed him to the back of the store where canned goods and sacks of flour, sugar, and rice were located.

"Let me know if you have any questions," Mr. Goodman said.

Nodding, she stared at the large pile of boxes standing in the corner. There must have been a dozen of them.

Goodman lifted one brow. "Is there a problem?"

"What? Oh, no, sir."

Looking dubious, he hurried to the front of the store when the bell over the door announced a customer.

It was close to eleven a.m. when Kade strolled into the Lazy Ace Saloon. He hadn't expected there to be more than a few people inside, but then he remembered the men worked in rotating shifts, which meant there was a good chance that a third of the miners would be in the saloon at any time of the day or night.

Catching the bartender's eye, he said, "Who's the boss here?"

"Barlow Jenks."

"Where can I find him?"

"This hour of the morning? Probably at the restaurant having breakfast."

"What time does he come in?"

The bartender jerked his chin toward the door. "Here he comes now."

Kade glanced over his shoulder. The owner was a short, stocky man, with a ruddy face and dark brown eyes that didn't miss a thing. He wore a pair of tan, whipcord trousers, a boiled shirt, a black string tie, and a flat-brimmed hat.

His eyes narrowed when he saw Kade. "You were in here last night."

Kade nodded. "I was wondering if you need a dealer?"

"You any good?"

"I walked away with four hundred dollars last night."

Jenks grunted. "I run an honest house. I catch you cheating once and you're out of here. You got a problem with that?"

"Suits me fine."

"We open at ten in the morning and close at two. My night man comes in at seven and stays until closing. If you can work mornings from ten until seven, you're hired."

"Obliged."

"Can you start today?"

"Sure."

"I'm Barlow Jenks."

"Kade."

"Take the table in the back corner. Cyrus will bring you a couple of fresh decks."

"You got a problem with me gambling in here on my own time?"

"Same rules apply. No cheating."

"Right."

Dealing for the house wasn't as satisfying or exciting as gambling with his own money. His was the only table with a dealer. A lot of men felt there was less chance of being cheated if someone with nothing to win or lose dealt the cards.

The time passed surprisingly fast.

Kade took a break at one to get something to eat. On the way to the restaurant, he stopped at the general store to see how Norrie was getting along. As luck would have it, she was also taking a break.

Hand in hand, they strolled down the street to the restaurant. Inside, they ordered beef stew and coffee.

"How do you like working?" Kade asked.

"It's harder than I thought. I must have stacked a hundred cans this morning, and I'm still not done."

Kade grinned at her. "I got a job at the saloon. Pays pretty good if you want to quit."

"Quit on my first day? I don't think so. Will you be working tonight?"

"No. I get off at seven."

"That's wonderful!" Norrie exclaimed. "We'll be able to have supper together every night!"

The next few days passed quickly. Norrie found she liked working in the store. It gave her an opportunity to meet the ladies in town. Most were friendly, though there were a few who snubbed her once they learned of her relationship with Kade. The people in town didn't know anything about him, only that he was a half-breed. All they saw was the color of his skin. It made Norrie wonder if Kade encountered distrust and suspicion everywhere he went.

She used her first week's pay to buy clothes—a dress, skirt and shirtwaist for herself, a pair of trousers and a dark blue shirt for Kade.

He grinned at her when she showed him what she'd bought. "Just like a woman," he said with a grin. "Spending your money on clothes."

She made a face at him. "I consider it a necessary purchase. You don't want to wear the same thing every day, do you?"

"Doesn't matter. All I do from ten to seven is sit behind a poker table. Nobody cares what I'm wearing."

"Well, I care."

Laughing softly, he pulled her onto his lap. "Buy all the clothes you want, darlin'."

"I love you, Kade," she murmured as she rested her head on his shoulder.

"Are you happy here?" He frowned when she didn't answer right away. "I guess you'd rather be back home."

"I miss Seth," she said quietly. "I miss the ranch."

"I know."

"Don't you miss having a home of your own?"

"You're all the home I need, darlin'."

Kade glanced at the four men at the table as he shuffled the cards and dealt a new hand. They came in about the same time every day. Joe Moss owned the blacksmith shop. He was a big, burly man with skin the color of ebony and arms like tree trunks. Barton Sims, who owned the barber shop, was his opposite in every way. Deacon Sorenson owned the hotel, Obadiah Johnson owned the livery. From the way they interacted, it was obvious they'd been friends for a good long while, four men who didn't care if they won or lost, but gambled because there wasn't much else to do.

Kade listened as they made desultory conversation about the gold strike and how it was good for business.

Of the four, Joe Moss was the best player. Kade had watched him carefully the first few times Moss had been at his table. He was either cheating, or the luckiest gambler Kade had ever seen. After a week, he'd come to the conclusion that it wasn't that Moss was so good, but that the other three were so bad.

But, winner or loser, it was all the same to him.

Kade looked up as Sheriff Jennings strolled into the saloon. The lawman had questioned Kade the first night he'd worked at the saloon. His questions had been friendly enough, but Kade hadn't missed the suspicion in his eyes as he asked if he was planning to stay in town. Now, he felt himself tensing as the sheriff ambled toward his table.

"Evenin', gents," he said. "Mind if I sit in?"

"Well, hell, Sheriff, gonna put a cramp in my game," Joe Moss said good-naturedly.

Jennings laughed as he settled into the empty seat across from Kade. "How are you enjoying our town?" he asked as Kade shuffled the cards.

Kade shrugged. "I've got no complaints. Pot's right, gentlemen," he said as he dealt a new hand.

There was a moment of silence as the men studied their hands.

"Cards?" Kade asked.

Sims and Johnson each took one, Sorenson took two.

"I'll play these," Moss said.

Kade sat back as the men upped the ante. He didn't miss the way Jennings repeatedly looked his way, or the speculation in his eyes. Damn. He told himself he was worrying for nothing. It had been years since he'd killed Matozi's murderer. What were the chances anybody here would have heard about it? Or seen that damn wanted poster?

He breathed a sigh of relief when Jennings cashed in and left the game.

Maybe it was time to move on.

The next morning at work, Norrie found herself thinking about Kade's encounter with the sheriff. Did the lawman suspect him of anything? Would they have to leave town?

She had just started sorting through a pile of men's longjohns, stacking them on a shelf according to size, when she spied Sheriff Jennings coming down the aisle toward her. Feeling a surge of panic, she glanced around, but there was nowhere to go, and avoiding him would likely make him think she had something to hide.

Smoothing a hand over her hair, she forced a smile. "Good morning, Sheriff."

"Mornin', Miss Norrie."

"Is there something I can help you with?"

"Indeed there is. How long have you known Kade?"

"He used to work on our ranch for us," she said.

"Where was that?"

"Clayton's County."

"Why did you leave?"

"My father was killed and we lost the ranch."

"I'm right sorry to hear that."

She nodded.

"I don't mean to pry, but are you married?"

"Not yet. He's been looking out for me since my father died."

"Admirable, I'm sure."

"Is Kade in trouble?"

"Not that I know of. I just like to get acquainted with new folks when they come to town."

"Of course."

He regarded her a moment, then tipped his hat. "Good day to you, Miss Norrie."

Feeling suddenly weak, Norrie took hold of the side of the shelf and let out a deep breath.

Kade paced the floor as Norrie relayed her encounter with the Sheriff that night over dinner. She finished by saying, "Maybe he was just being friendly."

"Yeah, maybe."

"But you don't think so?"

He lifted one shoulder and let it fall. "I haven't met too many friendly lawmen."

"You don't really think the sheriff knows who you are, do you?" she asked. "How could anyone have heard about you way out here?"

"Beats the hell out of me." Pausing in front of the window, he scrubbed a hand over his jaw. "I'm probably worrying for nothing."

Sighing, Norrie went to him and rested her head on his chest. "If you think we should leave..."

He stroked her hair as the old bitterness rose up inside him. If the man who'd seen what happened at the trading post that day had told the truth, he'd be a free man. If he'd been a white man, no one would have accused him of murder for trying to save his brother's life.

Kade paced the floor long after Norrie had gone to bed. Stay or go? He couldn't keep dragging Norrie from town to town. She deserved better than that. On the other hand, his gut was warning him to get out while he could.

He stood at the window hours later, still undecided, as he watched the sun rise over the distant mountains.

CHAPTER TWENTY-THREE

Seth glanced at Truvy as she bustled about the kitchen, clearing the table, putting the dishes in the sink. He still found it hard to believe she was his wife and that they were expecting a baby in only a few months. A baby. He shook his head, wondering what kind of father he'd be. He supposed his own father had loved him, though he couldn't recall ever hearing Connor say the words out loud. He couldn't help feeling his old man had been disappointed in him. For his part, Seth had been disappointed that Connor hadn't been more understanding. Seth had done his best to help out, but working on the ranch hadn't been easy with only one arm. There had been so many things he couldn't do, chores that required two strong arms, two good hands. Thank the Lord for Truvy. She never made him feel like he was less of a man.

He smiled as his gaze settled on her swollen belly. He had no doubt that she would be a wonderful mother. She was kind and sweet and infinitely patient. He hoped the baby would be a girl with her mother's golden-blonde hair and sky-blue eyes.

Truvy lifted one brow when she caught him staring at her. "Did you want something, Seth?"

"No," he said, his voice warm with affection. "I've got everything I want."

"Me, too." After wiping her hands dry, she sat on his lap. "It's been a while since Norrie and Kade left town. Do you think they're doing all right?"

"I don't know. I hope so."

"I wonder where they are. You'd think Norrie would write and let us know."

"Yeah," Seth agreed. And then he frowned. Maybe they were afraid to write, worried that he or Truvy might inadvertently tell someone where they were. Still, it was hard, not knowing if the only kin he had left was doing all right. He had seen Burdett in town a couple of days ago, strutting around like he owned the world.

Seth swore under his breath. Burdett certainly owned a good chunk of ground in Clayton's Corner, damn his eyes, including Seth's old home. Burdett's men now lived in the house, Burdett cattle grazed on McDonald land. Dammit, it wasn't right, but there wasn't anything he could do about it. Not a blessed thing.

"I'm sure Norrie's okay," Truvy said, stroking his cheek. "I have to believe Kade would let us know if she wasn't."

Seth nodded, thinking that if anything happened to Kade, Norrie would surely come home.

CHAPTER TWENTY-FOUR

It was Saturday night and the saloon was crowded with cowboys from the neighboring ranch, and miners who'd come into town to raise a little hell. Kade found it hard to believe it had been over a month since they moved here, but then, every day was pretty much like the last. He had contemplated moving on, but finally decided against it. Newcomers were few and far between and the chance of being recognized seemed pretty slim.

He sat at his usual table, idly shuffling a deck of cards. It was early evening and most of the men were more interested in drinking and flirting with the doves than gambling, although he knew that would change as the night wore on. For now, he was content to sit and watch.

Joe Moss and Obadiah Johnson sauntered in together. Moss ordered a bottle from the bar and the two men headed for Kade's table.

"Just the two of you tonight?" Kade shuffled the deck one more time, and dealt the cards.

"Yeah," Moss said as he uncorked the bottle. "Mrs. Sims and Mrs. Sorenson insisted their husbands stay home tonight. Said they was tired of spending every Saturday night alone."

Johnson grunted. "Hell to be tied down."

Moss filled two shot glasses and handed one to Johnson. "Sometimes," he agreed. "But if you're married long enough, the old lady don't care if you're home or not."

Johnson raised his glass. "I'll drink to that."

"Hell," Moss said, "you'll drink to anything."

Kade grinned as he listened to their banter. He was in the midst of dealing a new hand when a sudden silence fell over the saloon. Looking up, he saw two men facing off at the bar.

"Uh-oh," Moss said. "Looks like trouble."

"Yeah," Johnson said. "Young Rawlins don't like Jenny dancing with anybody else on Saturday night. Especially not Roscoe Downs. Don't help that Rawlins is drunk as a skunk."

A moment later, the batwing door swung open and Sheriff Jennings came in.

Sensing a showdown of some kind, Kade eased his chair away from the table, one hand resting on the butt of his Colt.

"What's going on?" Jennings asked.

"None of your business, Sheriff," Rawlins hissed.

"I'm making it my business unless you take your hand off that hogleg."

"Tell Downs to get the hell out of here."

"I ain't goin' nowhere," Downs said. "Not until I get my dance."

Kade gained his feet as Jennings took a step forward. He knew Rawlins saw the movement out of the corner of his eye. No doubt thinking the sheriff was drawing on him, Rawlins went for his gun.

But Kade was faster. The two gunshots blended together, but it was Rawlins who hit the floor.

Jennings glanced over his shoulder, then crossed the room toward Kade. "Reckon I owe you my life."

Kade shrugged. "Reckon so."

"I'll need you to come down to my office and fill out some paperwork," the Sheriff said. "Moss, you and Johnson take the body down to Doc Henley's."

Grumbling, the two men moved toward the bar.

"Can I buy you a drink before we go?" Jennings asked.

Kade shook his head. "No need." Grabbing his hat, Kade followed the lawman down to his office.

Inside, the sheriff pulled a sheet of paper from a desk drawer. "Just write down what you saw and what you did and then sign your name."

All too aware of the sheriff standing behind him, Kade scrawled a few lines describing what he'd seen and signed his first name.

"I'll need your last name, too," Jennings said, reading over his shoulder.

Kade swore inwardly. Damn, he'd never known his old man's name. He'd used Smith at the hotel, and he used it again now.

"You're mighty quick on the draw," Jennings remarked.

Kade shrugged. "Lucky for you that I was faster than Rawlins."

"Reckon so," Jennings said with a wry grin.

"Anything else?"

"No. Thanks, again."

With a nod, Kade left the office. Outside, he drew in a deep breath and let it out in a long, slow sigh.

Norrie stared at him, eyes wide, as he related what had happened. "Do you think that was wise?" she asked. "I mean, I'm glad you saved his life, but…"

"Hey," he said, pulling her into his arms. "It's okay."

"I hope so," she murmured, resting her cheek against his chest. "I kind of like it here."

Kade held her close, then brushed a kiss across the top of her head. "But?"

"I miss Seth."

"I know."

"Do you think we'll ever be able to go back home?"

"I don't know, darlin'," he said quietly. "But if you want to go and spend some time with your brother…"

She pressed her fingertips to his lips. "Not without you."

Leaning back, Kade's gaze searched hers. "I asked you to marry me awhile back. Are you still willing?"

She blinked at him. "Do you mean it?" It had been so long since he proposed, she'd been afraid he had changed his mind.

He nodded. "I can't think of any reason to wait any longer."

"Me, either!" she exclaimed, and threw her arms around his neck.

"Norrie!" He hugged her tight. "I'll try to make you happy."

"You just did. I love you, Kade. I think maybe I loved you from the minute I saw you, all shot up and bleeding."

He huffed a laugh. "Got a thing for shot-up outlaws, do you?"

"Just one."

He rested his forehead against hers. "I'll talk to the preacher tomorrow."

Norrie closed her eyes on a sigh, happier than she had ever been in her life. Kade loved her.

"Well, you're looking mighty happy today," Mr. Goodman remarked when Norrie arrived at the general store the next morning.

"Oh, I am!" Norrie replied. "I'm getting married!"

"Well, congratulations! When's the big day?"

"We haven't decided yet. He just asked me last night."

"Well, he's a lucky man," Mr. Goodman said, and turned away to wait on a customer.

Since there was only one customer in the store, Norrie made her way to the Ladies' Wear department in search of a new dress to wear to the wedding. The choices were slim and not particularly appealing, but she found a pale pink dress with a dark pink sash, a square neck and a full skirt. Carrying it into the back, she tried it on. It hadn't looked like much on the hangar she thought as she looked at herself in the mirror, but it fit well and flattered her figure. After taking it off, she carried it up front and laid it on the counter.

Smiling at Mr. Goodman, she asked, "Would you hold this for me until I get off work?"

"Why sure, Miss Norrie. And don't forget to let me know when you decide on a date."

Kade regarded Norrie through narrowed eyes as she folded her napkin and placed it on the table. She had fidgeted all through dinner. Unable to stand it any longer, he waited until the waitress came to collect their dishes before he asked what was wrong.

"Do you think I could write to Seth and tell him we're okay? I thought I could send it to Mrs. Minton and ask her to give it to Seth and not tell anyone."

A muscle twitched in Kade's jaw. He couldn't blame her for wanting to get in touch with her brother. Seth was all the blood kin she had left. Still, it was a risk. "I don't know, darlin'," he said and then, seeing the look of disappointment on her face, he said, "Joe Moss told me there's a good-sized town a two-day ride from here. I could mail it from there."

Norrie stared at him. A two-day ride? "Do you really think Sheriff Dawson is still interested in finding you?"

"I don't know." But it wasn't a chance he was willing to take.

After a moment, Norrie said, "I guess it's not a good idea."

"I'm sorry, sweetheart."

Smothering her disappointment, she summoned a smile and said, "I bought my wedding dress today."

With a wink, Kade said, "All we need now is a preacher."

Sundays were the best day of the week, Norrie thought. The General Store was closed and Kade didn't have to work.

After breakfast at the restaurant, they walked down to the church. Norrie was surprised to see people gathered outside. Somehow, she hadn't expected a town filled with miners, gamblers, and soiled doves to attend church services. Granted, a number of those in attendance were in business, like Mr. and Mrs. Horton, who owned the restaurant, and Deacon Sorensen who ran the hotel. The Goodman's were there, and the Sheriff and his wife.

Kade waited for the crowd to disperse before approaching the minister. Reverend Aaron Littlefield was a small, spare man with a thatch of graying brown hair and laugh lines around his eyes.

The reverend smiled as they drew near. "You must be the new couple I've been hearing about," he said. "Welcome to Moses. I'm sorry you missed our service this morning."

"We didn't know about it," Norrie said.

"Well, I hope you'll come next week. How can I help you?"

"We'd like to get married," Kade said.

The reverend nodded. "I would be happy to perform the ceremony. What day did you have in mind?"

Kade glanced at Norrie. "As soon as possible."

"I understand," he said, blue eyes twinkling. "Would tomorrow evening be convenient?"

"Oh, yes!" Norrie said.

"It'll just be us," Kade said.

"And Mr. Goodman," Norrie said.

"We'll need two witnesses," the reverend remarked. "I'll ask Doc Henley and his wife to stand up with you, if you have no objection. What time would be convenient?

Kade and Norrie exchanged glances. "How about seven tomorrow night?" Kade suggested.

"Fine," Reverend Littlefield said, shaking Kade's hand, "I'll see the two of you then."

Norrie couldn't stop smiling as they walked back to the hotel.

The next morning, after Norrie left for work, Kade went to look at the house he'd seen when they first arrived in town.

It was still for sale. A sign on the door directed him to talk to Doc Henley if he was interested.

He found Henley in his office bandaging a nasty cut on a miner's hand. Twenty minutes later, Kade shook the doc's hand and pocketed the key to the house, thinking that it would make a nice wedding present for his bride.

Monday mornings were quiet in the saloon. Kade found himself thinking about Reeves, the trader who had refused to tell the truth about what had happened at the trading post. He wondered if Reeves was still there and what the odds were that he could go back and persuade the trader to tell the truth. Slim and none, he thought ruefully, as a couple of miners came in and sat at his table.

Norrie glanced up as Mr. Goodman called her name. "It's five-thirty," he said, smiling. "And today's the big day. Why don't you head home? I reckon brides have a lot to do before the ceremony."

"Thank you so much," Norrie said, gathering her things.

"Don't mention it. Me and the missus will see you later."

Norrie's nerves were humming with excitement as she hurried down the street toward the hotel. In two hours, she would be Mrs.... Mrs. Who, she thought? She had no idea what Kade's last name was.

When she reached the hotel, she took a quick sponge bath, brushed her hair until it crackled, then tied it back with a pink ribbon before donning her dress. She thought briefly of her mother's bridal gown. She had hoped to wear it to her own wedding and hand it down to her own daughter, should she have one. She'd never had time to pack up the things in the attic. Now she never would.

She studied her reflection in the wavy mirror over the dresser. What would Kade think?

The thought had no sooner crossed her mind than he was there. Norrie stared at him, eyes wide. Clad in a pair of black trousers, a white shirt, and a black jacket, he looked even more handsome than usual. Removing his hat, he drew her into his arms.

"You're beautiful, Norrie."

"So are you. Where did you get those clothes? I've never seen anything like that in Goodman's."

"Believe it or not, they belong to Jacob Horton."

"The man who owns the restaurant?"

"Yep. It's what he wore when he got married. What do you think?"

"You look very handsome."

"They're coming to the wedding."

"Oh."

"Are you ready to go?"

Feeling suddenly shy, she nodded.

Kade settled his hat on his head, then took her hand in his.

When they reached the church, Norrie was surprised at how many people were inside. Besides Mr. and Mrs. Horton, there were several men she didn't know, but assumed knew Kade. Mr. and Mrs. Goodman sat side by side on the second row.

Reverend Littlefield waited for them at the altar. A buxom woman with iron-gray hair sat at a small organ.

A man and woman Norrie didn't recognize stood to one side of the Reverend. She guessed they were Doctor and Mrs. Henley, the witnesses.

The organist began to play as Kade walked her down the aisle.

When the song ended, the Reverend said, "We are gathered here this evening to join this man and this woman in holy matrimony, an honorable estate and not to be entered into lightly. Kade, do you take this woman to be your lawfully wedded wife? Will you love and protect her and keep yourself only for her as long as you live?"

"I will."

"Norrie, do you take this man to be your lawfully wedded husband? Will you love and honor him and keep yourself only for him as long as you live?"

"I will."

"Then, by the power vested in me I now pronounce you man and wife. Kade, you may kiss the bride."

Norrie's heart skipped a beat as Kade drew her gently into his arms, felt herself blush as there were hoots and hollers as he claimed his first kiss as her husband.

"Drinks on the house at the Lazy Ace!" Barlow Jenks bellowed.

Norrie looked up at Kade. Did he intend to spend their wedding night drinking with the men in town?

Seeing the worry in her eyes, he slipped his arm around her waist. "The Hortons have invited us to a wedding supper at their restaurant."

Her relief was palpable.

"We're not done yet," the Reverend Littlefield said. "You need to sign this here marriage license to make it official." He pulled a pot of ink and a pen from behind the altar and handed the pen to Kade, who signed his name and handed it to Norrie. The Reverend also signed it. "Now you're good to go," he said, grinning.

"Is Smith your real name?" Norrie whispered as they left the church and followed Mr. and Mrs. Horton down the boardwalk toward the restaurant.

"Not likely, but it's as good as any. I never knew my old man's name. The Indians called him *Matoskah*. It means White Bear. That's the only name I ever knew."

CHAPTER TWENTY-FIVE

Norrie looked at Kade askance as they left the restaurant. Instead of turning left toward home, he turned right at the corner. "Where are we going?" she asked.

"I thought we'd take a walk," Kade said.

"A walk?"

"Something wrong with that?"

"No." She made a vague gesture with her hand. "I just thought... never mind."

Kade grinned inwardly. He knew what she thought, that he would be eager to carry her to bed. Which he was. But when they made love tonight, it would be in their own home, in their own bed. It had taken some dickering, but he'd managed to obtain a bed and a small chest of drawers, a second-hand sofa, a kitchen table and two chairs. The house had a fireplace and a wood stove for cooking. Water had to be pumped from a well, but at least they had water.

"Are we visiting someone?" she asked as he turned down the narrow dirt path to a small, square house that had been freshly white-washed.

Pulling the key from his pocket, Kade said, "Welcome to your new home, Mrs. Smith," as he unlocked the door. Lifting her into his arms, he carried her across the threshold.

"You bought a house?" she asked, eyes wide with surprise. "Oh, Kade! Thank you."

He lowered her slowly to her feet, his body humming to life as her body slid along his. "I love you, Norrie," he said fervently.

Tears sparkled in her eyes as she murmured, "And I love you."

"Do you like it? If not, we can look for another one."

Norrie glanced around. It was a rough-hewn house, but seemed well-built. "All it needs is a woman's touch. Some curtains for the window. A rug for the floor." She walked from room to room. She found a table and two chairs in the kitchen. There was a dry sink at one end of the room, shelves on another. The bedroom had also been white-washed. It held a brass bed and a chest of drawers. "Curtains in here, too. And a rug, of course."

"It's nothing like your old home," Kade remarked, somewhat apologetically. "But one day I'll build you the kind of house you deserve."

"Someday," she murmured as she boldly slid his jacket over his shoulders and let it fall to the floor. "But we're here now."

"And what would you like to do, here, now?" he teased as he pulled her into his arms.

"I was hoping you might have an idea or two."

"Honey, I've got ideas you've never thought of."

She smiled up at him, her body quivering with anticipation as he began to undress her. Hands trembling, she unbuttoned his shirt and tossed it aside. In less time than she would have believed, they were naked and lying side by side on the bed. And the state of the house and the future and everything else ceased to matter, and there was only Kade, whispering that he loved her, his hands caressing her, arousing her, until she saw only him, wanted only him, here, in her arms, forever.

✤   ✤   ✤

In the morning, Norrie's first thought was that she was lying naked in Kade's arms and that the windows were bare and anyone passing by could look inside. First order of the day—buy material for curtains before she did anything else.

"Good morning, wife."

At the sound of his voice, Norrie smiled from ear to ear. *Wife.*

She turned in his arms. "Husband." Was there ever a more beautiful word?

When he reached for her, she shook her head.

"We've only been married a few hours and you're already refusing to fulfill your wifely duties?" he asked with mock consternation.

"No, but…" She gestured at the window. "Anyone can see us."

"Ah."

Sliding out of bed, he grabbed the sheet and draped it over the curtain rod. "Problem solved," he said as he climbed back in beside her.

"What a clever man I've married," she said, then let out a gasp as his hand cupped her breast. And there was no more time for talk.

It was early afternoon before Kade left for work. A few minutes later, Norrie walked to the General Store, even though Mr. Goodman had given her the day off.

"I didn't expect to see you today," he said with a grin.

"Kade had to go to work."

He grunted softly.

With a whole day ahead of her, Norrie wandered through the store. She found some blue-and-white checked material for the windows in the bedroom and the kitchen, a pretty flowered print for the living room. Her basket was soon filled with a packet of needles and thread, scissors, a tape measure, a bar of soap, a box of matches, salt and pepper, a loaf of bread, a dozen eggs, a box of baking powder.

Mr. Goodman helped her carry the rest of her purchases—some canned goods, dishes, silverware, a cook pot and frying pan, cups, a coffee pot, a sack of coffee, another of flour, a bag of potatoes, two oil lamps and oil. She also found a blanket for the bed, and two large braided rugs, one for the living room, the other for the bedroom.

"Can you please put all this on my bill?" she asked as Mr. Goodman added up her purchases.

"Of course, Miss Norrie. Is there anything else you need?"

"A way to get all this home?"

With a chuckle, he said, "I'll bring the buckboard around and give you a ride to your place."

Norrie thanked Mr. Goodman for his help as he carried the last box into the house. He had closed the store so he could drive her home, and when she mentioned she needed to pick up her clothes from the hotel, he had obligingly stopped there on the way out of town. She stood in the doorway a moment, thinking what a kind man he was.

She spent the rest of the day scouring the kitchen, stacking canned goods on the shelves, putting away the rest of the food, folding their clothes and laying them in the chest of drawers, making the bed. Lastly, she measured all of the windows for curtains.

She was hemming the curtains for the bedroom when Kade entered the house, whistling softly.

"You've been busy," he said.

"Very. I'm afraid we owe Mr. Goodman a great deal of money."

Kade nodded. "I'll take care of it later."

"I wish I could think of something nice to do for him. He not only stopped by the hotel so I could get our things, but he drove me home and carried everything into the house for me. How was your day?"

He shrugged. "Same as always. I could use something to eat. Let's go to the restaurant for some chow."

"Good idea." She hadn't bought any meat, since there was no place to store it.

Norrie sighed as they left the restaurant. Her first day as Kade's wife had been wonderful. Funny, how being married had changed everything. Making love last night and this morning had seemed sweeter, more meaningful, now that they were wed. Not that being in his arms hadn't always been wonderful, she thought, but it was even better now.

They were passing the jail when a shot rang out.

Before she quite knew what was happening, Kade had pushed her into an alley and told her to stay there.

Heart pounding, she watched him dart across the road, gun in hand. From inside the jail, someone bellowed, "Stop that man!" There was another shot and a man ran out the door. He came to an abrupt halt, the gun in his hand coming up when he saw Kade. Norrie screamed "No!" as the man and Kade fired at the same time.

When the smoke cleared, Kade stood tall and straight in the middle of the road. The other man lay face-down in the dirt.

Doors opened up and down the street as people rushed outside.

She saw Mr. Goodman go inside the jail. When he came out a few minutes later, he said, "The sheriff's dead and so is his deputy."

"Looks like his prisoner is dead, too," Doc Henley muttered. "Guess we won't be having a hangin', after all. Sims, Moss, come give me a hand with these bodies."

Norrie stepped out of the alley as all eyes turned in Kade's direction.

"Looks like we need a new sheriff," Barlow Jenks remarked.

"I say we found one," Jacob Horton said, giving Kade a slap on the arm.

There was a cheer from all the men present.

"What do you say, Kade?" Matthew Goodman asked. "You up for the job?"

Kade glanced at Norrie over the top of Goodman's head as he holstered his Colt. She didn't look happy, but she nodded.

"Looks like I'm your man," he said. "As long as I can still gamble at the saloon."

"Drinks on me," Jenks said.

In moments, the street was empty save for Norrie and Kade. She hurried toward him. "Are you all right?"

"Fine. Are you sure you're all right with this?"

"Not really, but I'd rather have you on the right side of the law than working in a saloon. And who knows, maybe one day it will work in your favor."

CHAPTER TWENTY-SIX

Norrie stood at the window of the General Store, staring into the distance. It had rained the last two days, keeping most of the women inside. Not that there were that many women in town. She thought longingly of Clayton's Corner and the friends she had left behind, the church bake sales and holiday dances, baby showers… Truvy's baby was due next month…

Biting down on her lower lip, Norrie placed a hand over her belly, wondering how to tell Kade she was pregnant. Would he be pleased?

Was he happy here? She told herself she was, and it was partly true, but only because she was with Kade. She worried about him every day, although there hadn't been any trouble in town since he became the sheriff. She had decorated the house as best she could. The curtains and the rugs helped, and they had bought an easy chair for the living room, and a wardrobe for the bedroom. Every payday, she bought a new dress for herself and a shirt and trousers for Kade. She had embroidered a sampler for the wall in the living room.

Sighing, she turned away from the window when the bell over the front door announced a customer.

❧   ❧   ❧

Kade was sitting in the Sheriff's Office, his feet propped on the scarred walnut desk, when a cowboy pushed the door open.

"You the law?" he asked breathlessly.

Kade tapped his finger on the badge pinned to his shirt. "What do you think?"

"Marshall over in Custer asked me to give this to ya," he said, thrusting a Wanted poster at Kade. "Said the guy used to live here and might be headed back this way."

"Obliged."

With a tip of his hat, the cowboy stomped out the door.

Kade grunted softly as he read the flyer.

WANTED
FOR MURDER AND ROBBERY.
Big Red Murdock
Six feet tall, black hair
brown eyes, scar on his left cheek
Last seen in Custer, Wyoming
$1500.00 Reward
Dead or alive.

He had tangled with Murdock over a game of poker in a Rapid City saloon a few years back. Murdock had been drunk, but he wasn't stupid and he'd backed down when push came to shove. Like the flyer said, he was a big man, over two hundred pounds, but he hadn't been packing a gun that night and something in Kade's eyes must have warned him to back off. Kade had bought him a drink and that had been the end of it.

Pushing away from the desk, he tacked the flyer on the bulletin board hanging outside the office, then strolled down the street. He kind of liked being a lawman. The men in town respected his gun if nothing else, a nice change from being called half-breed, and worse.

He thought about Norrie as he passed the General Store. She put up a good front, but he knew she wasn't really happy here. She missed Seth, but that wasn't the only thing bothering her. From time to time, he caught her staring at him, then quickly looking away. He thought she was hiding something, but he couldn't imagine what it was.

Tonight, after supper, he would ask her again and she had better, by damn, give him an answer this time!

It was a lovely night, Norrie mused as they walked home from the restaurant. Their lives had quickly fallen into a pattern. She spent her days working at the General Store while Kade took care of business at the jail, or walked through the town. There was little crime here, other than drunken fist fights at the saloon. He took her to dinner in the afternoon and out for supper in the evening. Mornings, they dined at home. But in a few months, the pattern of their lives would change dramatically.

She slid a sideways glance at Kade and found him watching her, a curious expression in his eyes—an expression she had seen often in the last several days.

When they reached home, he lit one of the lamps, then took her by the hand and pulled her down on the sofa beside him.

"What's going on with you?" he asked, his gaze searching hers.

"I don't know what you mean."

"Yes, you do, dammit. Something's wrong. Are you unhappy here? Are you sick? Why the devil won't you confide in me?"

She bit down on her lower lip, thinking she might as well tell him. She wouldn't be able to hide it much longer. Taking a deep breath, she blurted, "We're going to have a baby."

He blinked at her. Stared at her belly. Looked up at her again. "A baby?"

Hardly daring to meet his eyes, she nodded. What if he didn't want it? What if he left her?

"A baby," he said again. "When?"

"I'm not exactly sure. Six or seven months from now I guess."

A slow smile spread over his face. "Why didn't you tell me sooner?"

"I was afraid."

"Afraid? Of what?"

"That you wouldn't want it."

"Ah, Norrie," he murmured as he folded her into his arms. "Of course I want it." *A father*, he thought, stunned. *I'm going to be a father.*

It changed everything.

Later that night, after Norrie had gone to bed, Kade strolled through the town. Norrie was pregnant and this was no place to have a baby, let alone raise one. It was a great place to hide out. Not many strangers passed through and those that did were usually on the run. But he didn't want to raise his son or daughter in that hovel they called home, or in a town where fist fights happened on a daily basis.

Home. In his mind, he pictured the Black Hills, the air fragrant with the scent of pine, the cry of a red-tailed hawk soaring overhead, the vast blue sky that stretched away into forever. Did any of his people still make their home in the Sacred Hills? Or had they all gone to Canada after the massacre at the Little Big Horn?

Did his mother still live?

Too restless to sleep, Kade walked down to the Lazy Ace. It was late and the crowd was light. At the bar, he ordered a whiskey, then eyed the tables. After downing the last of his drink, he joined a game. One of the men looked vaguely familiar, but he couldn't place him until the stranger mentioned Clayton's Corner. After a few minutes, it came to him. His name was Charlie Farrell and he had worked for Burdett's outfit.

"What brings you to Moses?" Kade asked during a break in the game.

Farrell shrugged. "Just passing through."

Kade grunted softly. "You're a long way from home."

"Yeah. Quit my last job. Guy I rode for was no good. Didn't have no regard for the rights of others. Dropped his loop on more than one cow that weren't his." Farrell shook his head. "Ain't right. Man owned the biggest spread in the valley and it wasn't enough."

"Yeah. I've known men like that. I don't suppose you know Seth McDonald."

"Happens that I do. We spent many a night at the Three Queens swapping stories."

"Is he all right?"

"Last time I saw him, he was fit as a fiddle. Wife's gonna have a baby any day now."

"Dawson still the sheriff?"

"Nah, he retired and moved to Boston. His deputy took his place. Bradshaw ain't cut out for the job. Just don't have the right temperament for it. Know what I mean?"

"Yeah. So, where you headed now?"

"Wyoming. Lot of cattle ranches up that way."

"Take care." Gathering his winnings, Kade headed home, an idea percolating in the back of his mind.

Sitting at the breakfast table, Norrie stared at Kade. "You met Charlie Farrell?"

"Yeah, he was at the saloon last night. He said Seth and Truvy are doing okay. I was thinkin', maybe we should go back."

"Do you mean it?"

"Yeah, but it's a helluva risk."

"You're right." She sat back in her chair, shoulders slumped.

Reaching across the table, Kade took her hand in his. "We can't stay here, darlin'. This is no place to raise a baby."

"What about Burdett? And Sheriff Dawson?"

"I can handle Burdett. Dawson retired and moved to Boston. With Dawson out of the way…" He shrugged. "It should be safe enough."

"What about Bradshaw?"

"He's not much of a threat."

Norrie glanced around the kitchen. Kade was right. This was no place to raise a child, and it was sweet of him to worry about her, but going back home … Everyone in town knew Kade had been arrested and escaped jail, and that she had helped him. What would people say?

"It's up to you, darlin'," Kade said. "But whatever we do, we're not staying here."

Norrie sat in the living room, gazing into the starry night, after Kade left to make his evening stroll through the town.

The thought of going home filled her with equal amounts of anticipation and dread. It would be great to see Seth and Truvy, to be there when their baby was born, if it hadn't been born already, to have them there when her own child was born. But the thought of putting Kade's life in danger filled her with trepidation. Most of the people in town knew he was a wanted man, though, in reality, she hadn't heard anyone say anything against him.

But he was right about one thing. They couldn't raise their baby here.

Once Kade made up his mind they were leaving, he didn't waste any time. He found a buyer for their house and suggested that Joe Moss take over the job of sheriff until they could elect a new one. When Norrie refused to leave everything behind, he bought a wagon to carry their few belongings. Norrie insisted on taking the dishes, the silverware, the pots and pan, the coffee pot and the bedding, saying they could use them on the trail. Kade sold the furniture with the house.

"We might not have a place of our own for a while," he explained when she objected. "There's no point hauling it across country when we might not have anywhere to put it."

She couldn't argue with that. Two days later, she packed the last of their things, the food they were taking with them for their journey, and they were ready to go. The Appy mare stood in the traces, the mustang was tied to the back of the wagon.

Norrie sighed as they drove out of town. She wasn't looking forward to the long ride home, so she put it from her mind as best she could and concentrated on how good it would be to see Seth again, to renew acquaintances with people she had known most of her life.

Bowing her head, she sent a silent entreaty toward heaven, praying that, somehow, everything would work out for the best and that the Good Lord in His infinite mercy would send them a miracle.

Chapter Twenty-Seven

Norrie gazed up at the heavens, captivated, as always, by the mystical beauty of the moon, the endless number of stars that shone like tiny lights against the black velvet sky. Smiling, she pressed her hands against her belly where a new life rested. It was a miracle, she thought, but then, the world itself was a miracle of creation. Days and weeks that came and went, the changing seasons, seeds that sprouted and grew into fruits and vegetables, trees and flowers, the endless cycle of life, the wonder of life itself.

They had been on the trail for over a week and in all that time, they hadn't seen anyone else, only a herd of wild horses, a couple of deer, and once, a skunk.

She glanced at Kade, who was sitting with his back propped against a wagon wheel, his rifle at his side. He treated her as if she were made of glass, insisting they stop often so she could rest. It was endearing and a little annoying. She wasn't sick, only pregnant.

She worried about what would happen when they reached Clayton's Corner. How would the town's citizen react to his return? What would Elias do? What would they do? Kade had won a good deal of money playing poker, but it wouldn't last forever. And while they could stay with Seth and Truvy, they couldn't expect her brother to support them.

Maybe going home wasn't such a good idea.

She said as much to Kade in the morning.

"If you don't want to go home, where do you want to go?" he asked. "What do you want to do?"

"I don't know."

Brow furrowed, Kade stared into the distance. They could head north, to the Black Hills and look for his mother's people, or west, to Clayton's Corner. He left the decision to Norrie.

"Let's look for your people," she said after a long moment of deliberation. "If we can't find them, then we'll go home and hope for the best."

It took a week to reach the Black Hills, and another three days to locate a small band of Lakota. Norrie stared at the dozen or so hide lodges scattered in a small valley and wondered if Kade's mother was among the women. She glanced at Kade. His expression gave no hint of what he might be thinking or feeling as he urged the Appy down a narrow trail toward the encampment.

All activity came to a halt as the wagon pulled into the center of the village. Norrie counted over a dozen men, almost twice that many women, and a number of children. Recognition flickered in the eyes of some of the men as they came forward.

But Kade had eyes only for the woman who pushed her way through the crowd. She was tall, with long black hair just beginning to turn gray. Leaping lightly from the wagon, he took her in his arms. "*Ina.*"

"Chaska."

Norrie blinked back tears as they hugged. After a moment, the others gathered around them, all talking at once as they welcomed one of their own back home.

When the crowd moved away, Kade lifted Norrie from the wagon seat. "This is my mother, Wichapi," he said.

Norrie smiled uncertainly. "Tell her I'm happy to meet her."

With a nod, Kade spoke to his mother.

"Wel-come, *ch'unkschi,*" Wichapi murmured in halting English. "Let us … eat."

"Thank you."

Wichapi led them into her lodge and indicated they should sit. Many glances passed between Kade and his mother while she filled three bowls with stew, handed one to Kade and one to Norrie before dropping gracefully onto a blanket.

When they finished eating, Kade set his bowl aside. "Norrie, why don't you rest awhile?"

Sensing he wanted to speak to his mother alone, she nodded. She tired easily these days, she thought as she stretched out on a buffalo robe in the back of the lodge and closed her eyes, lulled to sleep by the lilting Lakota language.

"How have you been, my mother?" Kade asked.

"I am well, though my lodge has been empty." Her gaze searched his. "And you, my son?"

"I'm fine."

"Your woman is with child?"

Kade nodded. "Where are the rest of our people?"

"They scattered after the battle at the Greasy Grass. Many went north. Many were taken to the reservation." She paused, her gaze searching his. "How long will you stay?"

Kade shrugged. "I'm not sure. The *wasichu* are still after me for killing the one who killed my brother."

"Did you not know? The man, Reeves, is dead."

"Dead?"

She nodded.

"When did that happen?"

"Not long ago."

"How? Who?"

She glanced away. "He came here, wanting to trade cloth for furs. Someone slipped a knife into his back, and someone else took his body back to the post and dumped it where it was sure to be found."

Kade stared at her. "Someone, *Ina*? Would you happen to know who that someone might have been?"

Eyes twinkling, she murmured, "I could not say."

Kade grinned at her. With Reeves dead, there was no one to accuse him. The soldiers who had entered the store hadn't seen what happened that day, only the aftermath. "When you see this someone," he said fervently, "give them my thanks. And my love."

Late that night, Kade sat in front of his mother's lodge, lost in thought. Reeves was dead. The trader had been the only witness, the only one who actually saw what happened that fateful day. The two troopers who had tried to string him up had come in after the shots were fired. He needed a lawyer, he thought, a good one. With no witnesses to the crime and no evidence, there was a good chance the case against him would be dropped.

He told himself not to get his hopes up, that the chances were slim and none and yet he couldn't help thinking that coming home had been the best decision Norrie had ever made.

"Oh, Kade!" Norrie exclaimed the next morning when he told her about Reeves and what it might mean for their future. "Do you really think there's a chance the charges could be dropped?"

"I don't know, but it might be worth pursuing if I can find a good lawyer." And that wouldn't be easy, he thought. Not many whites were willing to defend an Indian. Or a half-breed.

"We have to try!"

He nodded. Last night, it had seemed like a great idea. In the bright light of day, he realized that he could still be convicted and find himself at the end of a rope.

Norrie stared at him, her brows rushing together when she saw the expression on his face. "What's wrong?"

"I was thinking of the consequences if I lost the case."

"Consequences? Oh! They could hang you."

"Yeah."

"We don't have to go home," she said. "We can stay here."

"Is that what you want?" Kade asked quietly.

Norrie glanced around. Did she want to live here, in a hide lodge, in the middle of nowhere? Raise her child here where he or she would never go to school or to church, never know his Uncle Seth? Never celebrate Christmas or Easter?

"Norrie?"

"I don't know," she said, her voice barely audible.

Drawing her into his arms, he said, "We don't have to decide right now."

In spite of Kade's words, Norrie couldn't think of anything else in the days and weeks that followed, though there were times, like now, when Wichapi was teaching her how to make *wasná*, that it wasn't in the forefront of her mind. *Wasná*, or pemmican, was a Lakota staple, made from a mixture of fat, dried meat, and berries. Wichapi had also taught her how to skin a deer—a rather unpleasant task—and how to stretch the hide. Lakota women cooked the food, made the clothes, gathered wood and berries, dried meat, raised the children, and were in charge of the lodge. Lakota warriors did the hunting and protected the village. In times of peace, the men seemed almost lazy compared to the women.

With winter coming on, Norrie began to have second thoughts about living with the Lakota. Once it snowed, food would be harder to come by and travel would be almost impossible.

That night, she realized Kade was having similar thoughts.

"We're leaving in the morning," he said. "I don't want you spending the winter here."

"But…"

"No arguments," he said. "I want you safe and warm this winter. And I want a doctor nearby when the baby comes."

Although she hated to admit it, Norrie was glad he'd made the decision he had. This was her first child and she didn't want to have it in a hide lodge. Maybe she was a coward. Indian women had their children here, but she wasn't an Indian woman. She wanted a doctor and family around her, a bed with a mattress.

Kade was as good as his word. In the morning, Wichapi helped him pack their belongings in the back of the wagon and gave them a supply of *wasná* and dried meat for their journey, as well as two buffalo robes.

Norrie hugged Wichapi and thanked her for her hospitality, then turned away as Kade bid his mother goodbye.

"Safe journey, *chaska*," she said.

"I'll come back in the spring, if I can," he said.

"Take good care of your woman. She loves you."

"Yeah. I know." Taking her in his arms, he said, "Stay well, *Ina.*" And turned away before she could see the tears in his eyes.

Norrie glanced at Kade. He had been quiet since they left the encampment, but she wasn't surprised. No doubt he was as worried as she was about returning to Clayton's Corner. What if he was arrested on sight? What if they couldn't find a good lawyer? She laid a hand on her swollen belly. The child would be born in the spring. For her baby's sake, she prayed that everything would work out.

They stopped only once that afternoon to eat and rest the horses before bedding down for the night. It was eerie, being out in the middle of nowhere, with only the flickering of the fire for light. Norrie found herself starting at every sound even as she chided herself for being so foolish. Her mother had always said there was nothing in the dark that wasn't there when the sun was up. As a child, Norrie had found that comforting, but she knew now that it wasn't true. There could be anything prowling around out there in the dark—wolves, bobcats, hostile Indians.

Only when Kade drew her into his arms did she relax. Only when he kissed her did the rest of the world fade away and there was just the two of them, reaffirming their love beneath the moon and the stars, his whispered words assuring her that everything would be all right.

Norrie was relieved when they reached Clayton's Corner. Their journey had been long but, thankfully, uneventful. They had passed through some beautiful country, and some so rugged she doubted if it would ever be settled.

The sun was setting when Kade pulled up in front of Truvy's boardinghouse.

Bone weary, she placed her hands on Kade's shoulders as he lifted her from the wagon.

"I'm going to take the rig down to the livery and look after the horses," he said.

"Don't be long."

"I won't."

Norrie ran a hand over her hair as she stepped into the boardinghouse, thinking that the first thing she wanted was a long soak in a hot bath.

Seth and Truvy had been busy, she mused. They had wallpapered the main room in a cheerful yellow and white flowered print and bought a new sofa, several new chairs and side tables. And a new check-in desk.

Seth looked up as the bell over the door sounded. "Norrie!" he exclaimed, his eyes widening with surprise. "How did you get here?" Hurrying out from behind the desk, he put his arm around her. "Where have you been all this time?" He glanced past her. "Where's Kade?"

"He took the horses down to the livery. It looks like you're doing well."

"Not bad. There's a new saloon in town, and a theater."

"Where's Truvy?"

"Upstairs, feeding my daughter."

"Congratulations, Seth. I'm so happy for you. What did you name her?"

"Truvy wanted to name her Nettie, after her grandmother so ..." Seth shrugged. "She spent ten hours in labor. How could I say no?"

"You did the right thing," Norrie said, and then she grinned at him. "You'll soon be an uncle."

"What?" Putting her at arm's length, his gaze ran over her. "Well, don't that beat all?"

"Is there any chance you have a room for us?"

"Of course." Returning to the desk, he plucked a key from the board. "Here you go. I'll bet you'd like nothing more than a bath right now."

"I'll bet you'd be right."

"Go up and make yourself at home. I'll heat some water. And after you get cleaned up, I'll have Truvy fix you something to eat."

Murmuring, "thank you," she gave her brother a hug before making her way upstairs. A hot bath. A real bed. She felt as if she had died and gone to heaven.

⚜   ⚜   ⚜

Kade didn't miss the changes in the town. The Three Queens had a new false front. A second saloon occupied the other end of the block. The Majestic Theater had a sign out front proclaiming that the Missouri Songbird would be performing on Saturday night at eight o'clock.

The livery also had a new coat of paint.

"Never thought we'd see you in these parts again," Lee Bailey remarked as he helped Kade unhitch the Appy.

"People still lookin' for me?" Kade asked.

Bailey shrugged. "Not that I know of. Although I reckon Bradshaw might make a play."

"He's got no proof that I did anything except break out of jail," Kade said with a wry grin. "And if he arrests me, he'll have to arrest Norrie, too."

Bailey grinned back at him. "I don't reckon he'll do that."

"I'm banking on it," Kade said as he scratched the mustang between the ears. "Feed 'em good, will ya? They've covered a lot of ground."

"Sure 'nough," Bailey said.

"If you hear anything, or if anyone comes around asking about me, I'd appreciate it if you'd let me know."

"Will do," Bailey promised.

With a nod, Kade left the livery and headed for the boardinghouse. It had been a gamble, coming back here, he mused, but what the hell, Lady Luck had always been on his side.

CHAPTER TWENTY-EIGHT

Norrie was in bed, asleep, when Kade returned to the boardinghouse. He guessed he couldn't blame her for turning in early. Their journey had been long and hard, especially for a woman in her condition. But she hadn't complained, not once.

He found Seth and Truvy in the parlor. Seth was reading a newspaper, Truvy was rocking the baby.

Truvy smiled at him. "It's good to have you back home," she said, patting the baby's back.

"Thanks." Removing his hat, Kade placed it on the hat rack in the corner, then dropped into one of the chairs.

"Are you here to stay?" Seth asked.

"I don't know. What's going on with Burdett?"

Seth snorted, a look of disgust on his face. "He's running cattle on our land. His men are living in our house. I'd like to get my hands on the sonofa…"

"Seth!"

"Sorry, Truvy. Just chaps my hide to see him strutting around like he owns the whole damn town."

"Did they ever find out who killed your old man?"

"No. But we all know who did it." Seth cleared his throat. "Don't take this the wrong way. We're both glad you and Norrie are here, but do you think it's wise? What if Bradshaw decides to arrest you?"

"Like I told Bailey, if Bradshaw wants to arrest me for escaping jail, he'll have to arrest Norrie, too. It was her idea."

"It sounds like something she'd do," Seth said with a laugh. "She was always turning wild things loose."

Truvy shot her husband a reproving glance. "What kind of thing is that to say about Kade?"

"It's okay," Kade said, grinning. "I've been called worse."

Norrie woke slowly. For a moment, she couldn't remember where she was—at the Lakota village? In the middle of the prairie? She opened her eyes a crack—a ceiling, four walls, a soft bed beneath her, a clock chiming the hour, the scent of coffee filling the air.

She was home. Pulling on the robe Truvy had lent her last night, she padded down the stairs.

She found the family in the kitchen, the remains of their breakfast on the table.

Sitting across from Kade, she said, "Why didn't you wake me?"

"You needed the rest."

"I saved some batter," Truvy said as she handed the baby to Seth. "How many flapjacks can you eat?"

"Maybe two. Or three."

"We've got bacon, too Would you like a cup of coffee?"

"Yes, please. But you don't have to wait on me."

"You just sit there and relax," Truvy ordered with a smile. "Today, you're a guest. Tomorrow, you can help."

Later, Norrie sat in the parlor and rocked the baby. Kade had gone out to look around. Seth was busy oiling a squeaky hinge on one of the doors, while Truvy was changing the sheets on the beds.

Stroking the boy's cheek with her fingers, Norrie imagined holding her own baby. Would it have Kade's dark hair and eyes, his copper-hued skin? Or would the baby take after her? Boy or girl? Not that it mattered, as long as it was born healthy and strong.

Her thoughts turned to Kade. It worried her that he was out wandering around the town. Just because Sheriff Dawson had retired didn't mean there was nothing to worry about, although she couldn't imagine that Elias—or anyone else in town—would have the nerve to confront Kade.

They never should have come here, and yet she was glad to be home with Seth and Truvy, to be in a town where she knew practically everyone.

Smiling, she closed her eyes, content to rock her niece and contemplate holding a child of her own. A little boy, she decided, with Kade's black hair and her father's brown eyes.

Kade strolled down the town's main street, all too aware of the curious glances that followed him. Several of the men nodded in his direction, a few of the women made it a point to give him a wide berth, but on the whole, he didn't detect any real animosity.

Until he came face-to-face with Lyle Burdett backed by two men who both wore Colts on each hip and looked like they knew how to use them. Not cowhands. Bodyguards, maybe. Or more hired guns.

Burdett pulled up short, eyes going wide with surprise. "Well, damn," he muttered. "I never thought I'd see you again."

"We have some unfinished business," Kade remarked, his hand resting lightly on the butt of his gun.

"Is that right?"

Kade nodded. "I haven't forgotten that you sent the Crowley brothers after me. You might want to think twice before you try pulling a stunt like that again." He jerked his chin at the two men flanking the rancher. "Especially with these two."

"Are you threatening me?" Burdett exclaimed, his voice rising so that those on the street could hear him.

"No." Kade's gaze darted at the two men standing behind Burdett. "I don't make threats. Stay out of my way." He stared at Burdett until the rancher moved aside, letting him pass. He didn't look back, but he could feel the icy gazes of the two hired guns on his back. He thought he knew one of them—a shootist from Abilene name of Hank Kirby. He was rumored to be fast, with nerves of steel. The other man was a stranger.

Kade blew out a breath when he reached the saloon. He paused in the doorway before moving to the bar where he ordered a whiskey.

"Well, look who's back in town," Clay Hamilton exclaimed as he stepped out of his office. "Never thought to see you in here again. Figured a rope had found you by now."

"Nice to see you, too."

Hamilton grinned. "You must have the devil's own luck."

Kade shrugged. "Let's hope it lasts."

"Does Bradshaw know you're back in town?"

"He probably does by now. I just ran into Burdett."

Hamilton muttered an oath. "He's buying up the whole damn valley. Won't be happy until he owns it all—ranches, businesses, hell, the whole damn shootin' match."

"Somebody should stop him."

"Yeah," Hamilton agreed. "Somebody."

"All I need is a reason," Kade drawled.

With a nervous laugh, Hamilton muttered, "Dammit, man, I hope I never see that expression on your face when you're looking at me."

Norrie looked up from the pie crust she was making when Kade entered the kitchen. She frowned, troubled by the taut lines around his mouth and eyes. "What's wrong?"

"Nothin'."

"No lies between us, remember?"

He pulled a chair from the table, turned it around, and straddled the seat. "I ran into Burdett."

"Oh."

"Yeah. He's got himself a new pair of hired guns."

"He can't have hired them for you," Norrie said. "He had no way of knowing we'd be coming back."

"Yeah. From what I hear, he's buying out anyone willing to sell."

"And probably those who aren't," Norrie said, her voice laced with venom.

"Clay Hamilton thinks someone needs to stop him."

"He didn't mean someone, did he? He meant you." Dusting the flour from her hands, she stood in front of Kade. "Promise me you won't go after him."

"He killed your father, Norrie. Have you forgotten that? I don't know if he did it by his own hand or hired someone to do it, but he was behind it. I'd bet my life on it."

"But we can't prove it. And if you kill him, they'll hang you. Please, Kade."

Rising, he pulled her into his arms. "I promise, darlin'. But if he comes after me ..."

Norrie pressed her fingertips to his lips. "Just stay out of his way. And Bradshaw's, too."

"Don't worry about Bradshaw, darlin'. He's not going to arrest me," Kade said with a wry grin. "If he did, he'd have to arrest you, too, for breaking me out of jail and I don't think he wants to do that. You're my insurance."

"I'm not sure he'll be so forgiving now," Norrie said seriously. "Don't forget, I chose you over him. I think I've lost whatever bargaining power I used to have."

CHAPTER TWENTY-NINE

Elias Bradshaw sat behind the Sheriff's desk, his booted feet propped on one corner. He'd heard Kade had come back to town but he hadn't believed it until he saw the proof with his own eyes. It made him sick, seeing Norrie with that outlaw. What she saw in that half-breed was beyond comprehension. The thought of the woman he loved carrying that man's baby turned his stomach.

He stared at the Wanted poster tacked to the wall. Even though the description fit Kade, he had no way to prove it was him. Sure, he could arrest the man for breaking out of jail, but that would implicate Norrie, and he couldn't do that, not when there was a chance that Kade might run out on her. Slim as that chance might be, he didn't want to do anything to ruin their friendship or make her hate him. Which was the other reason he didn't arrest Kade.

Damn. His best hope was to catch the 'breed breaking the law with plenty of witnesses so that he wouldn't have any choice but to arrest him.

Of course, the chance of that happening was pretty slim, too.

Damn, damn, and double damn. Norrie would be his wife now if that half-breed renegade had never come to town.

CHAPTER THIRTY

Kade sauntered down the street toward the saloon. Norrie had taken to helping Truvy at the boardinghouse—sometimes with cleaning the rooms or changing the sheets on the beds, sometimes with the cooking, sometimes with the baby. It left him with a lot of free time on his hands, time he spent at one saloon or another. He'd considered looking for a job, but he made more playing poker for a couple of hours a day than he could earn clerking at a store or mucking stalls at the livery.

The crowd in the Three Queens was light. He nodded at the regulars as he took a seat at one of the tables. He listened idly to the desultory conversation until one of the players mentioned Burdett's name.

"What was that about Burdett?" Kade asked.

"He's trying to buy the Oatman spread, offering the old man less than half of what it's worth. Said if Oatman won't sell, he'll buy up the mortgage."

"How much is the mortgage?"

"About a thousand dollars, I think. The old man had a bad year. Lost a lot of cattle. He swears Burdett's responsible, but he's got no proof."

Kade grunted softly. "Where's the Oatman ranch located?"

"Just east of town, out past what used to be the McDonald place."

"Thanks." Gathering his winnings, Kade pushed away from the table. "Deal me out."

Kade reined the mustang to a halt on the crest of a hill overlooking the Oatman spread. The rambling, two-story house was in bad shape, the barn needed a new roof and a new door. A few scraggly-looking chickens scratched in the dirt near a broken-down corral.

Clucking to the mare, Kade rode down the hill. He'd just pulled up in front of the house when the door banged open and an old man hefting a shotgun stepped out onto the sagging front porch.

"Tell Burdett I ain't sellin', and get the hell off my land!"

Kade lifted one hand. "Hold on, Mr. Oatman. Burdett didn't send me."

Doubt crossed the old man's face. "No? Then who the hell are ya?"

"My name's Kade."

"Kade? Seems I hear'd that name before."

"Probably. Can we talk?"

The shotgun in the old man's hand never wavered. "You can say what you want to say from there."

"I'd like to buy your place."

"Yeah?"

"Yeah. I'll buy your mortgage from the bank, and give you a thousand in cash in a few days."

Oatman looked him over. "How'd you come by that kind of money?"

"Does it matter?"

"No, I reckon not."

"How many cattle do you have?"

Oatman shrugged. "Maybe a hunnerd head, maybe a little more. They're strung out from here to the river. Got no one to help me round 'em up."

Kade nodded. "Do we have a deal?"

"Reckon so."

"I'll meet you at the bank tomorrow afternoon," Kade said. "Say, two o'clock? And let's just keep this between you and me until then."

With a curt nod, the old man lowered the shotgun. "Tomorrow. Two o'clock."

Kade divided the rest of his time that day between the Three Queens and the new saloon. He took a break for supper at the boardinghouse.

"Where have you been all day?" Norrie asked.

"I'll tell you tomorrow."

"Why not now?"

"Maybe it's a surprise," Truvy said, smiling at Norrie. "Is that it, Kade?"

Kade winked at Norrie. "You could say that."

"Will I like it?" Norrie asked.

"I hope so." He took a last bite of roast beef, drained his coffee cup. Rising, he grabbed his hat, then kissed Norrie on the cheek. "I'll see you later."

Norrie stared after him, her brow furrowed. Where had he been all day? And what was the surprise?

Kade met Oatman at the bank the next afternoon at two o'clock. It took a remarkably short time to pay the amount due and transfer the title to his name. Kade added Norrie's name to the deed and signed the necessary papers. The men shook hands all around and when Kade left the office, he was a landowner for the first time in his life.

"I'll need a day or two to pack up and move out, if that's all right," Oatman said as they left the bank.

"Sure. I'll need a couple of days to come up with the rest of the cash. Are you leaving town?"

"No. I reckon I'll move in with my daughter and her husband."

"How about if I meet you at the ranch in three days," Kade said. "I'll pay you what I owe you then."

The old man nodded. "Fine. I reckon my Bethy will be glad to see me when I've got a thousand dollars in my pocket."

"Reckon so," Kade agreed, and prayed his luck at the poker table would hold out another few days. And if it didn't? Well, hell, he'd cross that bridge when he came to it.

⚜ ⚜ ⚜

"When do I get to see my surprise?" Norrie asked. Feeling the need for some privacy, she had suggested they take a walk after dinner.

"In three days." Kade slid a glance at her, frowned when he saw the troubled expression on her face. "What's wrong, sweetheart?"

Not meeting his eyes, she asked, "Are you going to spend all your nights gambling in the saloon?"

"No. Just the next three days."

"What's happening then?"

"If I tell you, it'll ruin the surprise." And what a surprise it would be, he thought, for both of them, since he hadn't even seen the inside of the house. Stepping into the opening between two buildings, he drew her into his arms. "Just trust me a little longer."

Hoping to make the time pass, Norrie immersed herself in chores during the next few days. She dusted the boardinghouse from top to bottom, beat the dust from the rugs, washed the windows and the curtains, did the shopping for Truvy, watched the baby so Seth and Truvy could go out to dinner, swept the porch, and planted a garden in the backyard.

By the third day, she was bone weary and had a colossal back ache but when Kade told her it was time to see her surprise, she was ready to go.

He hitched the Appy mare to the wagon, lifted Norrie onto the seat, and they were on their way.

Norrie sent a longing glance toward her old home as they drove past. "Where are we going?" she asked as they turned left at the fork in the road. "There's nothing out here but the Oatman ranch."

Kade took a deep breath. Here goes, he thought. "It's now the Smith ranch, Mrs. Smith."

Norrie looked at him askance. "The Smith ranch?" she repeated, and then her eyes grew wide. "You bought it?"

"Yeah."

"Where did you get the money?"

"Gambling, of course. That's what I've been doing the last few nights. Fastest way I knew to earn the money," he said. "And before you ask, I won it all fair and square." It had been touch and go there for a while, he mused, but in the end, he'd won what he needed to pay Oatman what he'd promised.

Eyes filled with wonder, she said, "You really bought it?"

"Yeah. And I sure hope you like it, because I never saw the inside of the place."

Norrie grinned at him. "The outside is a mess but the inside...oh, Kade, the inside is lovely. Mrs. Oatman had quite a talent for decorating. Wait until you see it!"

Kade huffed a sigh of relief, thinking this could have turned out a lot differently.

Mr. Oatman was waiting for them on the front porch. A wagon loaded with his belongings was parked beside the house. A pair of horses stood in the traces.

"Right on time," the old man drawled.

Dropping to the ground, Kade helped Norrie alight from the seat.

"Afternoon, Miss Norrie," Oatman said. "I had no idea you'd be moving in. My Rachel would have been right happy about that. She always liked you."

"She was a wonderful, caring woman," Norrie said. "We all miss her."

"Thank you kindly." Oatman looked at Kade expectantly.

"I've got the cash right here." Reaching into his pocket, Kade withdrew a fat envelope and handed it to the old man. "One thousand dollars, as agreed."

Oatman held it tightly for a moment, then slipped it into the pocket of his overalls. "I left a lot of stuff in there," he said. "Just burn what you don't want." With a curt nod, he descended the stairs and climbed up on the wagon seat. He sat there a moment, looking out over the land. "Hope you and the Missus will be as happy here as we once were," he muttered.

Norrie's heart went out to Mr. Oatman as she watched him pick up the reins and cluck to the team. He looked like he'd aged ten years since his wife passed away.

"You okay?" Kade asked, seeing the sadness in her eyes.

"He looks so lost without her. I can't help feeling sorry for him," Norrie remarked as she watched Mr. Oatman drive away. She stared after him a moment and then blew out a sigh.

"How about showing me our new home?" Kade said, hoping to cheer her up a little.

Hand in hand, they walked toward the house. When they reached the front door, Kade lifted her into his arms. "Welcome to your new home, Mrs. Smith."

Norrie grinned as she pushed open the door with her foot and Kade carried her inside.

He stopped just inside the door, unable to believe his eyes. "Well, damn," he muttered. He'd thought Norrie was exaggerating about Mrs. Oatman's decorating skills, but, as she'd said, the inside was as lovely as the outside was ugly. Striped paper covered the walls, white lace curtains fluttered at the open windows. A high-backed sofa and a pair of easy chairs were arranged in front of a stone fireplace. A large, glass-fronted cabinet occupied one wall; the shelves were empty. He could see a dining room and a kitchen through a doorway to the right, a hallway opened on the left that he assumed led to an office or a sewing room. A staircase led to the second floor.

"How do you like it?" Norrie asked.

"Best deal I ever made," Kade remarked as he set her on her feet and kissed the tip of her nose. "I should have offered him more."

✤ ✤ ✤

The next few days were busy ones. Norrie packed their things, few as they were, and Kade transported them to the ranch. Seth and Truvy stopped by three days after they moved in. Truvy gave Norrie a lovely flowered table-cloth and a dozen matching napkins for a house-warming present.

Norrie had chosen the small bedroom upstairs for the nursery and often spent a quiet hour in there imagining what it would be like when her baby was born.

Mr. Oatman had left all his furniture behind, taking only his clothes and things that meant something to him personally.

Norrie bought new sheets, blankets, and a spread for their bed and, with Kade's help, rearranged the furniture in the room, making it her own.

She left the third bedroom as it was, thinking it would serve as a guestroom if the need ever arose.

Once they settled into the house, Norrie spent a couple of days a week helping Truvy at the boardinghouse. They got along well together, their friendship growing as the days passed by. It pleased Norrie to see her brother happy and feeling useful. He enjoyed working at the boardinghouse and meeting new people as travelers making their way back east or further west often stayed a day or two while waiting for the stage.

Kade, too, seemed happy, even relaxed, as the days passed. He spent most of his time working on the barn, repairing the roof, installing a new door, replacing the boards on the front porch. As she had when they first met, she loved to watch him work.

❧   ❧   ❧

Norrie was in the kitchen, preparing supper, when she felt the baby kick for the first time. At her gasp of surprise, Kade was at her side, his brow furrowed. "What's wrong?"

"Nothing." Taking his hand, she placed it on her rounded belly. "Wait. There! Did you feel it?"

He looked up at her with wonder in his eyes. "Does it hurt?"

"No. It feels wonderful."

"You're beautiful, you know that?"

"I'm glad you think so."

"I've never seen you looking so happy, so lovely. Being in the family way seems to agree with you."

"You agree with me," she said with a grin. "I never thought I'd ever be this happy. I love you, Kade."

Swallowing the lump in his throat, he drew her into his arms and held her close, praying that he would never let her down.

CHAPTER THIRTY-ONE

Elias Bradshaw stood at the window of the Sheriff's Office, idly watching the townspeople. It was Saturday and the streets were crowded with ladies who had come into town to do their shopping or visit with friends and family. Ranchers came in for supplies, or to have a bit of harness repaired, or to visit the blacksmith to see about new shoes for their horses.

He watched Truvy McDonald thread her way along the boardwalk, her baby in one arm, a wicker basket on the other. Seeing Truvy reminded him of Norrie. Not that he needed prompting to think about her. He didn't know why he couldn't get her out of his mind. She had never returned his affection, never really been more than a friend, but she was the only girl he'd ever liked. There were other women in town who had flirted with him. After all, he was a fair catch. He wasn't ugly, he had a job and a house. A girl could do worse. But it was Norrie who filled his thoughts, even now, when she was married to that renegade half-breed and carrying his baby. The thought of her in that man's bed, bearing his child, made him sick to his stomach.

But there was nothing he could do about it…at least nothing he had the courage to do. And that fact shamed him even as it made him hate Kade all the more.

He was about to turn away from the window when he saw Norrie strolling down the boardwalk looking as lovely as always. As she neared the Sheriff's Office, Elias stepped outside. "Afternoon, Miss Norrie."

"Good day to you, Elias."

He fell into step beside her. "Are you going shopping?"

"Yes," she said with a smile. "I need a few things for supper tonight."

"Mind if I walk with you?"

"Of course not. How do you like being Sheriff?"

He puffed out his chest a little. "I like it fine." He nodded toward the restaurant across the street. "Could I buy you a cup of tea, or something?"

"I don't think so, but thank you. Maybe another time?"

"Yeah, sure." He tipped his hat as she entered the General Store.

There had to be a way to get Kade out of the picture, he thought as he continued down the boardwalk. It wasn't right, that half-breed walking around town like he wasn't a wanted man.

Elias glanced at the men he passed by. Were they all laughing at him because he didn't have the nerve to arrest a wanted man? They probably figured he was scared shitless to go up against Kade, he thought glumly. And they'd be right. But who could blame him? He was just the local law, not some quick-draw artist like Kade, whose fast draw was like lightning.

A hired gun, he thought. That's what he needed. But he had no idea where to find one. And then he smiled. Lyle Burdett knew. He had two of them pretending to be cowboys on his ranch.

It was something to think about.

CHAPTER THIRTY-TWO

Kade wiped the sweat from his brow as he finished cutting the last rail for the new corral. As soon as he set it in place, he'd let the mustang inside to kick up her heels. He had repaired the old corral and then decided to build a new, larger one.

Heaving a sigh, he headed for the water barrel beside the barn, filled the dipper, and poured the contents over his head. Fall was around the corner, but you'd never know it, he thought. It had been hot as hell the last few days. Grabbing his shirt, he dried his face and chest. Standing there, he gazed at the house and the barn and felt a sense of pride for a job well done. He had never worked so hard in his life, but it had been worth it. There was just one more thing to do, but he needed to discuss it with Norrie.

He glanced at the few head of cattle grazing in the distance. He wasn't one for raising cattle. But horses … that was something else. All he needed was a good stallion and a couple of mares.

Hearing footsteps, he turned toward the house, smiled when he saw Norrie making her way toward him. She looked prettier every day. "Hey, darlin'," he said.

"Hi."

"Did you get your shopping done?"

She nodded. "You finished the corral."

"Yeah. Just one more thing to do."

"What's that?"

"Paint the house. What color would you like?"

"I don't know. I never thought about it." She glanced over her shoulder. "Maybe white with yellow shutters and a green door?"

"I'll pick up some paint next time I go to town."

"I saw Elias today."

"Oh?" Kade took her hand as they walked back to the house.

"He wanted to buy me a cup of tea."

"Is that right?"

"I said no," she said quickly.

'You don't have to stop seeing your friends because of me," he said quietly. "You knew him a long time before I came along."

"I don't want to encourage him," Norrie said.

"That's probably for the best. I'd hate to have to kill him."

"Kade! You wouldn't!"

Laughing, he pulled her into his arms. "No, darlin', I wouldn't kill him. I've put all that behind me."

Kade was scraping the old paint off the north side of the house when he saw three riders coming down the road. Climbing down from the ladder, he wiped off his hands, felt his insides tense when he recognized Burdett and his hired guns. Lifting his holster from the stump beside the ladder, he pulled his Colt from the leather and held it loosely at his side.

"Afternoon," Burdett said affably. "I heard Mr. Oatman had sold his property."

"Yeah?"

"It wasn't very neighborly of him to sell it to you after I made him an offer."

"Is that right?"

Nodding, Burdett reached inside his coat and pulled out a wad of cash. "I'd like to buy the place, here and now."

"It's not for sale."

"I'm willing to give you what you paid for the mortgage and the thousand dollars you gave Mr. Oatman."

"Perhaps you didn't hear me. It's not for sale."

A muscle clenched in Burdett's jaw. "I should have known trying to do business with you would be a waste of time."

"Tell your man to get his hand away from that hogleg or you'll be packing him home facedown on the back of his horse."

"McNally, don't be a fool."

McNally folded his arms over the pommel of his saddle.

"Get the hell out of here, Burdett," Kade said, his voice a low growl. "And don't come back."

Burdett backed his horse away, reined him around, and rode out of the yard, his head high.

The two hired guns glared at Kade.

"This ain't over," McNally said.

"I'm willing to finish it any time you are. Here and now, if it suits you."

The man's lip curled in a sneer before he wheeled his horse around and raced after Burdett. The second man followed, though he glanced over his shoulder several times, as though afraid of being shot in the back.

Kade huffed a sigh as he watched them go. He had a feeling in his gut that the next time he tangled with Burdett, only one of them would walk away.

"Who were you talking to earlier today?" Norrie asked when he went into the house later that afternoon to wash up.

"Burdett."

"Burdett!" She stared at him, eyes wide. "What did he want?"

"He made me an offer on the ranch. He didn't like it when I told him it wasn't for sale."

Face pale, she sank down on one of the kitchen chairs, her arms folded protectively over her stomach. "He's going to make trouble for us, isn't he?"

"Not if I can help it." But that was the question, wasn't it? Burdett was a fast talker. He was considered a respected member of the community by most of the folks who lived in town. Some of them even believed Burdett had done Norrie a favor by buying the ranch out from under her. After all, they said sympathetically, she couldn't have run the ranch by herself. But the ranchers saw Burdett for what he was, an ambitious man determined to buy all the property adjacent to his property. Some said he wouldn't be content until he owned the whole valley.

Kade stayed close to home the next few days, wary of leaving Norrie alone, but all was peaceful. He got in touch with a rancher in the next county who was reputed to raise some of the best breeding mares in the territory and after exchanging a few letters, Kade arranged to ride over and take a look at his stock.

In spite of her condition, Norrie insisted on going along. It was early on a lovely fall morning when Kade hitched the Appy to the buckboard and they drove over to meet with Calvin Warner.

The Warner Ranch was sprawled over many acres, divided into large pastures that housed about twenty-five brood mares, two dozen yearlings, and a couple of blooded stallions.

After introductions, Milt Warner showed them the mares that were for sale.

"Kade, how will you ever decide?" Norrie asked. "They're all so beautiful."

He nodded in agreement. Rarely had he seen such fine horse flesh, though he especially liked a long-legged, four-year-old bay mare.

"She is beautiful," Norrie said, "but look at that little dun mare. She's got beautiful eyes."

"Beautiful eyes, huh?" Kade said, grinning.

"And lovely conformation," Norrie pointed out with asperity.

"All right, you win," Kade said. "We'll take the dun mare."

They looked at stallions next. As far as Kade was concerned, there was only one choice—a flashy chestnut with three white socks and a narrow blaze.

"How much do you want for the stallion?" Kade asked.

Warner rubbed his hand over his jaw. "He's worth at least five hundred dollars."

"And the mare?"

"Three-fifty."

"Done. I can give you four hundred now and the rest in a few days, if that's all right."

Warner nodded. "I'll draw up the papers and they'll be waiting for you when you bring the balance."

Norrie smiled as the two men shook hands. They would breed the mare next summer for a spring foal. "Do you have a mare that's pregnant now?" she asked.

"As a matter of fact, I do. I sold her to a guy and bred her with one of my stallions, and then he couldn't come up with the balance of what he owed me. I gave him a four-month extension, but he never showed." Warner shrugged. "I can let you have the mare for two hundred, which is what he owes me."

"Let's have a look at her," Kade said.

Warner led the way to a large barn. A pretty little dapple-gray mare nickered softly when they entered.

"That's her," Warner said, gesturing at the gray.

Norrie's eyes lit up when she saw the mare. "Oh, Kade, can we buy her, too?"

"You heard the lady," Kade said. "We'll take both mares and the stud."

"Do you want to take the gray with you?"

Kade grinned at the look on Norrie's face. "I think so."

"Foal's due in the spring."

An hour later, the necessary papers had been signed, the gray was tied to the back of the buckboard, and they were on their way home, with the gray mare's bill of sale in Kade's pocket.

When they reached home, Norrie was ready for a nap. Kade dropped her off at the house, then drove the buckboard down to the barn, where he unhitched the Appy and turned her out into one of the corrals before leading the gray into the barn. He settled her in one of the stalls and tossed her a forkful of hay.

Two pregnant females on the place, he mused, with a grin. The mare's foal was due in the spring, about the same time Norrie was due. Not for the first time, he wondered what kind of father he would make. He had no experience with kids, no idea how to be a father. It was a sobering thought.

Kade shook his head. He thought briefly of Norrie's old man, cut down in his prime. Connor McDonald had been a good man who would never know his grandchildren because Lyle Burdett had coveted McDonald's land and had been willing to do murder to get it.

Kade swore softly. He had liked and respected McDonald. If there was any justice, the time would come when Burdett would pay the price for the misery he had caused Norrie and Seth.

Kade was on his way up to the house when he noticed the footprints. They weren't his and they weren't Norrie's. And they weren't Indian. They'd been made by a pair of boots, worn down at the heel.

Resting his hand on the butt of his Colt, he followed the prints as they circled the house. There were scuffs at the back door, indicating the intruder had paused there for a few moments before mounting his horse and riding out of the yard.

Kade followed the horse's tracks to the road, swore under his breath when they veered off toward Lyle Burdett's spread.

Later that night, lying in bed with Norrie in his arms, Kade stared up at the ceiling, trying to figure out how to warn

Norrie to be careful without causing her undo worry. He needed her to be cautious, to keep a gun close at hand when she was home alone, but he couldn't think of any way to warn her without alarming her.

Turning on her side, Norrie propped herself on one elbow. "What is it?" she asked. "Something's troubling you."

"What makes you think that?"

"You're as tense as a bow string. What's wrong, Kade?"

When did she learn to read him so well, he wondered, even as he searched for a way to tell her about the prints he'd found. "Let's talk about it in the morning."

"Let's talk about it now. I'm not going to be able to sleep for wondering what it is."

Huffing a sigh of defeat, he said, "I found some sign that someone was here while we were gone today."

"It was probably just one of the neighbors coming by."

"My gut tells me it was one of Burdett's men snooping around. I followed the tracks out to the road. They turned right, to his spread."

Sitting up, Norrie shivered. Darn Burdett. Why couldn't he leave them alone?

Kade tugged Norrie back down beside him, his arm going around her shoulders. "I want you to be careful when you're home alone. I don't think even a skunk like Burdett would do anything to hurt you, especially in your condition, but I'm not willing to take that chance. I'm not planning to leave you here alone, but I want you to keep a gun handy when I'm down at the barn. Norrie?"

"I hate that man!" she exclaimed, and burst into tears. Wasn't it enough that he had killed her father and driven her out of her home? What more did he want?

Murmuring, "Hush, now," Kade drew her into his arms and held her close while she cried. He stroked her hair, her back, kissed the tears from her cheeks. Gradually, her sobs subsided and she kissed him back, her hands warm on his bare skin.

He sucked in a breath when she raked her nails over his chest.

"Love me, Kade," she whispered.

"Norrie!" He rained kisses on her cheeks, her brow, the sweet curve of her breast as his hands caressed her. She was satin and silk in his arms and he worshipped her with every touch.

Norrie melted against him, his kisses and caresses driving everything else from her mind but her love, her need, for this man who had become her whole life.

She cried his name as he possessed her, his body melding with hers, filling her with peace and love and sweet release.

She fell asleep, smiling.

CHAPTER THIRTY-THREE

"Kade." Norrie stared at him. He was obviously lost in thought, his breakfast hardly touched. "Kade."

"What?"

"Do you want more coffee?"

"Oh. Yeah, thanks."

"Where were you?"

"I was just thinking. Oatman said he's got about a hundred head of cattle, give or take a few."

"And?" She refilled his cup, set the pot on the stove, and lowered herself into the chair across from him.

"Do you know where Jackson went?"

"Last I heard he was looking for work with one of the other ranchers. But that was months ago. I haven't seen him in town. Why?"

"I need to hire a couple of hands, at least temporarily, to help me round up the herd."

"I'll ask Seth next time I see him. Maybe he'll know."

"Let's go now," Kade said, pushing away from the table. "I need to order some wire so we can keep a few head close to home."

"But…" Norrie gestured at the dishes on the table and stacked in the sink.

"I'll help you clean it up later," he said with a wink. "Come on, grab your hat and let's go."

✤ ✤ ✤

They pulled up in front of the boardinghouse thirty minutes later.

"Well, this is a surprise," Seth said as Norrie and Truvy hugged. "What brings you into town in the middle of the week?"

"I need to hire a few hands," Kade said, "and I was wondering if you knew where I might find Jackson."

"I saw him about a month ago. He was leaving for Cheyenne looking for work. Said if he didn't find anything, he'd likely head back this way. How many men are you looking for?"

"Two or three," Kade said with a shrug. He waited until Truvy and Norrie went upstairs to check on the baby before saying, "Someone from Burdett's spread was sniffing around our place yesterday. I'm not sure, but it was likely one of his hired guns."

"Does Norrie know?"

"Yeah. I had to warn her to be careful. I need a couple of men to help me round up some cattle, but I really just want a couple of extra guns around, just in case. Burdett made me an offer for our place. He wasn't happy when I turned him down."

"He doesn't take no for an answer," Seth muttered. "We learned that the hard way."

"Well, he can't buy me out. And he can't scare me away. Is it okay if Norrie stays here while I take a look around and see if I can round up a couple of men?"

"Sure."

Both men looked up as Norrie and Truvy came downstairs.

"Seth, your daughter gets prettier every time I see her," Norrie said, lightly stroking the baby's cheek.

"I think that about Truvy every time I see her," Seth said, adoration in his eyes as he looked at his wife.

Norrie looked at Kade and smiled as she patted the baby's back.

Kade felt a rush of emotion as he imagined Norrie holding their child, knew he would do whatever it took to protect her from harm. Swallowing hard, he kissed her cheek. "I'm going out for a while to see if I can find a couple of men."

"Don't be long," she said, and he heard the worry in her voice.

"I won't." He kissed her again, sent a knowing look at Seth, and left the house.

Kade headed for the Three Queens, figuring that was the best place to find men who were out of work.

The saloon was fairly crowded for the middle of the day in the middle of the week. Going to the bar, he ordered a beer. Sipping it slowly, he perused the occupants– too old, a card sharp, a drummer likely just passing through. Three men playing a desultory game of poker looked like cowhands. Like most men, they wore guns. The question was, did they know how to use them?

He was about to head over to the table when Lyle Burdett and his hired killers strolled into the place.

Kade muttered under his breath when Burdett saw him. Wanting his hands free, he set his drink on the bar.

"Mr. Smith," Burdett said, flashing a fake smile, "just the man I was looking for."

Facing the rancher head-on, Kade said, "I can't imagine why."

"I believe we have some unfinished business."

"I don't think so. My place wasn't for sale the last time you asked, and it's not for sale now."

"Well, you might want to think it over. A ranch can be a dangerous place for a woman in the family way. She might fall down the stairs, or get snake-bit while working in the yard, or..."

Kade was across the room, his hands at Burdett's throat, before Burdett finished speaking. "I'm warning you, keep off my property. If anything happens to my wife, anything at all, I'm coming after you. You got that?" Kade glanced over the rancher's shoulder as Burdett's two hired guns started toward him. "Back off," he growled, "or your boss is dead where he stands."

"You heard him, boys," Burdett said, and there was no fear in his voice. "Do as he says."

The two men hesitated a moment before backing toward the door.

Kade drew his gun before releasing his hold on Burdett. "You ever seen what happens to a man staked out in the sun over an anthill?" he drawled. "Not a pretty sight."

"It that a threat?"

"Take it any way you want." Shoving Burdett aside, Kade made his way toward the door, turned and backed out onto the boardwalk. He stood there a moment, waiting to see if Burdett's men would follow. When they didn't, he cut down the alley and returned to the boardinghouse through the alley.

Norrie smiled at him as he came in the kitchen door. "Did you have any luck?"

"No. Are you ready to go home?"

"I guess so," she said. "Just let me tell Seth and Truvy goodbye."

❧ ❧ ❧

Kade was quiet on the way home. Norrie didn't know what had happened, but it wasn't good. His jaw was clenched so tightly she was surprised it didn't crack. A dozen questions popped into her mind, yet she hesitated to ask them. But something was definitely wrong. Of that, she had no doubt.

When they reached home, Kade sent her into the house. Going to the window, she watched him park the buckboard next to the barn, unhitch the Appy and turn the mare loose in the corral with the mustang.

Kade's mare trotted up to him but for once he ignored her. Instead, he stood there, staring off into the distance, his hand caressing the butt of his Colt.

The bleak look on his face, the hard set of his jaw, made Norrie go cold all over. She had seen that look before, when he killed the two bounty hunters. Suddenly frightened for the future, she wrapped her arms around her swollen abdomen, felt her baby's lusty kick, and prayed the child's father would still be alive when it was born.

CHAPTER THIRTY-FOUR

Norrie was filled with a growing sense of unease as the days and weeks went by. She found herself constantly going from window to window to make sure Kade was all right, to make sure there were no strangers lurking around the buildings, hiding in the shadows. She was cautious when she went out to milk the cow, feed the chickens and gather eggs, or when she went down to the barn to brush the Appy, or to work in the garden she had planted behind the house.

She went with Kade to the Warner ranch to pick up the dun mare and the stallion and for a day or two their presence distracted her. But only for a day or two.

When that paled, she decorated the baby's room—new curtains at the windows, a new rag rug for the floor, a rocking chair and a crib. She passed several hours with Truvy, sewing gowns and knitting booties.

She worried whenever they went into town, always on edge until they were safely headed back home. On one trip, Kade ran into Lee Jackson, who was more than happy to hire on. At first, Norrie was delighted to have someone she knew working on the ranch, but that was short-lived as she realized that now Jackson's life might also be in danger.

And always, in the back of her mind, was the nagging fear that Burdett would strike again when they least expected it.

Kade noticed, of course. He had eyes like a hawk and missed nothing. Only at night, in his arms, did she feel safe.

Kade sat on the front porch, his rifle at his side, as he stared into the darkness, his thoughts on Norrie. She was afraid for him. They never spoke of it, but he saw the fear in her eyes every time he left the house. He longed to comfort her, to assure her she was worrying for nothing, but he knew she would never believe him. Hell, he was worried enough for the two of them, not so much for his safety, but for hers. She had been through so much—losing her father and the ranch, breaking him out of jail, living in that squalid shack in Moses. He wasn't sure she could stand another loss, another heartache.

He'd seen fresh tracks out past the barn, tracks that led back to the Burdett ranch. He knew Burdett's gunnies were keeping an eye on him, but so far, they hadn't made a move.

Norrie had invited Jackson to stay in the house, but he'd elected to sleep on a cot in the tack room and Kade hadn't objected. He'd given Jackson a rifle and a shotgun and told him not to be afraid to use them if he caught anyone prowling around in the middle of the night.

He kept the horses close to home, either in one of the corrals or in the barn.

Blowing out a sigh, he glanced skyward. "*Wakan Tanka,*" he murmured. "Hear my cry. Watch over those I love and care for. Keep them safe. Weaken my enemies, strengthen my loved ones. Hear my cry. *Wakan Tanka.* Hear my cry. Hear my cry."

He rose at the sound of the door opening behind him. "Kade?"

"What are you doing up so late, darlin'?" he asked, turning to face her.

"I was going to ask you the same thing."

"Just feeling restless." His gaze ran over her, lingering on her belly, swollen large now with their child. "How are you feeling?"

She smiled as she placed a hand on her abdomen. "Your son is restless, too. I think he's trying to kick his way out."

"He probably just wants to see his mother," Kade remarked. slipping his arm around her waist, he gave her a hug. Aware of being an easy target, he picked up his rifle, followed Norrie into the house and closed the door behind them. "Go back to bed, love. You need your rest."

"Aren't you coming with me?"

Knowing she would worry if he refused, he nodded. "I'll be there as soon as I lock up."

In bed, she snuggled against him, her head pillowed on his shoulder. "We never talked about names for the baby."

"I thought I'd leave that to you."

She was quiet a moment. "Would you mind if we named him Connor, after my father?"

"Not at all. He was a good man." His fingers delved into her hair. "What if it's a girl?"

"I'm sure it's a boy. Truvy thinks so, too, because I'm carrying it high."

"What the heck does that mean?"

"High means up here," she said, placing her hand under her breasts. Moving her hand down toward her pelvis, she said, "Low means down here."

A son, Kade thought as he drifted off to sleep. He had always wanted a son.

He woke to the sound of someone pounding on the front door. Slipping out of bed, he grabbed his Colt and hurried down the stairs. He peered out the window beside the door, flung it open when he saw Jackson standing on the porch, shirtless and bare-footed.

"What's wrong?"

Face pale, Jackson said, "I killed a man."

"What? Who?"

"I don't know who he is. I found him sneaking around the barn carrying a can of kerosene and a box of matches. When I called out, he dropped the can and took a shot at me. I fired back and … he's dead."

"Where's the body?"

"I dragged it into the barn and covered it up."

"Are you all right?"

Jackson rubbed his left arm. "His bullet grazed me,"

"Come on inside and let me take a look at it."

"It's nothing."

"Don't argue with me," Kade said. "I'm not in the mood."

With a sigh of resignation, Jackson followed Kade into the kitchen, sat at the table while Kade set his Colt on the counter, then lit a lamp and filled a pan with water.

"You were lucky." Kade washed the wound, and bound it in a clean linen towel. "I think you're gonna need a couple of stitches. Go get dressed and I'll take you into town." He picked up his Colt as he heard the sound of soft footsteps coming down the stairs.

"What's going on?" Norrie exclaimed, her gaze darting from Jackson to Kade and back again as she stepped into the kitchen.

Jackson looked at Kade.

"There was some trouble at the barn. Jackson got shot. I'm gonna take him into town and have Doc take a look at him."

"I'm going with you."

"Damn right." No way was he leaving her home alone.

"Jackson, wait!" Norrie exclaimed when Jackson started to leave. "What if there's someone else out there?"

"If there was, I'm pretty sure he's gone by now," Kade said. "Get a move on, Jackson. We'll meet you down at the barn."

Knowing it was useless to argue, Norrie followed Kade upstairs. She had been worrying for weeks that something like this would happen, she thought as she stepped out of her nightgown. And now it had.

"I'm going down to hitch up the mare," Kade said, buckling his gunbelt. "I'll be back to pick you up."

"Are you sure Jackson's all right?" she asked as she pulled a dress from the wardrobe.

"Yeah. The bullet barely grazed his arm."

After hitching the Appy to the buckboard, Kade took a look at the body.

Coming up behind him, Jackson asked, "Do you think it's one of Burdett's men?"

Kade nodded. "Yeah. I saw him in town a while back. You're lucky it wasn't the other one."

Norrie sat between Kade and Jackson on the way to town. Kade was tense and watchful. Jackson, too. She was glad when the first buildings came into view.

Kade pulled up on the left side of the doctor's house where his office was located. "Norrie, you go in with Jackson."

"What are you going to do?"

"I'm going to get the sheriff and bring him back here."

"Is that a good idea?" she asked.

"Better he should hear what happened from Jackson than anyone else. I don't want him to think we've got anything to hide."

"But…"

"He's right, Miss Norrie," Jackson said, climbing down from the buckboard. "It was self-defense and if the dead man is one of Burdett's, I want to tell my side of the story before Burdett finds out."

"You're right, of course," she said as Kade helped her down.

Kade waited until Doc Williams, clad in his nightclothes, opened the door before making his way down the street to the Sheriff's Office.

Kade knocked twice before a sleepy voice called, "Who's there?"

"It's Kade."

There was a moment of silence, followed by a muttered curse before the door opened and Bradshaw stood there sleepy-eyed, clad in a pair of trousers, his shirt hanging open, his feet bare, his hair tousled. "What the hell are you doing here this time of night?" he asked sourly.

"My man, Jackson, killed one of Burdett's men tonight and got shot doing it. He's at the doctor's office and wants to make a statement."

"Did you see it happen?"

"No."

"Give me a minute," Bradshaw said, closing the door.

Kade glanced up and down the street. All was quiet.

Five minutes later, Bradshaw stepped outside, fully dressed. "All right, let's go."

Norrie sighed as Kade turned onto the road that led home. Dawn was lighting the sky. Elias had questioned Jackson and Kade for almost an hour. At the end of that time, he decided not to hold either one of them, pending further investigation and the coroner's findings. Since he had a prisoner in the jail, he said he would pick up the body in the morning after his deputy reported for duty.

When they reached home, Norrie went right to bed.

"Jackson, you go with her," Kade ordered. "You can bed down in the guestroom."

For once, the cowboy didn't argue.

Kade unhitched the horse and fed the stock before heading for the barn.

He cussed a blue streak when he opened the door and saw that the body was gone.

CHAPTER THIRTY-FIVE

Elias Bradshaw arrived late that morning. Kade was digging post holes behind the barn when the sheriff rode up.

"I'm afraid you made the trip for nothing," Kade said, peeling off his gloves. "The body's gone."

"Gone?" Bradshaw stared at him. "What do you mean, gone?"

"I mean it's not here."

Dismounting, Bradshaw checked every stall, climbed up into the hay loft, looked under a pile of straw, checked the tack room.

"Do you believe me now?" Kade asked, dryly.

"Who the hell steals a body?"

"Maybe the man who sent him," Kade suggested.

"I guess you think it was Burdett?"

"I don't know anyone else who has a grudge against me," Kade said, following him toward the door. "Besides, I saw the shooter with Burdett in town not long ago."

Bradshaw shook his head as he ambled out of the barn to where Jackson waited, his brow furrowed.

"Relax, Jackson. I don't doubt that you killed somebody, but until we have a body ..." Bradshaw shrugged. "As for you," he said, glancing at Kade, "You're damn lucky that Jackson came forward, cause if that body turns up somewhere, I'd sure as hell have come after you if he hadn't confessed."

"Yeah, I figured that."

Bradshaw glared at him. "Damn you, if it wasn't for Norrie…"

"I know. You'd arrest me now for breaking out of jail. Only it was her idea."

"You're forgetting that wanted poster."

"That could be anyone. You can only hold me on suspicion for so long. Besides, you need some kind of evidence. Or a witness. And I happen to know that the only witness is dead."

"Have you got proof of that?"

"Just my mother's word."

"Yeah. And where's she?"

"With her people."

Bradshaw snorted. "You expect me to take the word of…" Seeing the ominous look in Kade's eyes, the lawman changed his mind about whatever he'd been about to say. Swinging into the saddle, he said, "You'll slip up one of these days, and when you do, I'll be there."

"In the meantime, you might go question Burdett," Kade suggested.

"I don't need you to tell me how to do my job," Bradshaw retorted. Giving his horse a hard kick, he rode out of the yard.

"That man surely hates you," Jackson remarked.

"I can't argue with that," Kade agreed, pulling on his gloves. "Hand me that shovel, wall ya?"

Kade forced himself to concentrate on fixing up the ranch when all he wanted to do was confront Burdett. With Jackson's help, they strung miles of barbed wire and when they had a big enough area fenced in, Kade asked Seth to come and stay with Norrie while he and Jackson rounded up fifty head of cattle.

The days grew shorter, the nights longer and colder, and he grew increasingly nervous as the weeks sped by and the time for the baby's birth grew closer.

Kade relaxed a little with the coming of winter weather. It was nigh impossible for anyone to sneak up on the house without leaving tell-tale tracks in the snow, and equally difficult to make a quick getaway through the drifted snow. He refused to let Norrie do anything more strenuous than fix their meals, something she objected to daily.

"I'm not sick or an invalid," she argued on more than one occasion. "I'm just expecting a baby. Women have been having them for thousands of years, you know."

"Yeah? Well, you haven't," he retorted, and refused to hear any more about it.

Norrie stood at the living room window. It was a beautiful day. For the first time in weeks, the sky was blue and clear. The yard lay under a blanket of white. Kade and Jackson had gone down to the barn to turn the horses out for some exercise and she was thinking about what to prepare for the mid-day meal when the first contraction hit. At first, she thought it was nothing, but the next one was harder and the next harder still.

Sinking into the easy chair by the living room window, she wrapped her arms around her middle, took a deep breath as she fought off a sudden rush of fear as all the horror stories she'd heard of childbirth rushed to the forefront of her mind. It had been easy to put up a brave front with Kade, but now, with delivery so near, her courage deserted her. Mrs. Minton had delivered a stillborn son. Mr. Blackburn's first wife had died in childbirth and the baby with her.

Between contractions, she made her way to the front door and out onto the porch.

Where was Kade? Her gaze swept the yard, the barn, the corral, her anxiety growing every second. *Please, Lord, don't let me have this baby alone.*

She shrieked his name as another contraction threatened to tear her in two.

Kade dropped the harness he was holding at the sound of Norrie's cry. Racing out of the barn, he headed for the house, his heart in his throat when he saw her slumped on the front porch, her face as pale as the snow.

"Norrie! What is it?"

"The baby," she gasped. "It's coming."

"Come on," he said, lifting her into his arms, "let's get you into the house."

He carried her inside and up the stairs, removed her clothing, and settled her into bed. "I'm going to send Jackson into the town for the doctor. I'll be right back."

She nodded, her whole body tensing with pain.

Muttering an oath, he ran down the stairs, hollering for Jackson, who came on the run.

"I need you to ride into town and get Doc Williams right quick. Norrie's having the baby. Tell him to hurry. If you can't find him, send Truvy. But hurry, dammit!"

Thinking he would rather face a band of angry Comanche than go back upstairs, Kade took several deep breaths before returning to the bedroom.

Norrie looked up at him through pain-filled eyes, her hands clutching the sheets so tightly her knuckles were white.

"Relax, darlin'," Kade said, brushing her hair back from her face. "I know it hurts, but it'll hurt worse if you fight it. Think about the baby and how happy you'll be once he's born."

"Have you … ever delivered … a baby?"

"Not a human one."

"I think you're … about to," she said.

"So soon?" he asked, unable to keep the panic out of his voice. He'd always heard that first babies took their time. Why was this one in such an all-fired hurry?

A glance at Norrie told him he wasn't the only one worried.

"Animals or people, it's all pretty much the same," he said, forcing a smile. "Take slow, deep breaths." Taking a deep breath of his own, he glanced beneath the sheet.

Five minutes passed. Ten. Her contractions were coming harder, faster. Going to the cupboard in the hallway, he grabbed a handful of towels and spread them out under Norrie's hips.

She was panting now, her brow beaded with sweat. Never had time passed so slowly, and yet so quickly.

Kade reached for her hand, let out a groan of his own as her fingers tightened around his. He wiped the sweat from her brow, then went to the window and peered outside. Dammit, where was the doctor?

"It's coming!"

Kade moved to the end of the bed and lifted the sheet once more. He could see the baby's head. Damn. "Push, darlin'. Push with the contractions."

One last, harsh cry, a flood of liquid, and the infant slipped into Kade's waiting hands. "You were right," Kade murmured, his voice tinged with awe. "It's a boy."

It was then that Doc Williams and Clara James, the young woman who sometimes served as his nurse, arrived.

Kade surrendered the baby to more expert hands and went to stand by the head of the bed. "You did fine, darlin'," he murmured, bending down to kiss her cheek. "Just fine."

"Is he all right?" she asked, her gaze anxiously searching his face.

"Perfect," he assured her. "Ten fingers. Ten toes. Lots of black hair."

"I want to see him."

"Soon. Newborn babies of any kind are kinda wet and messy, you know. They need a lot of cleaning up."

Feeling like he was in the way, Kade went to look out the window while the doctor examined Norrie and the nurse looked after the baby. *I have a son*, he thought, and wished his mother was there to see her first grandchild.

"Here you go, Mrs. Smith," the nurse said as she placed the blanket-wrapped infant in Norrie's arms.

"Is he all right, Doctor Williams?" Norrie asked anxiously.

"Perfectly fine, my dear," Williams said. "You get some sleep now. He'll be wanting something to eat soon. I'll look in on you tomorrow. Miss James, I'll wait for you downstairs."

"I'll see you out." Kade gave Norrie a kiss on the cheek and then followed the doctor downstairs.

"Thanks for coming, Doc," Kade said, shaking Williams' hand. "Is there anything I need to do for her?"

"Just be sure she eats and that she drinks plenty of fluid. And no … uh … intimate relations for a while."

Kade nodded. Abstinence seemed like a damn good idea. How could he even think of putting the woman he loved more than his own life through the pain of childbirth again?

CHAPTER THIRTY-SIX

Norrie sighed as she lightly stroked her son's downy cheek. All the pain and fear had been forgotten the minute she held him in her arms. He was beautiful, perfect, from the top of his head to the soles of his tiny feet. If only her father was here to share this moment with her. Holding her son to her breast, she gazed out the bedroom window, wondering if they would ever find out who had killed her father. Deep in her heart, she knew it had been Burdett, but there was no way to prove it now, after so much time had passed.

At Kade's insistence, she had spent the last week in bed. Truvy had come over for a couple of hours each day to help out and it had been much appreciated, but Norrie was tired of being treated like an invalid. When Truvy came by this afternoon, she would let her know she was ready to resume her normal duties and care for the baby, too. After all, pioneer women had given birth on the trail and been on their feet again the next day!

Kade treated her as if she were made of spun glass. It had amused her at first, but enough was enough. As much as she loved spending all her time with the baby, she missed caring for Kade and the house. She even missed cooking and cleaning. She could hear him downstairs now, rattling the pots and pans as he prepared breakfast.

Throwing the covers aside, she stood and placed the baby in the crib, pulled on her robe, and padded down the stairs to the kitchen.

"Norrie!" Kade exclaimed when he saw her. "What are you doing out of bed?"

"I'm bored. Sit down while I fix breakfast."

"You should be resting."

"I've had enough rest to last a lifetime."

"The boy…"

"He's asleep. Now sit!"

Taking the knife from his hand, she sliced the bacon, scrambled half a dozen eggs, buttered four slices of toast, and filled two cups with coffee.

"I could have done it," he said as she set a plate in front of him.

"I know, and I appreciate all you've done, but I'm fine. You have enough to do looking after the ranch without waiting on me, too." Leaning down, she kissed his cheek. "I need to be busy."

Slipping his hand around the back of her neck, he drew her closer. "I love you, Norrie."

"I love you, too. Now eat your breakfast before it gets cold."

Kade strapped on his gunbelt on his way down to the barn after breakfast. Jackson was already there, mucking out one of the stalls, his Winchester propped against the barn door. Kade had insisted Jackson be armed whenever he was outside. He wasn't taking any chances on either one of them being surprised by one of Burdett's hired guns.

He felt a renewed sense of satisfaction as he looked around the yard. All their hard work had paid off. The wire was up. The corrals were in good shape. The barn had been repaired. The house had a new coat of paint. In a week or so, he would see about rebuilding the spring house and maybe putting up another corral.

The gray mare was due to foal any day. In a few weeks, he would breed the dun mare to the stallion. Perhaps he'd breed Norrie's Appy, as well.

He gazed into the distance, torn by a sudden need to visit his people so his mother could see the baby. Perhaps he might be able to persuade her to come home with him for an extended visit, if Norrie had no objection to having another woman in the house.

Norrie had just put Connor to bed when Kade came into the house calling her name.

"What is it?" she asked anxiously. Even though it had been months since Burdett had made any threatening moves against them, she worried about it constantly.

"The gray mare is in labor. I thought you'd want to know."

"Oh!" After making sure Connor was covered, she hurried down the stairs and followed Kade out to the barn. "How long has she been in labor?"

"About four hours."

The mare lay in one of the stalls, sides heaving. Sweat glistened along her neck and flanks. During the next hour, she moved restlessly, rising and pacing the stall, then lying down again.

"Poor thing," Norrie murmured as the mare's water broke. "I know just how she feels."

The mare lay on her side now, legs outstretched, her muscles contracting.

"Look! I see the foal," Norrie exclaimed as the head and neck appeared enclosed in a bluish-white membrane that tore as the head slipped out. The shoulders came next. When the foal's hips appeared, the mare rested for several minutes.

One more contraction, and the rest of the foal slipped out of the birth canal. Mare and foal both rested for a time and then the mare nosed her baby.

"It's a colt," Kade said, kneeling beside the foal.

"He's adorable," Norrie said. For a few minutes, they stood there quietly watching the mare and foal. The colt lifted his head. The mare gained her feet. And for the next twenty minutes they watched the colt struggle to stand.

"A new life," Norrie murmured as the foal finally gained control of its long legs. "It's always a miracle, isn't it? And right now, I need to go check on our own little miracle."

"I'll be along in a little while." He needed to stay until the mare passed the afterbirth and make sure it was all there, as well as make sure the mare didn't reject the foal.

Kade grinned as he watched Norrie run back to the house. There were all kinds of miracles, he thought, and then there was Norrie, the greatest of them all.

Kade turned the gray mare and the colt loose in one of the corrals the next day. Norrie smiled from the kitchen window as she watched the colt run circles around his mother and kick up his heels. Was there anything as cute as a baby horse? Other than her son, she amended, as she glanced into the living room, where Connor lay sleeping on the sofa. She felt her heart swell with love as she looked at him, thinking she'd never been happier in her life than she was now.

The days and weeks flew by. Looking back, Norrie was amazed at how quickly life moved on. She was suddenly keenly aware of the endless cycle of life. Winter had turned to spring and spring to summer. The rivers ran high. Wildflowers made bright splashes of color against the greening hills. There were little yellow chicks everywhere. The barn cat had given birth to five kittens. Their herd had increased as a number of cows produced calves.

Filled with energy, Norrie turned to gardening. She planted carrots and potatoes and onions, cabbage and peas, while Connor played in the dirt at her side. By the time she finished, he was dirty from head to foot.

Later that day, while Connor was napping, she walked down to the barn. She found Kade and Jackson perched on the top rail of the corral, taking a break. Jackson had been cutting wood for the stove and Kade had been painting the barn. He'd removed his shirt and the sun glinted on his copper-hued skin and cast blue highlights in his hair. Just looking at him filled her with a sense of joy and happiness. He was the sweetest, most caring man in the world, she thought, remembering how reluctant he'd been to make love to her after Connor was born. When she finally demanded to know what was wrong, he'd confessed he was afraid of getting her pregnant again. She'd stared at him in disbelief. Had he really been willing to live like a monk the rest of his life to spare her the pain of childbirth?

She felt herself blushing as she recalled how she had teased and tempted him night after night until he'd finally succumbed. Later, when they lay side by side, she had assured him that Connor had been worth every moment of pain and that she was looking forward to having a daughter. He had been as ardent as a young stallion ever since.

Norrie sighed. She had never been happier or more content, she thought, as she took her son upstairs to change his diaper and put him down for a nap. Her only regret was how quickly he'd grown. It seemed like one day he was a helpless infant and the next he was gurgling and smiling and rolling over from his tummy to his back and suddenly he was crawling. He was a constant joy and she loved him more than she would have thought possible.

Norrie was in the middle of making a cake a few days later when Kade came through the back door.

"I'm going into town to pick up that bag of oats I ordered last week. Do you need anything?"

"Flour and sugar," Norrie said. "And some baking powder. And maybe a bag of peppermint sticks?"

"You and your sweet tooth," he said, giving her a quick kiss on the cheek. "I won't be gone long. Jackson's going to finish painting the barn while I'm gone."

"I'll miss you."

"You'd better."

"Don't forget the candy," she called as he went out the back door. As she listened to the sound of hoofbeats and the rattle of the wagon as he left the yard, she wished she had gone with him.

✤ ✤ ✤

Kade parked the wagon in front of Minton's Groceries and Dry Goods and swung down from the seat. He cast a longing glance at the saloon, thinking it had been a while since he'd had a shot of whiskey or passed a few hours playing poker. But today was not the day.

After Mr. Minton filled his order, Kade drove down to the feed store to pick up a fifty-pound bag of oats.

He was on his way out of town when a quick movement to his right caught his eye, followed by a flash of sunlight on a rifle barrel. He rolled off the seat, drawing his Colt as he fell. He fired at the same time as the man who stepped out of the alley.

Kade felt a searing pain in his upper arm as he gained his feet. He recognized the man lying in the street as Hank Kirby, one of Burdett's hired guns.

Holstering his Colt, he clamped his hand over his bleeding arm. Seconds later, the street was crowded with men, all talking at once.

Kade swore as Bradshaw came running toward him, a smug smile twisting his lips. "What's going on here?"

Kade jerked his chin at Kirby. "He took a shot at me and I fired back. My aim was better than his."

Bradshaw grunted. "Anybody else see what happened?"

"It was self-defense, Sheriff," Kade said dryly. "Or do you think I killed him and then shot myself in the arm?"

Bradshaw glared at him as Doc Williams came hurrying toward them.

The doctor knelt beside the dead man a moment, then stood and walked toward Kade. "Better let me have a look at that arm."

"Sure, Doc."

"Where the hell do you think you're going?" Bradshaw asked. "I'm not through with you yet."

"If you've got questions, go talk to Burdett," Kade retorted. "That's one of his hired gun lying in the street."

"If you need Mr. Smith, he'll be in my office," the doctor said in a tone that brooked no argument. "Can't you see the man's bleeding."

Stifling the urge to laugh in Bradshaw's face, Kade followed Williams to his office.

Wide-eyed, Norrie stared at Kade's bandaged arm. "What happened?"

"One of Burdett's men took a shot at me."

"In town?"

"Yep. Bold as brass."

"Is he …?"

"'Fraid so."

"I can't believe that even a man like Burdett would be that brazen. Are you sure the man who shot you worked for him?"

"Yeah. I recognized him, but I'm sure Burdett will come up with a good alibi. Probably insist he fired the man weeks ago and doesn't know a thing about it."

"You could have been killed." Fighting tears, Norrie rested her cheek against his chest and closed her eyes. What would she do if she lost him?

"Hey," he said, wrapping his uninjured arm around her, "I'm fine."

It could have been worse, Kade thought. Burdett could count his lucky stars that Norrie had stayed home with Connor. If Norrie and their son had been with him, they would both have been in the line of fire, and Lyle Burdett would be dead now.

Bradshaw rode out to see Kade later that day. "I went to see Mr. Burdett," the lawman said. "He denied having any knowledge of the incident. Said Kirby acted on his own. Probably hoping to collect the bounty on that reward poster."

"Maybe you should take the damn thing down," Kade suggested, a hard edge to his voice.

"I'll think on it," Bradshaw said. "Anyway, you've got no case against Burdett. Like you told me a while back, without proof, I can't hold him on suspicion for very long. Give my best to Miss Norrie."

Kade scowled as he watched the sheriff ride away. Damn the man. No doubt Bradshaw was just waiting for Burdett to put a bullet in his back so he could come courting Norrie.

"It'll be a cold day in hell before that happens," Kade muttered.

Elias scowled as he rode back to town. He hadn't hated many men in his life, but he sure as hell hated that damn half-breed. If not for Kade, Norrie would be Mrs. Bradshaw now. He knew it was wrong to wish harm to anyone, but in a dark corner of his heart, he wished Hank Kirby had succeeded. It shamed him that he felt that way, but there it was.

When he got back to town, he was going to sit down and go through all the old wanted posters. If he was lucky, he just might find Kade's name on one of them.

CHAPTER THIRTY-SEVEN

Lyle Burdett paced the parlor floor. Kirby had failed him, damn the man. It had taken some fast talking to convince Bradshaw that he'd had no idea Kirby had ambushed Kade. He wasn't sure if the sheriff had believed his story, but there was no proof that he was involved.

Muttering an oath, he poured himself a glass of bourbon and downed half of it. Maybe he was going about this all wrong. He'd hired four of the best fast guns in the territory and they had all failed him. Maybe it was time he confronted the half-breed instead of sending one incompetent fool after another. Or maybe…

Going to the window, he stared out into the gathering twilight. The 'breed had a pretty young wife and a kid… Perhaps he'd be willing to sign over the deed to the ranch in exchange for the lives of his family.

He would have to plan carefully, time it perfectly. There would be no room for mistakes. He mulled it over for several minutes, weighing the pros and cons of such a plan.

In the end, he rejected it. Even if he successfully swapped the woman's life for the deed to the ranch, he would still have Kade to contend with.

There had to be a better way, but damned if he knew what it was.

Chapter Thirty-Eight

After weeks of sticking close to home, Kade decided it was time for a change of scenery. Knowing how worried Norrie had been after the incident in town, he hadn't strayed far from the ranch, but enough was enough.

"Get your coat and bundle up Connor," he said one night after dinner.

"Where are we going?"

"Wherever you want. I've been cooped up long enough."

He saw the doubt in her eyes, and then she sighed. "We haven't seen Seth and Truvy in a while."

"Get Connor ready. I'll get the buckboard."

Norrie dressed Connor while Kade was gone, packed a few diapers and Connor's favorite blanket, and they headed for town.

It was a beautiful night for a drive. Norrie blew out a sigh, glad that Kade had suggested they go to town. She'd let her fears keep her home long enough.

Seth and Truvy greeted them with smiles. Truvy dished up the apple pie she'd made that afternoon and they gathered around the kitchen table, making small talk.

Kade and Seth endured an hour of listening to the women brag about their children and exchange recipes before deciding to go to the Three Queens for a drink in spite of the disproving looks from their wives.

"We won't be long," Kade assured Norrie.

"No gambling, Seth," Truvy admonished. "Remember your promise."

"I remember," he muttered as he followed Kade out the door. "Sometimes she treats me like I'm a kid," he groused when they were outside.

"Women are like that," Kade said, slapping Seth on the back. "Always worrying about something. Forget about it," he said as they pushed through the saloon's batwings doors. "I'll stake you to a couple of hands of poker. If you lose, it won't matter. If you win …." He lifted one shoulder and let it fall. "You can buy her a new dress."

Inside, Kade ordered two whiskeys. He sipped his as he perused the tables. "Come on," he said, "let's try our luck."

At the table, he staked Seth to twenty dollars in chips, bought the same amount for himself, and sat back. It wasn't a high stakes game, just a few of the businessmen passing a little time.

The talk at the table was mostly about the rising cost of beef and a recent bank robbery in the next town. Kade paid little attention until he heard Burdett's name mentioned.

"He's at it again," Perkins, the banker, remarked. "He just bought out Graham."

A muscle twitched in Kade's jaw. If he remembered rightly, Colby Graham owned one of the small ranchers to the north of town.

"Did he buy up the man's mortgage?" Lee Bailey asked. "That seems to be how he operates."

"That's not what I heard," Deke Larsen said, lowering his voice. "Graham hisself told me Burdett sent one of his hired guns over. Made some kind of threat against Colby's family."

Kade swore under his breath. The man had to be stopped, but how?

They played another couple of hands and when they walked away from the table, Kade was ahead close to forty dollars.

"Not sure if I should tell Truvy I've been gambling," Seth said ruefully.

"You didn't wager any of your own money," Kade remarked. "Why should she be upset?"

Seth shrugged. "Who knows why women behave the way they do? I sure haven't figured it out. Don't know if I ever will. Don't get me wrong, I like being married," he said with a grin. "Most of the time."

Kade slapped his brother-in-law on the back. "Just do what you think best. She won't hear it from me."

Truvy had cake and coffee waiting for them when they returned to the boardinghouse.

Kade and Norrie took their leave a short time later.

"Did you win?" she asked as Kade turned the buckboard toward home.

"What do you think?"

"Did Seth?"

He slid a sideways glance at her. "What makes you think he played?"

"Because I know my brother. And I know you. How much did you give him?"

"Twenty."

"Did he win?"

"I think he walked away with about thirty dollars over the twenty I gave him. Don't be angry, love. He had a good time."

"How much did you win?"

"Maybe I lost."

She looked at him, one brow raised. "How much?"

"I came away with a hundred over what I started with," he said with a wink. "If you're a good girl, I'll give you half."

Norrie snuggled against Kade, one hand lightly exploring his chest. Sometimes it embarrassed her, how much she enjoyed touching him, having him touch her in return. She knew some of the women in town looked on intimacy as a chore, something to be gotten over with as quickly as possible. Others endured it only for the sake of having children. She sometimes wondered if there was something wrong with her, that she took such pleasure in sharing her bed with her husband. But if it was a fault of some kind, she didn't want to be cured.

She moaned softly as his hands caressed her breasts, her thighs, felt a wave of anticipation as his mouth covered hers. And then there was no more time for thought as he rose over her, save for a fleeting sense of pity for all those women who would never know how wonderful it was to be loved by a man like Kade, to feel his hands on her flesh, hear his voice, husky with desire, as he whispered that he loved her.

Kade stared up at the ceiling, his fingers playing with a lock of Norrie's hair. She slept beside him, her head pillowed on his shoulder, her breath soft against his neck. Sometimes, as now, he wondered what he'd ever done to deserve her. Without her, he'd still be drifting from town to town, spending his days and nights in two-bit saloons, with no hope of any kind of a future other than a rope around his neck or a bullet in the back. And then he'd met Norrie. She had saved his life in more ways than one.

Drawing her body closer to his, he closed his eyes and sent a silent prayer of thanks to *Wakan Tanka* for bringing her into his life.

Kade woke with a start. For a moment, he lay there, wondering what had roused him. And then he heard it again…a cow's plaintiff cry.

Slipping out of bed, he yanked on his pants, grabbed his Colt, and ran down the stairs. He paused at the front door, opened it warily before stepping cautiously outside.

His gaze swept the yard. At first, everything seemed still and then he heard it, the faint sound of hoofbeats.

Gun in hand, he made his way to the barn. The doors were closed. He checked inside but all was quiet. He eased open the door to the tack room where Jackson spent his nights.

"Who's there?"

Kade froze. "Don't shoot, it's me."

"What's wrong?"

"I thought I heard something, but there's no sign of trouble. Go back to sleep."

After closing the door, Kade headed back to the house. He paused every few feet, his gaze sweeping the moonlit darkness. Deciding he must have imagined it, he went back to bed.

Kade was in the middle of breakfast when Jackson came through the back door. "I found out what woke you last night."

Norrie looked at Kade. "What's he talking about?"

"I thought I heard something outside."

"You did," Jackson said. "Someone killed two of the calves in the middle of the night. I guess you scared whoever it was off before they got all of 'em."

"I think we both know who did it," Kade muttered. "Sit down and eat and then we'll go bury the carcasses."

Kade's anger grew when he saw the slaughter of the calves. It was such a cold-hearted act. He'd never thought of cattle as having emotions but it fed his anger when he saw one of the cows standing over her dead calf, mooing softly.

They dragged the calves away from the ranch, buried them deep to keep predators from digging them up.

When they were done, Kade sent Jackson up to the house to keep an eye on Norrie and Connor. Still fuming, he saddled the mustang and went looking for trail sign.

He found the prints of two shod horses near the fence line. He followed the tracks to the road leading to town.

Dismounting, Kade tried to sort out the two sets of prints he was following but it was no use. They were lost among dozens of other hoof prints and wheel tracks. Muttering under his breath, he swung onto the mustang's back and headed back to the ranch. Whoever the culprit or culprits were, they hadn't turned toward Burdett's ranch. Not that that proved anything, he thought irritably. They could still have been hired by Burdett.

Maybe he needed to hire a few men of his own.

Or just confront Burdett face-to-face and get it over with.

❧ ❧ ❧

Lyle Burdett paced the parlor floor, his outrage growing with every step. "Fools!" he shouted. "I'm surrounded by incompetent fools!"

"We did the best we could," Yates said, not meeting the boss's eyes. "The 'breed came out of the house before we finished and we hightailed it outta there."

"Did it ever occur to you to cut him down?"

Yates shuffled from one foot to the other. "I ain't no hired gun. And I don't cotton to the idea of killing cattle, either."

"Pack your gear and get out!" Burdett roared. Turning to face the second cowhand, he said, "What's your story?"

Hat in hand, the cowboy known as Browning cleared his throat. "I ... uh ..."

"What?" Burdett snarled impatiently.

"If you want any killin' done, Mr. Burdett, I'm not the man for the job. Cows is one thing. But gunnin' a man, even a dirty half-breed ..." Browning shook his head. "Best find yourself another hand."

"Get out!" Burdett fumed as Browning left the house. Unable to contain his rage, he grabbed a bottle of whiskey from the sofa table and hurled it against the wall.

Hands clenched, he stared at the shattered crystal. Maybe it was time to do the job himself. All he had to do was pick the time and the place.

CHAPTER THIRTY-NINE

Kade glanced over his shoulder as Norrie stepped out onto the porch, their son balanced on her hip. It seemed only days ago that Connor been a helpless infant. How quickly he had turned into a sturdy little boy with a mind of his own. Thankfully, there had been no further threats from Burdett. Instead of putting Kade's mind at ease, it only served to put him more on edge as he wondered what trouble Burdett could be planning that took this much time.

"It's a beautiful night," Norrie remarked, coming to stand beside him. The sky overhead was midnight blue sprinkled with millions of twinkling stars and a bright, yellow moon. "What are you thinking about?"

"My mother."

"Oh?"

"What would you think if she came to live with us?"

"I don't know," Norrie said, surprised by the question. "Do you think she would want to?"

"I don't know. Would you mind if she did?"

She hesitated a moment, her brow furrowed, before she said, "No, not at all. Your mother is our son's only living grandparent. I think he should get to know her."

Kade smiled, his heart filled once again with love and gratitude for the woman who had changed his life and given it meaning. "How soon can you be ready to go?"

Norrie glanced at Connor, who was wriggling in her arms. "I don't think we should go." She lifted her hand to still the protest she saw in his eyes. "It's a hard journey, and sometimes dangerous. Connor and I would only slow you down. And distract you if there was trouble."

Kade grunted softly. "You're probably right. But I can't help thinking the two of you might be in more danger staying here alone than going with me."

"We could go and stay with Seth and Truvy."

It was something to think about, Kade mused. He had recently hired four cowhands, ostensibly to help Jackson with the chores when, in fact, he'd hired them to keep an eye out for Burdett and his men. Three of them were just cowboys looking for work. Cody Lane hailed from Texas. He was the youngest, just eighteen years old. Lucky Montoya had some Mexican blood in him. Jed Walker was a seasoned cowhand who'd worked for one of the other ranches before Burdett bought the place.

The fourth man, Link Sumner, was a fast gun Kade had met in Kansas City a few years back. Sumner was tall and thin and the most unlikely trigger man Kade had ever seen, with his mild blue eyes and curly brown hair. But he was deadly with a six-gun. The man had been passing through Clayton's Corner when Kade ran into him. Sumner had been down on his luck and willing to hire on, temporarily, at least. Kade didn't think Burdett would try anything in town. Norrie had a lot of friends there. If he rode hard, he could make the trip to the Lakota and back in eight or nine days. Still, he didn't like the idea of leaving Norrie and his son for that long.

Staring into the distance, Kade dragged a hand across his jaw. Maybe he should write a letter to his mother and have Sumner deliver it. If she agreed to come here, Sumner could bring her.

Yes, indeed, it was something to think about.

Three weeks later, Kade sat down and wrote a letter to his mother, asking her if she would like to come for a visit to see her first grandson, and perhaps stay with them permanently. He read through the letter twice, sealed it in an envelope, and gave it to Sumner.

"I'm counting on you to bring her here safely," Kade said. "Don't let me down."

"Don't worry," Sumner said, tucking the envelope into his shirt pocket. "I'm looking forward to that bonus you promised me if I can get her back here in two weeks."

"Be careful."

Touching his fingers to his hat brim, Sumner rode out of the yard, one saddlebag filled with supplies, the other with gifts for Kade's mother.

Kade stared after him. It was going to be a long two weeks.

Needing to spend some time alone with Norrie, Kade asked Mrs. Minton to come and stay with Connor while he and Norrie went on a picnic. With her children grown, she happily agreed.

Norrie fussed a little at leaving Connor behind, but Kade begged so sweetly, she couldn't refuse.

She packed a lunch while he saddled their horses. The Appy and the mustang were eager for a run and Norrie felt all her cares fall away as they raced across the prairie. She had almost forgotten what it was like to feel the wind in her hair, to feel the freedom that came with losing herself in the exhilaration of riding across the prairie to the sound of her horse's hooves.

Riding beside her, Kade threw back his head and let out a wild war whoop that spooked the birds in the trees and sent them scattering.

Laughter bubbled up inside Norrie as the horses gradually slowed to a trot and then a walk. "I'm so glad you talked me into this," she said as Kade reined the mustang to a halt in the shade of a tree.

"Me, too," he said as he lifted her from the back of her horse and into his arms. "It's been too long since I had you all to myself."

"And what will you do, now that we're here all alone?"

"What do you think?" he murmured as he lowered his head and claimed her lips with his.

Norrie closed her eyes as she surrendered to his kisses. Still locked in each other's arms, they sank to the ground. She gloried in his touch as his hands moved over her, sliding under her shirt to caress her bare skin. Between kisses, they undressed each other.

Kade left her only long enough to grab the blanket tied behind his saddle and spread it on the ground before taking her in his arms again.

The sun was warm against her bare skin, but not as hot as Kade's kisses. She ran her hands over his shoulders and chest, along his hard-muscled arms and belly, laughing when he groaned as if he was in pain.

When he couldn't take her teasing any longer, he tucked her beneath him, his eyes filled with love and desire as he claimed her for his own.

Norrie sighed as she gazed up at the sky through the leaves of the tree, thinking she had never been happier or more content. Propping herself on one elbow, she looked at Kade. His eyes were closed, his breathing slow and easy. Just looking at him sent a thrill through her. She traced her fingertips lightly over his lower lips, let out a yelp when he bit her.

"What are you doing, woman?" he growled. "Can't you see I'm trying to sleep? You wore me out."

Norrie laughed softly. "I guess you're too tired to make love to me again," she said with a heavy sigh. "I guess we should eat."

"I'll never be *that* tired," he said as he pulled her on top of him and kissed her until she was breathless, her whole body yearning for his touch.

It was hours later when Norrie unpacked the picnic basket.

They rode back to the ranch side by side. Norrie's body ached in places that had never hurt before but it was a wonderful reminder of a wonderful day.

As soon as they reached home, Norrie jumped off her horse and ran into the house, eager to see Connor. She found him upstairs, sound asleep in Mrs. Minton's arms. "Did he give you any trouble?"

"Goodness, no. What a sweet thing he is," Mrs. Minton said, smiling. "Fair reminds me of my own Jonathan, himself now a father of three." Apparently sensing how eager Norrie was to hold her son, Mrs. Minton rose and placed Connor in Norrie's arms. "Any time you need me, I'll be glad to come and stay with him. After all, a young couple needs some time alone now and then."

"Thank you so much, Mrs. Minton. One of the men is bringing the buckboard up to take you home."

Mrs. Minton dropped a kiss on Connor's cheek, then hurried downstairs.

Norrie sank into the rocking chair, wondering if it was possible for Connor to have grown while she was gone. She missed the baby days, when she was the most important person in his life. He was already trying to walk on his chubby little legs, eager to explore the world around him, a world that would grow larger as he did.

With a sigh, she put those thoughts aside. He would need her less and less as he grew up, but for now, he was hers.

Kade glanced over his shoulder as Jackson came up beside him. "Did you have any trouble while we were gone?"

Jackson shrugged. "Part of the fence was down and a couple of cattle were on the other side, but I couldn't tell if the fence was pulled down deliberate or if one of the cows knocked it over."

Kade grunted softly. "Doesn't seem like Burdett's work. He'd likely have killed the cattle, or stolen them."

"I reckon. Cody went into town to pick up some dry goods for Norrie. He hasn't come back yet."

"How long ago did he leave?"

Jackson shrugged. "Not long after you did."

"He should have been back by now."

"Yeah. You want me to go after him?"

"No. I'll do that," Kade decided. "You go up to the house and stay there. Take Jed with you."

"You think Cody ran into trouble?"

"I think he ran into Burdett."

Jackson shuffled from one foot to the other. "What'll I tell Norrie when she asks where you are?"

Kade shrugged one shoulder. "Make something up. Give me your gunbelt."

Jackson stared at him.

"What's wrong?" Kade asked.

"I don't think I've ever seen you without your Colt."

"I left it home," Kade said impatiently. "Took my rifle instead."

"Maybe I should go with you," Jackson muttered as he unbuckled his gunbelt and handed it over.

"No." Kade settled the Colt on his hip. "If I'm not back in an hour, you and Jed take Norrie and Connor to the boardinghouse and stay there."

Kade didn't take time to saddle the mustang. Swinging onto her bare back, he slammed his heels against her sides and lit out hellbent for leather toward town.

He found Cody lying face down in a patch of dry brush on the side of the road. Blood leaked from a bullet wound in his back. There was no sign of his horse.

Dismounting, Kade hunkered down on his heels beside him and turned him over. He was barely breathing, his face fish-belly white and twisted in pain. He wasn't going to make it.

"Did you see who shot you?" Kade asked, cradling the boy in his arms.

"One of … Burdett's … men," Cody gasped. He clutched Kade's arm. "Two of them … ambushed me. Tell my ma …" His hand convulsed around Kade's arm as his head fell back.

Kade sat there, his rage growing as he closed the kid's eyes. After a moment, he stood and draped the body over the mustang's withers. Whoever had killed Cody had left a clear set of tracks. An error in judgement on the part of the killer?

Or bait for a trap?

"It ends now," Kade muttered as he swung onto the mustang's back. "One way or another, it ends now."

The tracks led to the town. Kade made a brief stop at the undertaker's to drop off the kid's body, then followed the tracks down to the saloon. He paused at the swinging doors and looked inside. He spied two of Burdett's men standing at the bar, whiskey in his hand. A quick glance around the room showed two more of Burdett's men sitting at a poker table with another man whose back was toward Kade.

It was Burdett.

Figuring they'd be in there celebrating for a while, Kade hurried down to the sheriff's office.

Bradshaw looked up when he entered the room. "Something wrong?" he asked.

"Damn right. I want you to arrest two of Burdett's men for murder."

"Murder! Who's dead?"

"One of my hired hands. Cody told me who shot him just before he died."

"Is that right?"

"His body's at the undertakers," Kade snapped. "They shot him in the back and left him for dead. Now haul your ass down to saloon and arrest them. And Burdett, too, since I'm sure he was behind it."

"Burdett," Bradshaw muttered.

"I know you're afraid of him," Kade said, his voice laced with scorn, "but it's time to earn your keep."

Bradshaw's cheeks flushed bright red. "Let's go."

A sudden hush fell over the saloon when Bradshaw stepped inside with his gun drawn, and Kade at his heels. "Everybody stay right where they are," the lawman said, his voice overly loud. "Point 'em out, Kade."

"The fella in the red shirt at the bar, and likely the man with him."

"See here," Burdett exclaimed, rising. "What's this about?"

"Your men have been accused of killing one of Kade's hired hands."

"That's ridiculous," Burdett scoffed.

"Kade claims the boy identified the man who shot him before he died."

Burdett made a dismissive gesture with his hand. "That half-breed will say anything to get back at me, even though I've never done anything to him."

"You damn liar!" Kade snarled.

"That's enough!" Bradshaw jerked his chin toward the men Kade had pointed out. "You two, come with me. You're under arrest until we can sort things out." Bradshaw cleared his throat. "You, too, Mr. Burdett."

"This is nonsense!"

"I'm sure it will all be cleared up," Bradshaw said. "Let's go."

A sudden tension filled the room as Burdett glanced at his men.

Kade watched Burdett's eyes, knew the moment the decision had been made. In one of those rare moments where time seemed to slow, he watched Burdett's men draw and fire at Bradshaw. At the same time, Burdett reached inside his jacket and withdrew a pistol. Dropping to one knee, he fired at Kade as Kade pulled his Colt and fired back.

Time sped up again and Kade experienced it all through a red haze of pain. The sound of shattering glass as a shot went wild and hit the mirror behind the bar. The mingled scents of gun smoke and the acrid scent of gun powder. The coppery scent of fresh blood. Men's voices, all talking at once.

Burdett lying on the floor, a splash of crimson spreading over his shirt front. His men sprawled in a widening pool of blood.

Bradshaw looking badly shaken as he held a hand over his bleeding shoulder.

It was over, Kade thought as he sank to the floor and spiraled into a sea of blackness.

All over.

CHAPTER FORTY

Norrie smiled uncertainly when she opened the door and saw Elias standing on the porch with Mrs. Minton. "What happened to your arm?" she asked, eying the bandage on his shoulder.

"There was some trouble at the saloon and ..."

"Trouble?" Norrie glanced from Elias to Mrs. Minton. What was she doing here? What kind of trouble?""

"With Burdett."

"What's he done now?"

Elias shuffled from one foot to the other. "He's dead. Kade's been shot."

"What?" Feeling suddenly light-headed, she grabbed the edge of the door. "Is he ...?"

"Not yet. But he's bad hurt. Jackson's saddling your horse. Mrs. Minton came to stay with your boy."

Norrie stared at him, unable to believe what she was hearing. And then Jackson was there with her horse, lifting her into the saddle.

The ride to town passed in a blur. Kade had been shot. Her mind refused to believe it, refused to think he might be dead, even now.

When they reached the doctor's office, she jumped off her horse and ran inside.

"Where is he?"

Doc Williams jerked a thumb toward the room where he kept patients overnight.

"Is he..."

"Not yet."

Taking a deep breath, Norrie hurried across the floor and opened the door. She hesitated a moment before she stepped inside.

Kade lay on the bed, his eyes closed. The bandage wrapped around his chest looked very white against the coppery hue of his skin. There were taut lines around his mouth, his breathing was shallow and uneven. When she took his hand in hers, it was cool, almost cold.

Silent tears tracked her cheeks as she murmured his name. Falling to her knees bedside the bed, she prayed as she had never prayed before, begging and pleading for his life to be spared.

She stayed at his side all that day, refusing to leave him alone for a moment. He didn't stir, only lay there, as still as death. What would she do if she lost him? She couldn't imagine her life without him.

Day turned to night, and night to day and still there was no change.

Seth and Truvy came by but she was hardly aware of their presence. She had eyes only for Kade. He had always been so strong, so resilient, it broke her heart to see him so still, so silent.

On the third day, Seth insisted she come to the boardinghouse to get something to eat. Mrs. Minton was there, with Connor. She found a measure of peace when she held her son, followed by a fresh wave of grief as she realized Connor might grow up never knowing who his father was. The thought brought a fresh wave of tears.

She ate the meal Truvy prepared, though she tasted none of it.

She took a nap when Seth insisted.

When she returned to the doctor's office, she asked the question she hadn't wanted to ask. "Is he going to die?"

"To tell you the truth, I have no idea," Williams said. "I didn't expect him to last this long. The bullet did some internal damage. I did all I could, but the rest is up to him."

With a nod, she returned to Kade's bedside. "Please don't leave me," she whispered, taking his hand in hers. "I need you. Connor needs you. Please come back to me." Bending down, she kissed him lightly. "I love you, Kade. But if you die on me, I'll hate you the rest of my life!"

A deep shuddering breath stirred the blanket covering him. Eyes still closed, he murmured, "No, you won't."

"Kade!" Jubilant, she kissed him again. "Oh, Kade! I was so afraid I'd lost you."

"Never." His hand tightened on hers. "Never."

To Norrie's relief, Kade began to recover. It was slow going at first. He'd lost a lot of blood and he was weaker than he would admit, but he grew stronger with every passing day.

They were sitting on the front porch two weeks later, with Connor playing at their feet, when Kade stood abruptly. "I'm sick and tired of doing nothing," he muttered irritably. "I don't care what Doc Williams said, I'm going back to work."

"Oh, no you're not!" Norrie exclaimed.

"Yeah?" He stared at her, a challenge in his eyes. "Who's gonna stop me?"

Norrie looked up as two riders approached the house. With a broad smile, she pointed and said, "Your mother! That's who. She got here just in time."

The next few minutes passed in a flurry of hugs and questions as Kade asked Link Sumner about the trip and Wichapi asked about Kade's injury. There were oohs and aahs as Wichapi held her grandson.

"He is a fine boy," she said as she held Connor in her arms. "He looks much like his father."

"*Ina*, where did you learn to speak English?" Kade asked.

"A soldier came to our village. He had been wounded by the Crow. He spoke our language and taught me his."

Kade shook his head in amazement. She spoke English better than some whites he knew.

"Have you come to stay?" Norrie asked, smiling as Connor tugged on his grandmother's braids.

"If you do not mind."

"Of course not!"

"Then I will stay."

Kade sighed as he sat back, thinking that he had everything he had ever wanted. A wonderful woman who loved him. A healthy son. A ranch that could thrive now that Burdett was no longer in the picture.

He said as much that night, in bed, as he took Norrie in his arms.

"We have been blessed, you and I," she agreed as she ran her hands over his chest and belly, her fingers lingering on the nasty scar left by Burdett's bullet. An inch one way or the other, Doc Williams had told her, and she would have lost him. "Prayers are answered," she murmured. "The fact that you're lying here beside me proves that."

He caressed her cheek with his knuckles. "I heard you praying for me," he said quietly. "I felt myself slipping away and then I heard your voice, thick with tears, and I felt something tangible move through me … I don't know what it was … your voice, your prayers …" He shrugged. "I love you, darlin'."

Laying her head on his shoulder, Norrie whispered, "And I love you. And I'll show you how much just as soon as you're stronger."

"I'm strong enough now," he said with a wicked grin. "As long as you do all the work."

Laughing softly, happier than she had ever been in her life, she wrapped him in her arms and in her love, a silent prayer of gratitude rising in her heart as she showered him with kisses, and the hope and the promise of forever.

~*finis*~

About the Author

Madeline is one of those rare birds—a California native. She's lived in Southern California her whole life and loves it (except for the earthquakes). She and her husband share a home with a fluffy Pomeranian named Lady, a mischievous cat named Trouble, and a tortoise named Buddy.

Madeline and her alter ego, Amanda Ashley, have written over 90 books and short stories, many of which have appeared on various bestseller lists, including the New York Times Bestseller List, the Waldenbooks Bestseller list, and the USA Today list. Not bad for someone who started writing just for the fun of it.

Madeline loves to hear from her readers. You can contact her at **darkwritr@aol.com**.

For a list of all her books, including covers and chapter previews, visit her website at www.madelinebaker.net.

ABOUT THE PUBLISHER

This book is published on behalf of the author by the Ethan Ellenberg Literary Agency.
https://ethanellenberg.com
Email: agent@ethanellenberg.com

Made in the USA
Las Vegas, NV
01 July 2022

50957082R00174